BOLLINGEN SERIES LXXII

PUSHKIN

painted by Orest Kiprenski in 1827

Eugene Onegin

A NOVEL IN VERSE BY Aleksandr Pushkin
TRANSLATED FROM THE RUSSIAN, WITH
A COMMENTARY, BY Vladimir Nabokov

PAPERBACK EDITION

IN TWO VOLUMES

I

———————

Translator's Introduction

Eugene Onegin : The Translation

———————

Bollingen Series LXXII

Princeton University Press

To Véra

Foreword

The novel in verse *Eugene Onegin*, by Aleksandr Pushkin
(1799–1837), was begun in 1823 and completed in 1831.
It came out in parts between February, 1825, and
January, 1832; this accumulation of eight chapters (the
first two of which are represented by two editions of
their own) is considered to form a "first" edition. A
complete edition in one volume ("second" edition) ap-
peared in March, 1833, and was followed by the *editio
optima* ("third" edition) of January, 1837, published
less than a month before Pushkin's fatal duel.*

Can Pushkin's poem, or any other poem with a definite
rhyme scheme, be really translated? To answer this we
should first define the term "translation." Attempts to
render a poem in another language fall into three
categories:

(1) Paraphrastic: offering a free version of the origi-
nal, with omissions and additions prompted by the
exigencies of form, the conventions attributed to the
consumer, and the translator's ignorance. Some para-

---

* My thanks are due to the Houghton Library, Harvard Uni-
versity, for permission to reproduce its copy of this rare
edition. See vol. 4 in the 4-vol. edition.

phrases may possess the charm of stylish diction and idiomatic conciseness, but no scholar should succumb to stylishness and no reader be fooled by it.

(2) Lexical (or constructional): rendering the basic meaning of words (and their order). This a machine can do under the direction of an intelligent bilinguist.

(3) Literal: rendering, as closely as the associative and syntactical capacities of another language allow, the exact contextual meaning of the original. Only this is true translation.

Let me give an example of each method. The opening quatrain of *Eugene Onegin*, transliterated and prosodically accented, reads:

> *Moy dyádya sámïh chéstnïh právil,*
> *Kogdá ne v shútku zanemóg,*
> *On uvazhát' sebyá zastávil,*
> *I lúchshe vídumat' ne móg . . .*

This can be paraphrased in an infinite number of ways. For example:

> My uncle, in the best tradition,
> By falling dangerously sick
> Won universal recognition
> And could devise no better trick . . .

The lexical or constructional translation is:

> My uncle [is] of most honest rules [:]
> when not in jest [he] has been taken ill,
> he to respect him has forced [one],
> and better invent could not . . .

Now comes the literalist. He may toy with "honorable" instead of "honest" and waver between "seriously" and "not in jest"; he will replace "rules" by the more evocative "principles" and rearrange the order of words to achieve some semblance of English construction and retain some vestige of Russian rhythm,

arriving at:

> My uncle has most honest principles:
> when he was taken ill in earnest,
> he has made one respect him
> and nothing better could invent . . .

And if he is still not satisfied with his version, the translator can at least hope to amplify it in a detailed note. (See also Comm. to Eight : XVII–XVIII.)

We are now in a position to word our question more accurately: can a rhymed poem like *Eugene Onegin* be truly translated with the retention of its rhymes? The answer, of course, is no. To reproduce the rhymes and yet translate the entire poem literally is mathematically impossible. But in losing its rhyme the poem loses its bloom, which neither marginal description nor the alchemy of a scholium can replace. Should one then content oneself with an exact rendering of the subject matter and forget all about form? Or should one still excuse an imitation of the poem's structure to which only twisted bits of sense stick here and there, by convincing oneself and one's public that in mutilating its meaning for the sake of a pleasure-measure rhyme one has the opportunity of prettifying or skipping the dry and difficult passages? I have been always amused by the stereotyped compliment that a reviewer pays the author of a "new translation." He says: "It reads smoothly." In other words, the hack who has never read the original, and does not know its language, praises an imitation as readable because easy platitudes have replaced in it the intricacies of which he is unaware. "Readable," indeed! A schoolboy's boner mocks the ancient masterpiece less than does its commercial poetization, and it is when the translator sets out to render the "spirit," and not the mere sense of the text, that he begins to traduce his author.

In transposing *Eugene Onegin* from Pushkin's Russian into my English I have sacrificed to completeness of meaning every formal element including the iambic rhythm, whenever its retention hindered fidelity. To my ideal of literalism I sacrificed everything (elegance, euphony, clarity, good taste, modern usage, and even grammar) that the dainty mimic prizes higher than truth. Pushkin has likened translators to horses changed at the posthouses of civilization. The greatest reward I can think of is that students may use my work as a pony.

One of the complications attending the translation of *Eugene Onegin* into English is the necessity of coping with a constant intrusion of Gallicisms and borrowings from French poets. The faithful translator should be aware of every such authorial reminiscence, imitation, or direct translation from another language into that of the text; this awareness may not only save him from committing howlers or bungling the rendering of stylistic details, but also guide him in the choice of the best wording where several are possible. Terms that are stilted or antiquated in Russian have been fondly rendered in stilted or antiquated English, and a point has been made of preserving the recurrence of epithets (so characteristic of a Russian romanticist's meager and overworked vocabulary), unless a contextual shade of meaning demanded the use of a synonym.

I have tried to explain many special matters in the Commentary. These notes are partly the echoes of my high-school studies in Russia half a century ago and partly the outcome of many pleasant afternoons spent in the splendid libraries of Cornell, Harvard, and the City of New York. Nothing, of course, approaching an exhaustive study of the variants to *Eugene Onegin* could be accomplished without photostats of Pushkin's manuscripts, but for obvious reasons these could not be obtained.

In many instances it was necessary to quote the Russian text. Pushkin, and his printers, used, of course, the old orthography (an illustration of it is provided by the reproduction of the 1837 edition). A method of transliteration not only based on that spelling but also reflecting Pushkin's personal departures from it would have conformed better to my notion of accuracy in these matters; but in a work not intended to baffle the foreign student of Russian, I thought it wiser to base transliteration on the new orthography introduced after the Revolution of February, 1917 (especially since all Pushkin's texts, with no concession to scholarship whatsoever, are so printed in Soviet Russia). Some of his drafts lack punctuation, and this has been supplied. His deletions are always enclosed in pointed brackets, and I have square-bracketed my own explanatory intrusions.

The writing of the book now in the hands of the reader was prompted about 1950, in Ithaca, New York, by the urgent needs of my Russian-literature class at Cornell and the nonexistence of any true translation of *Eugene Onegin* into English; but then it kept growing—in my moments of leisure, with many interruptions caused by the demands of other, more complicated, pursuits—for about eight years (during one of which I received the support of a Guggenheim Foundation award). Since 1957, after most of the book was completed, I have had little contact with current Pushkiniana.

In connection with my translation and annotations, several papers of mine have appeared: "Problems of Translation: *Onegin* in English," *Partisan Review* (New York), XXII (fall, 1955); "Zametki perevodchika" (A Translator's Notes), I, *Novïy zhurnal* (New Review; New York), XLIX (1957); "Zametki perevodchïka," II, *Opïtï* (Essays; New York), VIII (1957); and "The Servile Path," in the collection *On Translation*, ed. R. Brower (Cambridge, Mass., 1959).

The two stanzas on pp. 9–10 of my Introduction, besides appearing in *The New Yorker*, were reprinted in my collected *Poems* (New York, 1959; London, 1961), likewise in my collected *Poesie* (Milan, 1962) *en regard* of an Italian translation. My version of stanza xxx of Canto Six of *Eugene Onegin*, with part of its commentary, was published in *Esquire* (New York), July, 1963. Appendix One, on Abram Gannibal, was published in a somewhat abridged form, entitled "Pushkin and Gannibal," in *Encounter* (London), XIX: 3 (September 1962). Appendix Two, my notes on prosody, was privately issued as an offprint by Bollingen Foundation in spring 1963.

I have always envied the writer who ends this kind of foreword with a glowing tribute to Professor Advice, Professor Encouragement, and Professor Every-Assistance. The extension of my own thanks is more limited, but their temperature just as high. I owe them to my wife, who suggested many improvements, and to my son, who made a preliminary index. For undertaking the publication of this work, I am grateful to the officers and staff of Bollingen Foundation and, in particular, for their choice of Mr. Bart Winer as copyeditor, to whom I am indebted for a meticulous and brilliant job.

Montreux, 1963   VLADIMIR NABOKOV

"*EO*" Revisited

The entire translation published in 1964, i.e., the basic text and all the variants and quotations in the Commentary (as well as a few notes therein, e.g., Two : XLI, Four : VII, Four : XLI, XLII, Five : II, Seven : XLVI, etc.) have now been revised. In correcting the verse, I set myself a double task: in the first place, to achieve a closer line-by-line fit (entailing a rigorous coincidence of enjambments and the elimination of verse transposal), and, in the second, to apply throughout, without a trace of halfheartedness or compromise, my method of "signal words" as represented in the Correlative Lexicon (to which see note). Otherwise, the 1964 translation remains intact and basically unassailable.

In an era of inept and ignorant imitations, whose piped-in background music has hypnotized innocent readers into fearing literality's salutary jolts, some reviewers were upset by the humble fidelity of my version; the present improvements will exasperate them even more. A detailed "Reply to My Critics" that appeared in *Encounter* (February 1966) has been republished in *Nabokov's Congeries* (Viking Press, 1968). It is included in my *Strong Opinions* (McGraw-Hill, 1973).

Besides the agonizing oneginization and reorganiza-
tion of the line structure in the established texts and in
all additional material, several revisions have been
made in the Commentary: a few notes have been
deleted, a few added, and several entries have been
altered. I am indebted to the following readers who
corrected my errors in the 1964 edition: to Mr. John
Bayley (*The Observer*, Nov. 29, 1964) for emending the
title of Goethe's poem as given in my note Two : IX :
5–6; to Mr. Carl Proffer (*in litt.*) for supplying the right
reference in connection with the nickname "Red
Rover" in note Eight : XXVI : 5–11; to Mr. Thomas
Shaw (*The Russian Review*, April 1965) for establishing
the correct civil rank in note Eight : I : 1; to Mr. K. van
het Reve (*in litt.*) for straightening out my Latin in note
Six : XI : 12; and, last but not least, to Mr. Aleksandr
Gershenkron (*Modern Philology*, May 1966) for
rectifying, on Mr. D. Chizhevski's behalf, a wrong
cardinal point and a wrong date in note Two : XXXVII : 9.

V.N.

Montreux, January 1972

*Contents**

VOLUME I
(*Volume I of 1975 Edition*)

Translator's Introduction

Eugene Onegin

A Novel in Verse by Aleksandr Pushkin

* The pagination of the 1975 edition has been retained for this paperback edition.

Contents

VOLUME II

Commentary, Part 1

(*Volume 2 of 1975 Edition*)

Commentary, Part 2

(*Volume 3 of 1975 Edition*)

Contents

Index

(Volume 4 of 1975 Edition)

Method of Transliteration

Except when otherwise stated, I have followed in all my transcriptions of Russian texts the new spelling adopted in Russia after the Revolution. The reform did not affect, or at least was not supposed to affect, anything in the pronunciation. Its main object was to get rid of certain superfluous ornamental letters. Thus (to mention a few of the changes), it retained only one of the vowels, identically pronounced but differently spelled, corresponding to the English *e* in "yes"; abolished the so-called "hard sign" that used to follow all nonpalatalized consonants at the end of words; and substituted for the nonaccented *a* in the *ago* of genitive endings (pronounced like the *a* in the *ava* of *Cavalleria*) an *o*, which, being unaccented, is pronounced, or should be pronounced, exactly like the *a* it replaces. Below is a table of the transliterations used in the present work.

Russian Character	Transliterated	PRONOUNCED
А а	a	Like the Italian *a*. Resembles the *a* of "art" (never pronounced as in "man" or "male").
Б б	b	As in "Byron." Exceptions: medial *b* before a voiceless consonant and final *b* tending to *p*. Thus *próbka*, "cork," rhymes with *knópka*, "tack,"

Russian
Character   Transliterated   PRONOUNCED

		and *lob*, "forehead," rhymes with *pop*, "priest" (but *volshébno*, "magically," and *velikolépno*, "splendidly," do *not* rhyme).
В в	v	As in "Victoria." Exceptions: medial *v* before a voiceless consonant and final *v* tending to *f*. Thus *bulávka*, "pin," rhymes with "Kafka," and *nrav*, "temper," rhymes with *telegráf* (but *svoenrávnïy*, "capricious," and *telegráfnïy*, "telegraphic," do *not* rhyme).
Г г	g	As the hard *g* of "go" (never as in "gentle" and never mute before *n*). Exceptions: medial *g* before a voiceless consonant and, in a few words, final *g* tending to aspirated *h* as in *myágkiy*, "soft," and *bog*, "god." Otherwise, final *g* tends to *k*. Thus *rog*, "horn," rhymes with *urók*, "lesson." In terminations of adjectives and pronouns in the genitive singular, *g* is pronounced *v*. Thus *nemógo*, "of the mute," rhymes with *slóvo*, "word."
Д д	d	As in "Dante." Exceptions: medial *d* before a voiceless consonant and final *d* tending to *t*. Thus *vódka* rhymes with *glótka*, "throat," and *sled*, "trace," with *let*, "of years" (but *ládno*, "all right," does *not* rhyme with *besplátno*, "gratis").
Е е	e	As *ye* in "yellow."
Ё ё	yo	As *yo* in "yonder" (never as in "yoke").
Ж ж	zh	As *s* in "measure" or *z* in "azure" (never as in "zeal") and as the French *j* in "Jacques" or the second *g* in

Russian Character	Transliterated	PRONOUNCED
		"garage." Exceptions: medial *zh* before a voiceless consonant and final *zh* tending to *sh*. Thus *lózhka*, "spoon," rhymes with *kóshka*, "cat," and *krazh*, "of thefts," rhymes with *karandásh*, "pencil" (but *lózhnïy*, "false," does *not* rhyme with *roskóshnïy*, "luxurious").
З з	z	As in "zebra" (never as in "mezzo-soprano" or "azure"). Exceptions: medial *z* before a voiceless consonant and final *z* tending to *s*. Thus *skázka*, "fairy tale," rhymes with *láska*, "caress," and *glaz*, "eye," with *nas*, "us" (but *ráznïy*, "different," does *not* rhyme with *prekrásnïy*, "beautiful").
И и		As the first *e* in "scene" (never as *i* in "mine"), but as *ï* (see p. xxi) after the three letters *zh*, *ts*, and *sh*.*
Й й	-y	A semivowel existing only in diphthongs: thus *táyna*, "mystery," in which *ay* is like an English long *i* or, more exactly, the French *aille*; *ey*, "to her," which sounds like the end of a long-drawn English "away!" in the mist and the distance; very close to the French *eille*; *kiy*, "billiard cue," in which *iy* is like the French *ille* in *quille*;

*In Pushkin's time, and generally before the new orthography was introduced (in 1918), и, when preceding a vowel, was replaced by the identically pronounced i. There were also other differences: thus е was written as ѣ in a number of words (this letter, although pronounced exactly as *e*, I have transliterated by *ye* whenever the necessity to mention it arose, for the sake of differentiation), and words terminating in consonants had the useless "hard sign," ъ, affixed at the end. When medial, it acts as a medial ь (see further) and is marked thus, '.

Russian Character	Transliterated	PRONOUNCED

boy, "battle," in which *oy* sounds like the *oy* in the English "boy" (in which, however, the *o* has greater duration and the *y* is not so strident);

duy, "blow" (imperative), in which *uy* sounds like the French *ouille* as in *andouille*; and

-*iy*, the ending of adjectives (masc. sing.), which sounds like the French *œil*.

| К к | k | As in English, but never mute before *n*. |

Л л	l ⎫	
М м	m ⎬ As in English.
Н н	n ⎭	

| О о | o | Like the Italian *o*; close to the first *o* in "cosmos" when accented and close to the second *o* when not (never as in "go"). In Moscow speech the unaccented *o* (as, for example, in *Moskva*) is pronounced in a manner about as "ah"-like as the accented *o* in New York English ("jahb," "stahp"). In ordinary good Russian the unaccented *o* (as, for example, in *koróva*, "cow") is pronounced like the final *a*, which sounds like the ultima of "Eva." |

| П п | p | As in English, but never mute before *n* or *s*. |

| Р р | r | A clean, clear vibration that is closer to the Italian than to the English (never amplifying the preceding vowel as it does sometimes in English). When burred (by old-fashioned Peterburgians), it is undistinguishable from a French *r* and then very annoying to the Moscow ear. |

Russian Character	Transliterated	PRONOUNCED
С с	s	Like the first *c* in "cicada" (never like the second).
Т т	t	As in "Tom" (but never as in "ritual" or "nation").
У у	u	As *oo* in "boom." Similar to the French *ou* (never as the *u* of "buff" or of "flute").
Ф ф	f	As in English.
Х х	h or kh	Close to *ch* in the German *ach* or the Scottish "loch." There is no *k* sound about it, as the usual *kh* transliteration unfortunately suggests to the English eye. I have used *kh* only in one or two cases when *s* precedes it (for example, *skhodíl*, "descended"), to avoid confusion with *sh*.
Ц ц	ts	As *ts* in "tsetse" or the German *z* in *Zermatt*. It should be observed, however, that in many words such as *otsyúda*, "from here," in which *ot* is a prefix, *kázhetsya*, "it seems," in which *sya* is the suffix, and *détskiy*, "childish," in which *skiy* is the suffix, the transcription *ts* corresponds to these two separate letters in Russian.
Ч ч	ch	As in English.
Ш ш	sh	As in English.
Щ щ	shch	A fusion of sibilants that can be imitated in English by such combinations as "fish chowder," "cash check," "hush child," "plush chair," and so forth.
Ы ы	ï	A medial or final nonpalatal vowel pronounced as a very blunt, short *i* by trying to say *ee* while keeping the tensed tongue back so as not to touch

Russian Character	Transliterated	PRONOUNCED
		the inner side of the lower teeth, as it would do in a palatal vowel. The result is a kind of cross between a dull short *i* and a grunt. (The character chosen to represent this difficult letter should not be mistaken for the sharp French *ï* bearing the same diacritical sign, as in *naïf*.)
Э э	e	As in "Edinburgh." Apart from foreign words and geographical names, it is found only in *étot*, "this," and its derivations and in a few interjections such as *e*, *ey*, *eh*, and so forth.
Ю ю	yu	As *u* in "use" but of less duration.
Я я	ya	As in the German *ya*.
Ь ь	'	A palatal sign modifying (softening) the preceding consonant, so that *t'* sounds somewhat like *ts*, *d'* like *tz*, and so on. A usual termination of infinitives (*govorít'*, "to speak"; *pet'*, "to sing"; *pisát'*, "to write"). When placed after a medial letter it indicates not only palatization but also a very slight pause. Thus the *n'e* of *pen'e* is like the *niè* of the French *dernièrement*. Consequently *Il'yá*, "Elijah," sounds very like the French *il y a* pronounced rapidly.

Although rigid consistency would require that in transliteration all Russian names ending in ий should end in *iy* (such as surnames—e.g., Vyazemskiy—and first names—e.g., Grigoriy—as well as the names of avenues, lanes, and boulevards, all of which are masculine in Russian), I have had to make certain concessions to accepted spellings as given in works of reference.

All surnames lose the *y* after the *i* in transliteration (e.g., Vyazemski). All first names retain the *y* (e.g.,

Grigoriy), except in the case of one or two Russian names that have lost it in English usage (e.g., Dmitri instead of Dmitriy). The same goes for the names of boulevards, avenues, and lanes, except in the case of the Nevski, or Nevski Avenue (instead of Nevskiy). The word "street," *ulitsa*, is feminine in Russian, and the feminine ending of the adjective to it is completely transliterated in English (e.g., Morskaya Street). All names ending in oй (Shahovskoy, Bolshoy) retain the *y* in transliteration.

Except for the surnames of female performers, such as dancers, singers, actresses, and so on, which traditionally retain these feminine endings (Istomina, Pavlova), all feminine surnames, although ending in *a* in Russian, take a masculine ending in transliteration (Anna Sidorov, Anna Karenin, Princess Vyazemski).

I omit the soft sign in Russian names (Bolshoy instead of Bol'shoy, Olga instead of Ol'ga, Gogol instead of Gogol'), unless such names appear in lines of Russian or in other phrases that require exact transliteration in my Commentary.

Not a few Russians have German surnames, and there occur borderline cases in which a transliteration is preferred to the German original. But, generally speaking, I use the simple German spelling of such names whenever this does not clash with tradition (thus, Küchelbecker instead of Kyuhel'beker).

No accents are used in Russian, but I use them to indicate the correct stress whenever it might help the reader in scanning a verse.

In capitalizing the first word of each line when quoting verse, given that it is capitalized in the original, I have adhered to the following principles: it is capitalized in translations when the lines render exactly the form of the original, including rhymes and rhyme pattern; it is also capitalized in lines that are metrically faithful translations of blank verse or rhymeless dactylic hexameters.

Calendar

The Julian calendar (Old Style), introduced by Julius Caesar in 46 B.C. and adopted by the First Council of Nicaea in A.D. 325, was used in Russia up to the Revolution of 1917. The Gregorian calendar (New Style), now in general use, was introduced by Pope Gregory XIII in 1582. The date October 5, 1582, was called October 15, 1582; thus ten days were dropped. In Great Britain, however, the Old Style lasted till 1752, when, in September, eleven days were dropped.

The years 1700 and 1800 were not leap years by the Gregorian rules (whereas 1600, being divisible by 400, was); therefore, the difference between the two calendars was increased in each of those years by one day, bringing it to eleven days from 1700 to 1800, twelve from 1800 to 1900, and thirteen from 1900 to 1917. Thus the middle of July in Russia would be the end of July elsewhere, while January 12, 1799, and January 13, 1800, in the world at large would both be New Year's Day in Russia.

In the present work all dates pertaining to events in Russia are Old Style unless stated otherwise. Dates pertaining to events in the rest of the world are New Style. When there exists a possibility of confusion, both styles are given thus: 1/13 January.

Acad 1937   A. S. Pushkin. *Polnoe sobranie sochineniy* (Complete Collected Works), vol. VI, ed. B. Tomashevski. Akademiya nauk SSSR (U.S.S.R. Academy of Sciences), Leningrad, 1937. (The so-called "akademicheskoe izdanie," or academic edition.)

Acad 1938   A. S. Pushkin. *Polnoe sobranie sochineniy* (Complete Collected Works), vol. XIII, ed. M. A. Tsyavlovski. Akademiya nauk SSSR (U.S.S.R. Academy of Sciences), Leningrad, 1938. (The so-called "akademicheskoe izdanie," or academic edition.)

Acad 1948   A. S. Pushkin. *Polnoe sobranie sochineniy* (Complete Collected Works), vol. V, ed. S. M. Bondi. Akademiya nauk SSSR (U.S.S.R. Academy of Sciences), Moscow and Leningrad, 1948. (The so-called "akademicheskoe izdanie," or academic edition.)

EO   *Eugene Onegin.*

Lit. nasl.   *Literaturnoe nasledstvo* (Literary Heritage), nos. 16–18. Moscow, 1934.

MA   Moscow Central Archives.

MB   Lenin Public Library, Moscow.

PB   St. Petersburg, later Leningrad, Public Library.

PD   Pushkinskiy Dom (Pushkin House), Leningrad.

P. i ego sovr.   *Pushkin i ego sovremenniki* (Pushkin and His Contemporaries), nos. 1–39. St. Petersburg, 1903–30.

Vremennik   *Vremennik Pushkinskoy komissii* (Annals of the Pushkin Commission), vols. I–VI. Moscow, 1936–41.

Works 1936   A. S. Pushkin. *Polnoe sobranie sochineniy* (Complete Collected Works), ed. Yu. G. Oksman, M. A. Tsyavlovski, and G. O. Vinokur. Akademiya nauk SSSR (U.S.S.R. Academy of Sciences), Moscow and Leningrad, 1936. 6 vols.

Works 1949   A. S. Pushkin. *Polnoe sobranie sochineniy* (Complete Collected Works), vol. V, ed. B. Tomashevski. Akademiya nauk SSSR (U.S.S.R. Academy of Sciences), Moscow and Leningrad, 1949.

Works 1957   A. S. Pushkin. *Polnoe sobranie sochineniy* (Complete Collected Works), vol. V, ed. B. Tomashevski. Akademiya nauk SSSR (U.S.S.R. Academy of Sciences), Moscow, 1957.

Works 1960   A. S. Pushkin. *Sobranie sochineniy* (Collected Works), vol. IV, ed. D. D. Blagoy. Gosudartsvennoe izdatel'stvo hudozhestvennoy literaturï (State publishers of belles-letters), Moscow, 1960.

[ ]   Translator's interpolations.

⟨ ⟩   Canceled readings.

> . . . *Il' k·devstvennïm lesam*
> *Mladoy Ameriki . . .*
> . . . Or to the virgin woods
> Of young America . . .
>
> PUSHKIN, from a rough draft of *Autumn*
> (1830–33)

Nowadays—an unheard-of case!—the foremost French writer is translating Milton word for word and proclaiming that an interlinear translation would be the summit of his art, had such been possible.

> PUSHKIN, from an article (late 1836 or early 1837) on Chateaubriand's translation *Le Paradis perdu*, Paris, 1836

Description of the Text

In its final form (1837 edn.) Pushkin's novel in verse (*Evgeniy Onegin, roman v stihah*) consists of 5541 lines, all of which, except a set of eighteen, are in iambic tetrameter, with feminine and masculine rhymes. The 5523 iambic lines (only three of which are incomplete) break up into the following groups:

	Lines
(1) Prefatory Piece, rhymed ababececediidofof	17
(2) Eight Cantos (termed "chapters," *glavï*), the basic component of which is a fourteen-line stanza rhymed ababeecciddiff:	
One: 54 stanzas numbered I–LX (IX, XIII, XIV, and XXXIX–XLI missing)	756
Two: 40 stanzas numbered I–XL (VIII : 10–14 and XXXV : 5–11 missing)	548
Three: 41 stanzas numbered I–XLI (III : 9–14 missing), with	568
"Tatiana's Letter to Onegin," freely rhymed, between XXXI and XXXII*	79
Four: 43 stanzas numbered I–LI (I–VI, XXXVI, XXXVII : 13 [in part]–14, and XXXVIII missing)	601
Five: 42 stanzas numbered I–XLV (XXXVII, XXXVIII, and XLIII missing)	588

*See below for "The Song of the Girls" between XXXIX and XL.

Thus, in all there are 5523 iambic tetrameters. To this should be added:

(*a*) A master motto in French prose (composed by the author but presented as "tiré d'une lettre particulière").

(*b*) A song consisting of eighteen lines, in trochaic trimeter with long terminals, "The Song of the Girls" (in Three, between XXXIX and XL).

(*c*) A set of forty-four authorial notes.

(*d*) An appendix with some comments in prose on the fragments of *Onegin's Journey*.

Moreover, there are the following chapter mottoes: Chapter One, a line from Vyazemski; Two, a venerable pun, slightly improved (*O rus!* Horace; *O Rus'!*); Three, a line from Malfilâtre; Four, a sentence from Mme de Staël; Five, two lines from Zhukovski; Six, two (not adjacent but printed as such) lines from Petrarch; Seven, two lines from Dmitriev, one from Baratïnski, and two from Griboedov; Eight, two lines from Byron.

Most of the dropped stanzas are found in early editions or in MS. In some cases their omission may be regarded as a deliberate structural gap. A large mass of *EO* material rejected by Pushkin comprises dropped stanzas, variant stanzas, expunged continuations, samples from "Onegin's Album," stanzas referring to *Onegin's Journey* (the latter expanded into a chapter that was to come after Seven, thus turning the established Eight into a ninth chapter), fragments referring to a tenth chapter, and numerous canceled lines found in drafts and fair copies. I have translated in my notes all the most important and interesting rejections as given in various publications, but I am fully aware that no adequate study of original texts can be accomplished before *all* Pushkin's MSS preserved in Russia are photographed and made available to scholars, and this, of course, a cagey police state cannot be expected to do without some political reason—and I can see none yet.

For the basic text I have relied as completely as possible (that is, with the correction of obvious misprints, the worst of which are pointed out in my notes) on the last edition published in Pushkin's lifetime. This "third" edition, now exceedingly rare, was printed under the supervision of Ilya Glazunov, bookseller, and brought out in January, 1837—certainly before January 19, when it was advertised for sale in the *St. Petersburg Gazette* (supp. 14, p. 114). This miniature volume (32mo) was praised in the "New Books" section of the literary review *The Northern Bee* (*Severnaya pchela*, no. 16, pp. 61–63), on January 21, for its pretty pocket format.

The fifth page of this edition reads:

Evgeniy
Onegin
roman v stihah.
Sochinenie
Aleksandra Pushkina.
Izdanie tretie.

5

Sanktpeterburg.
V tipografïi Ekspeditsïi zagotovleniya Gosudarstvennïh bumag.

(*EO*, a novel in verse. The work of Aleksandr Pushkin. Third edition. St. Petersburg. In the printing shop of the Office of Purveyance of State Papers.)

The sixth page bears the master motto ("Pétri de vanité," etc.), the seventh, the beginning (ll. 1–12) of the Prefatory Piece, and the eighth, its end (13–17).

The numbered pages contain eight chapters, headed by mottoes (One, pp. 1–40; Two, pp. 41–69; Three, pp. 71–105; Four, pp. 107–38; Five, pp. 139–69; Six, pp. 171–202; Seven, pp. 203–40; Eight, pp. 241–80); Pushkin's "Notes," pp. 281–93; and "Fragments of *Onegin's Journey*" with some comments, pp. 295–310.

After this come two blank pages and the cover, with the modest line, *Izdanie Glazunova*, "Published by Glazunov."

For further details on this edition see "The Publication of *EO*," item 24.

The novel is mainly concerned with the emotions, meditations, acts, and destinies of three men: Onegin, the bored fop; Lenski, the minor elegiast; and a stylized Pushkin, Onegin's friend. There are three heroines: Tatiana, Olga, and Pushkin's Muse. Its events are placed between the end of 1819, in St. Petersburg (Chapter One), and the spring of 1825, in St. Petersburg again (Chapter Eight). The scene shifts from the capital to the countryside, midway between Opochka and Moscow (Chapter Two to the beginning of Seven), and thence to Moscow (end of Seven). The appended passages from *Onegin's Journey* (which were to be placed between Chapters Seven and Eight) take us to Moscow, Novgorod, the Volga region, the Caucasus, the Crimea, and Odessa.

The themes and structural devices of Eight echo those of One. Each chapter has at least one peacock spot: a

young rake's day in One (xv–xxxvi), the doomed young
poet in Two (vi–xxxviii), Tatiana's passion for Onegin in
Three, rural and literary matters in Four, a fatidic night-
mare and a name-day party in Five, a duel in Six, a
journey to Moscow in Seven, and Onegin's passion for
Tatiana in Eight. Throughout there is a variety of roman-
tic, satirical, biographical, and bibliographical digressions
that lend the poem wonderful depth and color. In my
notes I have drawn the reader's attention to the marvel-
ous way Pushkin handles certain thematic items and
rhythms such as the "overtaking-and-hanging-back" de-
vice (One), interstrophic enjambments (Tatiana's flight
into the park and Onegin's ride to Princess N.'s house),
and the little leitmotiv of a certain phrase running
through the entire novel. Unless these and other mecha-
nisms and every other detail of the text are consciously
assimilated, *EO* cannot be said to exist in the reader's
mind.

Pushkin's composition is first of all and above all a
phenomenon of style, and it is from this flowered rim
that I have surveyed its sweep of Arcadian country, the
serpentine gleam of its imported brooks, the miniature
blizzards imprisoned in round crystal, and the many-
hued levels of literary parody blending in the melting
distance. It is not "a picture of Russian life"; it is at
best the picture of a little group of Russians, in the sec-
ond decade of the last century, crossed with all the more
obvious characters of western European romance and
placed in a stylized Russia, which would disintegrate at
once if the French props were removed and if the French
impersonators of English and German writers stopped
prompting the Russian-speaking heroes and heroines.
The paradoxical part, from a translator's point of view,
is that the only Russian element of importance is this
speech, Pushkin's language, undulating and flashing
through verse melodies the likes of which had never

been known before in Russia. The best I could do was to describe in some of my comments special samples of the original text. It is hoped that my readers will be moved to learn Pushkin's language and go through *EO* again without this crib. In art as in science there is no delight without the detail, and it is on details that I have tried to fix the reader's attention. Let me repeat that unless these are thoroughly understood and remembered, all "general ideas" (so easily acquired, so profitably resold) must necessarily remain but worn passports allowing their bearers short cuts from one area of ignorance to another.

The "Eugene Onegin" Stanza

Here are two samples I have written after the meter and rhyme sequence of the *EO* stanza. They first appeared (with a different last line) in *The New Yorker* for Jan. 8 1955.

What is translation? On a platter
A poet's pale and glaring head,
A parrot's screech, a monkey's chatter,
And profanation of the dead.
The parasites you were so hard on
Are pardoned if I have your pardon,
O Pushkin, for my stratagem.
I traveled down your secret stem,
And reached the root, and fed upon it;
Then, in a language newly learned,
I grew another stalk and turned
Your stanza, patterned on a sonnet,
Into my honest roadside prose—
All thorn, but cousin to your rose.

Reflected words can only shiver
Like elongated lights that twist
In the black mirror of a river
Between the city and the mist.
Elusive Pushkin! Persevering,
I still pick up your damsel's earring,
Still travel with your sullen rake;

I find another man's mistake;
I analyze alliterations
That grace your feasts and haunt the great
Fourth stanza of your Canto Eight.
This is my task: a poet's patience
And scholiastic passion blent—
Dove-droppings on your monument.

The *EO* stanza, as a distinct form, is Pushkin's invention (May 9, 1823). It contains 118 syllables and consists of fourteen lines, in iambic tetrameter, with a regular scheme of feminine and masculine rhymes: ababeecciddiff. The abab part and the ff part are usually very conspicuous in the meaning, melody, and intonation of any given stanza. This opening pattern (a clean-cut sonorous elegiac quatrain) and the terminal one (a couplet resembling the code of an octave or that of a Shakespearean sonnet) can be compared to patterns on a painted ball or top that are visible at the beginning and at the end of the spin. The main spinning process involves eecciddi, where a fluent and variable phrasing blurs the contours of the lines so that they are seldom seen as clearly consisting of two couplets and a closed quatrain. The iddiff part is more or less distinctly seen as consisting of two tercets in only one third of the entire number of stanzas in the eight cantos, but even in these cases the closing couplet often stands out so prominently as to cause the Italian form to intergrade with the English one.

The sequence itself, ababeecciddiff, as a chance combination of rhymes, crops up here and there in the course of the rambling, unstanzaed, freely rhymed verse that French poets used for frivolous narrative and badinage in the seventeenth and eighteenth centuries. Among them by far the greatest was La Fontaine, and it is to him that we must go for Pushkin's unconscious source. In La Fontaine's rhymed *Contes* (pt. III, Paris, 1671), poems of the licentious fable type, I have found two passages—and no doubt there are more—where

among the rills and rillets of arbitrarily arranged rhymes
the ababeecciddiff sequence chances to be formed, much
as those mutations that evolution pounces upon to create
an insular or alpine species. One such sequence occurs
in the pentapodic *La Courtisane amoureuse*, ll. 3–16
(*miracles, Catons, oracles, moutons, même, Polyphème,
assis, soucis, joliette, eau, fuseau, fillette, un, commun*),
the other is represented in the tetrapodic ll. 48–61 of
Nicaise, a slightly salacious piece of 258 lines. The open-
ing "Que" refers to "trésors" in l. 47—these being
masculine good looks and youth:

> Que ne méprise aucune dame,
> Tant soit son esprit précieux.
> Pour une qu'Amour prend par l'âme,
> Il en prend mille par les yeux.
> Celle-ci donc, des plus galantes,
> Par mille choses engageantes,
> Tâchait d'encourager le gars,
> N'était chiche de ses regards,
> Le pinçait, lui venait sourire,
> Sur les yeux lui mettait la main,
> Sur le pied lui marchait enfin.
> A ce langage il ne sut dire
> Autre chose que des soupirs,
> Interprètes de ses désirs.

To a Russian ear the last two lines are fascinatingly like
Pushkin's clausules.

La Fontaine's free alternations had a tremendous
impact on Russian techniques; and long before the
sporadic ababeecciddiff sequence became fixed as a
species in the *EO* stanza Russian versificators, when fol-
lowing their French masters, would now and then, in the
process of literary mimicry, evolve that particular pat-
tern. An irregularly rhymed poem in iambic tetrameter,
Ermak, composed in 1794 by Ivan Dmitriev (whom his
good-natured friend, the historian Karamzin, extrava-
gantly called the *russkiy Lafonten*), is a case in point. In

this Siberian eclogue we find the sequence ababeecciddiff at least twice: ll. 65–78 (the beginning of the Ancient's sixth speech in his dialogue with the Young One) and ll. 93–106 (part of the Ancient's seventh speech). Twenty-five years later (1818–20) Pushkin used the same sequence in his very Gallic, freely rhymed tetrametric fairy tale, *Ruslan and Lyudmila* (e.g., Canto Three, ll. 415–28), finished in 1820, three years before *EO* was begun.

In choosing this particular pattern and meter for his *EO* stanza Pushkin may have been toying with the idea of constructing a kind of sonnet. The stanza, indeed, may be regarded as (1) an octet consisting of two quatrains (abab and eecc) and a sestet consisting of two tercets (idd and iff), or (2) three quatrains (abab eecc iddi) and a couplet (ff). French tetrapodic sonnets and English tetrametric ones were, of course, common beginning with the end of the sixteenth century; the form has been termed the Anacreontic sonnet. It was parodied by Molière in *Le Misanthrope* (1667; act I, sc. ii); Shakespeare handled it once (Sonnet CXLV), and Charles Cotton a number of times. The French rhyme scheme might go, for instance: abba ecce ddi fif (Malherbe's *A Rabel, Peintre, sur un livre de fleurs*, 1630, referring to MS illustrations of flowers made by Daniel Rabel in 1624); the English one: bcbc dfdf ggh jjh (Cotton's "What have I left to doe but dye," pub. 1689).

Shakespeare's tetrametric rarity has the sequence: bcbc dfdf ghgh jj; make–hate–sake–state, come–sweet–doom–greet, end–day–fiend–away, threw–you.

In the *EO* stanza the only departure from an Anacreontic sonnet is the arrangement of rhymes (eecc) in the second quatrain, but this departure is a fatal one. One shift back from eecc to ecec would have the *EO* stanza remain within the specific limits of the Anacreontic sonnet. Actually, ll. 5–8 of the *EO* stanza are not a quatrain at all, but merely two couplets (of which the masculine one, 7–8, is sometimes a discrete element, similar in intonation to 13–14). The intrusion of these two adjacent couplets and the completely arbitrary interplay of phrase and pause within the eecciddi part of the *EO* stanza combine to make it sound quite different from the most freakish tetrametric sonnet, even if, as in a number of cases, the cut is that of a sonnet (e.g., three quatrains and couplet, as in st. II and eight others in Chapter One; octet and two tercets, as in One : VI; two quatrains and two tercets, as in One : XVI, a rare case); or if, as in one striking case, the rhymes of the octet are limited to two, as in the Petrarchan typical subspecies of the sonnet (see Four : XXXI: *pishet–molodóy–díshet–ostrotóy*, *uslíshit–pishet–zhivóy–rekóy*, *vdohnovénnïy–svoegó–kogó–dragotsénnïy–tebé–sud'bé*; see also Commentary).

A device introducing a good deal of variation is the enjambment, which can be intrastrophic or interstrophic. In the first case, we find an extreme example in which the usually autonomic first quatrain is unexpectedly and brilliantly run into the second, with the phrase sometimes stopping abruptly in the middle of l. 5 (e.g., Five : I, XXI; Six : III; Seven : XV). In the second case, the whole stanza is run into the next one, and the phrase is pulled up short in the very first line (see Three : XXXVIII–XXXIX, and Eight : XXXIX–XL).

On the other hand, we find certain stanzas in which our poet takes advantage of the couplet intonation to make a mechanical point, or he overdoes the tabulatory device by listing emotional formulas, or cataloguing objects, in monotonous sequences of three-word verses. This is a drawback characteristic of the aphoristic style that was Pushkin's intrinsic concession to the eighteenth century and its elegant rationalities.

The only approach to the *EO* rhyme scheme that I can

think of in English poetry is the sequence in the first fourteen lines of the stanza of eighteen unequal lines in which Wordsworth wrote the *Ode to Lycoris* (three stanzas) of May, 1817. The rhymes go: bcbcddffghhg-iijjkk. Here are the first fourteen lines of the middle stanza:

> In youth we love the darksome lawn
> Brushed by the owlet's wing;
> Then, Twilight is preferred to Dawn,
> And Autumn to the Spring.
> Sad fancies do we then affect,
> In luxury of disrespect
> To our own prodigal excess
> Of too familiar happiness.
> Lycoris (if such name befit
> Thee, thee my life's celestial sign!)
> When Nature marks the year's decline,
> Be ours to welcome it;
> Pleased with the harvest hope that runs
> Before the path of milder suns . . .

The Structure of *"Eugene Onegin"*

When, in May, 1823, Pushkin began *EO*, he probably had some idea of the kind of picture that the rural frame of Chapter Two might provide; a dim heroine no doubt haunted the avenues of his thought; but we have reason to assume that he reached the middle of Chapter Two before that dim figure split into two distinct sisters, Olga and Tatiana. The rest of the novel was a mere cloud. Chapters and parts of chapters were planned one way and came out another. But when we say "structure" we are not thinking of the workshop. Rough drafts, false scents, half-explored trails, dead ends of inspiration, are of little intrinsic importance. An artist should ruthlessly destroy his manuscripts after publication, lest they mislead academic mediocrities into thinking that it is possible to unravel the mysteries of genius by studying canceled readings. In art, purpose and plan are nothing; only the result counts. We are concerned only with the structure of a published work, for which the author is alone responsible insofar as it was published within his lifetime. Last-minute alterations or those forced by circumstances—no matter what motives affected him—should stand if he let them stand. Even obvious misprints should be treated gingerly; after all, they may be supposed to have been left uncorrected by the author. Why and wherefore he did this or that is beside the point. We can invoke a change of plan, or an absence of plan, and—instead—the teleological intuition of genius; but these are matters of a metaphysical order. It is, let me repeat, the structure of the end product, and of the end product only, that has meaning for the student—or at least this student—confronted with a master artist's work.

The structure of *EO* is original, intricate, and marvelously harmonious, despite the fact that Russian literature stood in 1823 at a comparatively primitive level of development, marked by uncontrollable and perfectly pardonable leanings toward the most hackneyed devices of Western literary art still in use by its most prominent exponents. I have already discussed the basic brick of its structure, the stanza especially invented for *EO*, and shall return to it in my Commentary. Intrastrophic and interstrophic enjambments are often functional enough in *EO* to merit a place in our catalogue of structural items. But it is in the distribution of the subject matter, the balance of parts, the switches and swerves of the narrative, the introduction of characters, the digressions, the transitions, and so forth that the technique of our artist is fully revealed.

EO, as published in its final form by Pushkin, is a model of unity (despite certain structural flaws *within* this or that chapter, e.g., in Four). Its eight chapters form an elegant colonnade. The first and the last are linked up by a system of subthemes responding to each other in a pleasing interplay of built-in echoes. The St. Petersburg of Chapter One is antiphonally doubled by the St. Petersburg of Chapter Eight (minus the ballet and the good cheer, plus a melancholy love and a faro deal of motley memories). The Moscow theme, richly adumbrated in Chapter Two, is developed in Chapter Seven

The entire set of chapters is felt to consist of two parts, with four chapters in each, these parts consisting of 2552 and 2676 iambic tetrameters respectively (the actual center is Five : v : 6–7, "mysteriously all objects foretold her something"). Onegin's speech to Tatiana in the last chapter of the first batch is answered by Tatiana's speech to him in the last chapter of the second batch. The bloom–doom, heart–dart Lenskian theme is commenced and concluded, respectively, in the second chapters of both batches, and there are other symmetrical combinations of a less striking, though not less artistic, kind. For example, the lyrical letter of Tatiana to Onegin in Chapter Three not only is answered in Chapter Eight by Onegin's letter, but finds its subtle counterpart in Lenski's elegy to Olga in Chapter Six. Olga's voice is heard only three times, every time in brief interrogation (Five : XXI : 12–14; Six : XIV : 1; Six : XIX : 13).

This "classical" regularity of proportions is beautifully relieved by the "romantic" device of prolonging or replaying a structural theme in the chapter following the one introducing it. This device is used for the theme of The Countryside in One and Two; for the theme of Romances in Two and Three; for the theme of The Meeting in the Avenue in Three and Four; for the theme of Winter in Four and Five; for the theme of The Name Day in Five and Six; for the theme of The Poet's Grave in Six and Seven; and for the theme of The Social Whirl in Seven and Eight, which clinches the circle, since this last theme reoccurs (for the rereader) in One. It will be noted that these dovetailings and overlappings repeat, in terms of chapters, the device of enjambment from stanza to stanza, which in its turn repeats, in terms of strophes, the functional and ornamental run-ons from verse to verse.

Turning to structural devices within the chapters, we should examine first of all Pushkin's handling of transition; i.e., the complex of devices a writer uses for switching from one subject to another. When examining the transitions in the structure of a work, and in passing esthetic and historical judgment upon them, we must distinguish, of course, between the what and the how, between the kind of transition chosen for this or that purpose by the artist and the way it is applied by him. In the study of transition a clear perception of matter and manner leads to an appreciation of one of the most important elements of a story in verse or prose.

Roughly, there are two main types of transition, the narrational, or natural, and the authorial, or rhetorical. No rigid distinction is possible. The extreme type of rhetorical is the abrupt apostrophization by the author, and the most natural transition is a logical flow of thought from one thing to a related thing. Both types are used by Pushkin, and both had been used before him, from the day of the most ancient romances to the era of Byron. I purposely select a poet rather than a prose novelist because the fact that a novel is written in verse affects the manner of the transitions in it, even though the cantos are called chapters. Thus the rhetorical type (e.g., "Let us return to our hero," "Allow me now, reader,") is emphasized by its being transposed from prose to verse and in the process may acquire a tinge of parody; or, conversely, the new medium, evocative music, may restore the freshness of the ancient term; and the natural narrative forms of transition in verse often seem more delicate and even more "natural" than in prose.

The simplest transitions are from the general to the particular or vice versa: they are transitions from a general statement to a specific instance (often brought in by means of a "but") or from a specific case to a didactic generalization (often brought in by means of a "thus"). A favorite formula is the temporal transition, which introduces a new subject with the phrase "meanwhile" or "time passed." If we replace the notions story, character, landscape, recollection, and didactic digression by the letters S, C, L, R, and D, then we can define all types of transition as more or less distinctly expressed switchings from S to C, from C to S, from S to L, from S to R, from S to D, from C to D, and so forth, in all possible combinations and successions, with inner or outer doors and natural or artificial bridges providing passages from one theme to another.

The term digression is inevitable, I suppose; and Pushkin himself employs the term (*otstuplenie*), and does so in a more or less disparaging sense (Five : XL : 14). Actually, digression is only one form of authorial participation. This digressive participation may be a brief intrusion hardly distinguishable from a conventional rhetorical transition ("Let me now turn"), or, at the other extreme, it may be an elaborate functional treatment of "I" as a character in the novel, a stylized first person enjoying all the rights of expression and confession that the third-person characters have. Stylized Pushkin conversing with imagined Onegin and sharing recollections with him, or Pushkin's stylized Muse quietly admiring a St. Petersburg rout to which the poet escorts her—while Prince N. escorts thither his wife—are as much part of the plot as Onegin and Tatiana are. When we break Pushkin's Participation into its various components we find: autobiographical matters (more exactly, stylized autobiographizations) that can be classified under such headings as musings, lyrical, amorous, nostalgic; matter-of-fact remarks on the author's mode of life at the time of writing or at former times; melancholy or jocose allusions to real circumstances and real people; promises or memories of fictional events; and assumed friendships with invented characters. Autobiographizations merge and mingle with professional matters, which include remarks on the author's actual work of composing, on his characters as characters, on his other products, past, present, or anticipated, on his habits of writing, on the writings of others, and so forth. Finally, a form of participation is presented by "philosophizings," which are more or less didactic, serious, semiserious, or facetious asides, sometimes in the form of parenthetical remarks, often in that of brief aphoristic formulas. Pushkin was a brilliant wit (especially so in his correspondence); but he did not shine in the didactic genre, and his indebtedness to the elegant generalities of his time, or more exactly of a period just previous to his time, is sometimes painfully evident in the rather trivial observations of the Social Whirl, Women, Custom, and Mortality that occur throughout *EO*.

Let us now examine the chapters one by one.

CHAPTER ONE

Chapter One consists of fifty-four stanzas: I–VIII, X–XII, XV–XXXVIII, and XLII–LX (the gaps denote dropped stanzas, of which XXXIX–XLI are not known to have ever existed). The main characters are "I" (a more or less stylized Pushkin) and Eugene Onegin. The focal point of the chapter, its bright, rapid hub, is represented by twelve stanzas (XV–XVII, XXI–XXV, XXVII–XXVIII, XXXV–XXXVI), sixteen hours in the town life of Onegin, a twenty-four-year-old dandy. The historical time is the winter of 1819, and the place, St. Petersburg, capital of Russia. It is Onegin's eighth year of fashionable life; he is still fond of foppish dress and rich food, but is getting bored with the theater and has already abandoned ardent love-making. This Day of a Dandy is interrupted at three points (XVIII–XX, XXVI, XXIX–XXXIV) by Pushkin's recollections and reflections and is inserted between an account of Onegin's education and a description of his spleen. The former is preceded by a glimpse of Onegin's posting to his uncle's countryseat (in May, 1820), and the latter is followed by an account of the friendship between Onegin and Pushkin and of Onegin's arrival in the country—to find his uncle dead. The chapter ends with another set of "Pushkin" stanzas (LV–LX).

Development of Themes in One

I: Onegin's mental monologue while on his way from St. Petersburg to his uncle's estate.

II: A conventional transition, "Thus a young scapegrace thought." Pushkin introduces his hero (this "informal" introduction will be supplemented much later by a kind of "formal" one, the parody of a belated preamble in the last stanza of Chapter Seven). St. II also contains some professional matter—namely, an allusion to *Ruslan and Lyudmila* (1820)—and the formula "The hero of my novel" (this formula will be repeated, with a slight change, in Five : XVII : 12, where Tatiana sees with emotion "the hero of our novel" presiding at the feast of ghouls in her dream). The autobiographical strain is represented in II : 13–14 by a jocose allusion to the author's own banishment from the capital.

III–VII: This description of Eugene's childhood and youth is permeated by the theme of desultory education and forms a more or less continuous flow. A philosophizing note can be distinguished in the various facetious references to Onegin's upbringing (V : 1–4, "All of us"; IV : 13, "what would you more?" VI : 2, "to tell you the truth"), and a professional intrusion comes in the quatrain of VII, where "we" could never make Onegin master the mysteries of prosody. The theme of Onegin's indifference to poetry will be taken up again in the sestet of Two : XVI (when Lenski reads Ossian to Onegin), and Onegin will almost understand at last "the mechanism of Russian verses" in Eight : XXXVIII : 5–8. The picture of Onegin's youth is that of a Frenchified Russian dressed like an English fop, who at sixteen or seventeen is out in the world. He is a drawing-room automaton. The brilliancy of his epigrams is noted, but none are quoted in this chapter, and later samples of his wit do not live up to its description.

VIII, X–XII: A rhetorical transition from the mental to the sentimental part of Onegin's general education is represented by the "but" of VIII : 5. The "art of soft passion" in 9 leads to Ovid, and there is an obvious autobiographical allusion in the parenthetical digression on his exile in Moldavia with which VIII closes. Pushkin cut down to three stanzas (X–XII) his final account of Onegin's philanderings.

XV–XXXVI: This is the centerpiece of the chapter, an account (interrupted by digressions) of one day in Onegin's life in St. Petersburg. The absence of any technically distinct transition between the account of Onegin's way with women and the beginning of his day in XV is curiously compensated for by the artificial pause owing to the cancellation of the two stanzas between XII and XV. This brings into proper narrational relief the "Time and again" or "It happened" (*Bïvalo*) formula introducing the story of Onegin's day.

XV–XVII: There is an uninterrupted flow of themes here (XV : 9–14, morning stroll; XVI, dinner; XVII, departure for the theater).

XVIII–XX: Pushkin's participation. A nostalgic digression on the theater starts with the opening of XVIII, which ends with a lyrical recollection of green-room dallyings in the forbidden city ("there, there . . . my young days swept along "—echoing in a more melancholy key the closing couplet of II). This is followed by the autobiographical XIX, with its nostalgic evocation of stage nymphs and the anticipation of change and disillusion. We can consider XX as a crystallization of these theatrical memories.

Pushkin forestalls Onegin and is first to enter the theater, where he witnesses Istomina's performance, which is over by the time Onegin arrives in the next stanza. This is the overtaking device (to be repeated in XXVII). The natural transition from Pushkin to Onegin is beautifully timed and toned here.

XXI–XXII: The account of Onegin's movements continues. The theater bores him. French cupids and Franco-Chinese dragons are still in full swing, but Onegin leaves the playhouse and drives home to change.

XXIII–XXVI: Pushkin, still an incorporeal participant, inspects Onegin's dressing room. The theme is formally introduced with the time-honored rhetorical question, "Shall I . . .?" A parenthetical piece of facetious philosophizing in XXIV : 9–14 deals with Rousseau, followed by more of the same in the quatrain of the next stanza ("Custom is despot among men," a banality that is to crop up in various forms here and there throughout the novel). St. XXVI presents a professional digression turning on the criticized use of foreign-born words in Russian. The author's self-conscious fondness for Gallicisms will be referred to again in the preliminaries to "Tatiana's Letter" in Three and in Eight : XIV : 13–14.

XXVII: The overtaking device is repeated. Pushkin has lingered too long in the fop's dressing room that he has been describing to his readers, and Onegin is first to set out for the mansion where a ball is already in progress. There is the rhetorical transition, "we'd better hurry to the ball," and then Pushkin, in a batlike, noiseless dash, overtakes his hero (XXVII : 5–14) and reaches the illuminated house first, as he was first to reach the theater.

XXVIII: Now Onegin arrives. His actual presence at the ball is mentioned only here, and later retrospectively, in XXXVI.

XXIX–XXXIV: This set of six stanzas, full of stylized

autobiographical matters, is the most conspicuous digression in the canto. It shall be known as the Pedal Digression. A natural transition leads to it from XXVIII : 10–14, in which two themes are adumbrated: (1) ardent glances following pretty ankles, and (2) whisperings of fashionable ladies. Pushkin, in XXIX, takes the second theme first and develops it in a rather conventional little picture of amorous intrigue in ballrooms. After a nostalgic evocation of those St. Petersburg festivities, the pedal theme proper is taken up in XXX : 8, and goes on through XXXIV, with references to Oriental rugs (XXXI), Terpsichore's instep (XXXII : 2–8), feminine feet in various environments (XXXII : 9–14), a celebrated seascape (XXXIII), a happy stirrup (XXXIV : 1–8), and a disgruntled ironical conclusion (XXXIV : 9–14).

XXXV: The Pedal Digression is closed: "And my Onegin?"—this is the typical rhetorical transition here. Pushkin hastens to keep up with him as he goes home from the ball, but is delayed by the description of a fine frosty morning.

XXXVI: In the meantime Onegin has reached his bed and is fast asleep. A rhetorical and didactic question follows in 9–14: "But was my Eugene happy?" It is answered in the negative in the first line of the next stanza.

XXXVII–XLIV: A set of five stanzas (XXXIX–XLI do not exist) describing Onegin's spleen. The gap left by the omission of XXXIX–XLI produces the impression of a tremendous yawn of ennui. Onegin has lost interest in society belles (XLII) and in courtesans (XLIII : 1–5). He now shuts himself up and, to no avail, tries writing (XLIII : 6–14) and reading (XLIV). Onegin, who could not versify, cannot write prose either and does not join the mettlesome profession to which Pushkin belongs. The theme of Onegin's reading, which began in One : v and vi (Juvenal, two lines from the *Aeneid*, Adam Smith), is treated in a general way without names or titles in One : XLIV and will be taken up again in Seven : XXII and Eight : XXXV.

XLV–XLVIII: Here more details concerning Onegin's "chondria" are given, but the main structural significance of these stanzas is their bringing together of the two main characters of the canto. Here (XLV) starts their friendship. Up to this stanza Pushkin had been haunting the canto but not actually appearing in it as a person in a novel. Pushkin's voice had been heard and his presence felt, as he flitted in and out of the stanzas in a ghostly atmosphere of recollection and nostalgia, but Onegin was not aware of his fellow rake at the ballet or in the ballroom. Henceforth Pushkin will be a full-fledged character, and he and Onegin will actually appear as two persons for the space of four stanzas (XLV–XLVIII). The similarities between the two are emphasized in XLV (the differences will be pointed out later—although we already know that Onegin is no poet); Onegin's caustic charm is described in XLVI, and both are seen enjoying a lucent Northern night on the Neva embankment in XLVII–XLVIII. Nostalgic memories of past loves and a burst of music on the Neva now lead to an especially fine digression of two stanzas.

XLIX–L: This is a third sustained lyrical digression (see my notes, in the Commentary, to the Venetian allusions in these stanzas). It amplifies in plangent strains the notes of nostalgia and exile in II, VIII, and XIX. Moreover, it stresses anew the difference between the two characters—between the dry eighteenth-century prosaic hypochondria of free Onegin and exiled Pushkin's rich, romantic, inspired *toska* (a spiritual yearning rather than the dyspepsia of a hypped rake). Especially to be marked is the urge to fly to a country of exotic liberty, Blueland, fabulous Africa, for the express purpose of excruciatingly regretting *there* sullen Russia (the very country one had abandoned), thus blending new experience and redeemed memories in the synthesis of an artistic revaluation.

Pushkin in 1823 in Odessa (see his own note to L : 3) still dreams of visiting Venice (XLIX) and Africa (L), as he apparently had dreamed during his walks with Onegin in the first week of May, 1820, judging by the very natural transition opening LI: "Onegin was prepared with me to see alien lands; but . . ."

LI–LIV: We are now ready to resume the theme of I–II. Pushkin and Onegin part, and, rich with all the information gathered in regard to Onegin's childhood, youth, and dissipated life in St. Petersburg, we again join Onegin in his journey from the capital to his uncle's manor. "And with this I began my novel," observes Pushkin in a professional aside (LII : 11). Onegin arrives to find his uncle dead (LII : 12–14). He is now installed in the country (LIII : 9). At first he is amused, then ennui assails him again. The pleasures of the country, listed in LIV as provoking boredom in Onegin, afford a natural transition to the autobiographical and professional digression of the six stanzas that close the chapter (LV–LX).

LV–LVI: Pushkin opposes to his friend's spleen his own creative love for the countryside, which he lauds as the best habitat for his Muse. In LVI the difference between a stylized Pushkin, blissfully dreaming in idyllic wilds, and Onegin, moping in the country, is used to mark the fact that our author does not share the Byronic fad of identifying himself with his hero. A reference to an "ironic reader" and to a reviewer engaged in "complicated calumny" is another professional note in this stanza.

LVII–LIX : 1–12: A semilyrical, semiliterary digression, in the course of which Pushkin explains the way inspiration works with him. St. LVII (which will be marvelously echoed and amplified in Eight : IV and *Onegin's Journey*, XIX) adds, by implication, two more bibliographic references—namely, to *The Caucasian Captive* and *The Fountain of Bahchisaray*, composed by Pushkin in the intervening years between *Ruslan and Lyudmila* (finished 1820) and *EO* (begun 1823).

LIX : 13–14 and LX : 1–2: A rather unexpected professional aside. Pushkin promises to write a big narrative poem unconnected with *EO* (a somewhat similar promise —this time of a novel in prose— will be made in Three : XIII–XIV).

LX : 3–14: In the meantime he has finished the first chapter of the present novel and, to the pseudoclassical accompaniment of injunctions and anticipations, sends it forth to those "Neva's banks" whose Northern remoteness he had invoked in II, thus elegantly closing the canto.

CHAPTER TWO

Chapter Two consists of forty stanzas; of these, two stanzas (VIII and XXXV) are incomplete, one having only the first nine lines, and the other only the first four and last three. The time is June, 1820; the place, a region of forests and grasslands situated some 250 miles SSE of St. Petersburg and 200 miles W of Moscow, approximately at the intersection of long. 32° and lat. 56° (thus about 150 miles SE of Mihaylovskoe, where Pushkin was to arrive from Odessa, in August, 1824, for a two-year stay while composing the next canto). The constellation of fictional countryseats in *EO* consists of four properties (with villages inhabited by serfs), each separated from the other by a few miles: Lenski's rich estate (Krasnogórie, as it is named in Chapter Six), the estate of Zaretski (a reformed rake in Chapter Six) some three miles away, Onegin's château and extensive lands, and the Larins' comparatively modest country place with a manor house that is qualified as a humble shelter but can bed fifty guests.

Pushkin saw Chapter Two as dedicated to Lenski, the Göttingen graduate and minor poet, and it is true that the whole canto is swarmed, as it were, around Onegin's country neighbor; but architectonically its central part —although depending on Lenski, proceeding from Lenski, and returning to Lenski—is not Lenski himself but the Larin family. Fifteen stanzas (VI–XX) are devoted to a characterization of Lenski and to his association with Onegin, and this is followed by a kind of stepping-stone sequence of seventeen stanzas (XXI–XXXVII): from Lenski's Olga to her sister Tatiana; from Tatiana's favorite novels to a characterization of her parents; from her mother's sentimental education to the Larins' life in the country; from that to Brigadier Larin's death; from his death to Lenski's visit to the cemetery; which in its turn leads to an eschatological and professional epilogue in three stanzas. All this intricate matter turning on the Larin-Lenski theme, which links Arcadia with death and madrigals with epitaphs (thus foreshadowing through a misty but accurate crystal Lenski's own death in Chapter Six), is prefaced by an idyllic description of Onegin's situation in the country (I–V).

Development of Themes in Two

I–V: The story of Onegin's removal to the country (One : LII–LIV) is continued; the generalization of *rus* (One : XLIV–XLVI) grades now into the specific features of a stylized *Rus'*. Sts. I–II take us to and into the castle; III characterizes Onegin's late uncle; IV illustrates Onegin's attempt to cure his ennui by improving the conditions of the peasants; and this leads to V, which depicts the attitude of the neighboring squires toward the young fashionable from town and his newfangled liberalism.

VI–XX: The same severe criticism (thus goes the transition to the next theme) is applied to Lenski, another young liberal who has just returned to his country estate from a German university. Sts. VII–XII deal with his nature, his ways, his studies within the same frame of rural gentry. In XIII–XVIII Lenski and Onegin are brought into contact and juxtaposition. And in XIX–XX Lenski's love is sung in an imitation of Lenski's lines—which leads us to Olga and her family, the centerpiece of the chapter.

Pushkin's participation in this chapter is mostly philosophical: he sides with Onegin; both are blasé, bizarre beaux in their attitude to what moves Lenski. In XIII : 13–14 and XIV : 1–8, friendship, a favorite theme of the day, is commented on by Pushkin's voice. Lenski's discussions with Onegin in XV–XVII lead Pushkin to a philosophic passage concerning the passions (XVII–XVIII). The intonations of XVII : 6–14 will be repeated in the authorial dirge following upon Lenski's death in Six. A series of professional remarks on the moon, heroines of novels, and feminine names are instrumental in switching to the central theme of the chapter, the Larin family. Except for a commentary on doll play at the end of XXVI and a couplet on habit at the end of XXXI, the author's voice is hardly heard until the very end of the chapter.

XXI–XXXIII: The structural hub of this chapter consists of the thirteen consecutive stanzas depicting the Larin family.

XXI: Eighteen-year-old Lenski is in love with a maiden of sixteen named Olga, his childhood playmate. Their fathers, both of whom died while Lenski was at Göttingen, had foreseen a match.

XXII: A stanza in Lenski's own elegiac strain describing the poetical love Olga inspired.

XXIII: Olga's type of beauty bores Pushkin in Chapter Two as much as it will bore Onegin in Chapter Three. The stanza parodies the manner in which a novelist might start to describe his heroine. A rhetorical transition follows.

XXIV: A switch from the sentimental to the romantic,

from Olga the rosy romp to pale, brooding Tatiana. Despite her Frenchified mind, Tatiana will soulfully live up (in Chapter Five) to the folksy associations of her name.

XXV–XXVII: Tatiana's pensive childhood is described. (Note the enjambment from XXVI to XXVII, a technique felt by Pushkin to be characteristic of the new, and thus "romantic," approach. Additional, even more striking, interstrophic enjambments will be given Tatiana in Three : XXXVIII–XXXIX, when she flits into the park to avoid Onegin, and Five : V–VI, when a heavenly portent causes her to shiver in a technically impeccable run-on.)

XXVIII: Although a casement is not specifically mentioned here, this stanza prepares the image of Tatiana (to be later perceived in retrospect by Onegin at the end of Eight : XXXVII, as constantly sitting by the window and peering into a misty remoteness full of fancies).

XXIX: Here comes the first throb of a theme that will be fully developed in Three : IX, that of Tatiana's beloved books. Her library, if not actually dated, is definitely pre-Byronian, with a strong stress on the eighteenth-century sentimental epistolary novel. At this point Pushkin introduces the theme of novels, only to use it as a transition from Tatiana to her mother, who, if not such a voracious reader as her daughter, had also looked in "real life" for the heroes of Richardson's novels. A transitional enjambment takes us to the next stanza.

XXX: Mme Larin's youth is described. She was in love with a dashing young guardsman.

XXXI: But was made to marry a plainer person, a quiet squire.

XXXII: Her practical occupations in the country . . .

XXXIII: . . . have replaced the fads of her young years in Moscow. The transformation of a mannered miss into a mobcapped squiress should be compared to Lenski's potential future (a comfortable sinking into rural routine after an idealistic youth), as suggested by Pushkin in Four : L and especially in Six : XXXIX.

XXXIV–XXXV: A description of the Larins' old-fashioned habits and customs.

XXXVI: "And thus they both declined." This intonation leads us in a beautiful transition to the theme of death and doom, which is the Lenskian leitmotiv. Larin is dead; it is his epitaph that tells us his first name. It is Lenski who reads this epitaph.

XXXVII: The inner circle is completed. Through a series of structural transitions (from Lenski to his love, Olga, from Olga to Tatiana, from Tatiana's books to her mother's beau, from the beau to the husband, from maturity to death, from dead Larin to still living Lenski) we are brought back to Lenski. Lenski quotes a footnote from the French version of *Hamlet*, and inscribes a "gravestone madrigal," which combination of terms renders perfectly the merging of his two themes: early death and fugitive poetry.

XXXVIII : 1–3: He also makes an inscription for his parents' monument.

XXXVIII : 4–XL: These stanzas, which close the chapter on a personal, strongly emotional note, are in keeping with the themes of doom and oblivion that give transcendental pathos to Lenski's insipid image.

CHAPTER THREE

Chapter Three consists of forty-one stanzas plus a freely rhymed piece of seventy-nine lines—"Tatiana's Letter to Onegin"—and an eighteen-line song in trochees. "Tatiana's Letter" is the centerpiece of the chapter. It is preceded by a set of twenty-five stanzas (VII–XXXI) gradually leading up to it and is followed by six stanzas dealing with its dispatch and the ensuing wait. Thus thirty-one stanzas in all, and the central letter, are devoted to the depiction of Tatiana's love for Onegin, and this main part of the canto is symmetrically enclosed between Onegin's two visits to the Larins' countryseat. The visit with which the chapter begins takes up the first six stanzas (I–VI), and the visit with which it ends takes up the last four stanzas (XXXVIII–XXXIX, XL–XLI), with the song in the middle of the final set. It will be noted that the actual sermon addressed by Onegin to Tatiana during this second visit is given only in the middle of the next chapter (Four : XII–XVI). It should also be noted that Chapter Three is the first one in the novel in which conversations are rendered: these are five dialogues, two between Onegin and Lenski, two between Tatiana and her old nurse, and a short exchange between Mme Larin and Lenski.

Development of Themes in Three

I–II and beginning of III : 1: We have heard Onegin's voice in the soliloquy beginning Chapter One, in his bored comment at the theater (One : XXI : 12–14), and in his reflections on Lenski's enthusiasms (Two : XV : 8–14). We have heard Lenski's voice in his little monologue pronounced on the grave of his fiancée's father. Now the two voices, Onegin's and Lenski's, are brought together in the first dialogue of the novel. This is also the outset of Lenski's sad fate: the first knot of doom is tied. Onegin, in an attempt to alleviate boredom, decides to accompany his friend to the Larins', and thenceforth fate takes over. The time is midsummer, 1820.

III: Description of their visit. Pushkin, for reasons of his own, left out the last six lines of the stanza.

IV–V: The second dialogue between Onegin and Lenski on their way home. Onegin's boredom is, if anything, worse. Lenski compares Tatiana to Zhukovski's Svetlana. Onegin is dreadfully rude in his remarks about

Olga. Lenski goes into a huff. It is presumed that this first little unpleasantness is soon patched up (no trace of it remains six months later, at the end of Chapter Four, when another dialogue between the two young men is reproduced, with Olga freely mentioned).

VI: The general impression produced by Onegin's visit to the Larins'.

VII–VIII: The impression produced on Tatiana. It is passionate love at first sight. Note that she has not even spoken to Onegin; she just sits silently by the window.

IX–XIV: This set of six stanzas represents an important professional digression: Pushkin uses Tatiana's state of mind and heart as a natural transition (IX : 1, "With what attention . . . now") to a discourse on novels. In X the theme of the letter to the hero (which will be specifically developed in XXI–XXXVI) is introduced. In IX–X the books Tatiana reads in the original French or in French translation are mentioned (the theme has already been inaugurated in Two : XXIX). These favorite novels are Rousseau's *Julie*, Mme Cottin's *Mathilde*, Mme de Krüdener's *Valérie*, Mme de Staël's *Delphine*, Goethe's *Werther*, and Richardson's *Grandison* and *Clarissa* (both already alluded to in Chapter Two : XXIX–XXX). As the adolescent reader she is, Tatiana identifies herself with the heroines of these novels and identifies Onegin with their heroes, but the author of *EO* points out that his Onegin is a very different person from Sir Charles Grandison (X : 13–14).

After listing these characters in IX and X, Pushkin, in XI, sums up the Sentimental Novel of the eighteenth century, still read by provincial Tatiana in 1820, and transfers his attention (in XII) to the Romantic Novel read by more sophisticated young ladies "nowadays," i.e., in 1824. These are the works of Byron, in French translation; the novel *Melmoth*, by Maturin, also in French translation; and the novel *Jean Sbogar*, by the

French imitator of Byron, Nodier. In the following stanzas, XIII–XIV, Pushkin promises his readers that in his old age he will write a family novel in prose with a Russian background (instead of the imported stuff). At the end of XIV, a lyrical autobiographical recollection of a past love closes this digression on novels.

XV–XVI: "Tatiana, dear Tatiana!"—with this rhetorical apostrophe Pushkin turns again to his heroine and describes her rambles in the garden avenues, her daydreaming, her obsession with Onegin. This leads us to nightfall and to the third dialogue in the canto.

XVII–XXI: This conversation, in her room, with her old nurse, leads, in its turn, to Tatiana's asking for paper and pen. The letter to Onegin begins to take definite shape. In the course of the dialogue comes the contrast between Tatiana's romantic "falling in love" and the widowed nurse's recollection of her routine wedding in terms of peasant habitus. (It should be noted that from a purely psychological point of view there is not much difference between the nurse's marriage and the equally "traditional" union between Pauline and Squire Larin, as depicted in Two : XXXI, or Tatiana's conventional marriage to wealthy Prince N. at the end of the novel.) The letter to Onegin is actually written by the end of XXI; whereupon Pushkin asks the rhetorical question, "Whom, then, is it for?"—a transition toward a long professional digression.

XXII–XXXI: This set of ten stanzas, leading up to the text of Tatiana's letter, is one of the longest digressions in the novel. It has a twofold purpose, two problems, one of matter and one of manner: in XXII–XXV the purpose is to explain Tatiana's action by contrasting her candid and ardent soul with that of cold fashionable belles (XXII) or freakish flirts (XXIII), whom Pushkin (and Onegin) had known in St. Petersburg (an autobiographical note recalling One : XLII, in which Onegin became bored by those capricious ladies); and in XXVI–XXXI the purpose is to explain that the text to be produced presently is only a paraphrase in Russian verse of Tatiana's French prose.

Professional matters of translation are discussed (XXVI–XXXI). Tatiana, like other gentlemen's daughters of her day, "knew Russian badly" and spoke it in a "negligent patter" with an admixture of Gallicisms that our poet finds much more charming than the pedantry of bluestockings. In XXIX he evokes the imitation of light French verse in Bogdanovich's *Little Psyche* (*Dushen'ka*) and the tender poetry of Evariste Parny (whom he has closely imitated in XXV). St. XXX is a dedication to the poet Baratïnski, whom Pushkin deems (quite wrongly) a better expert than himself in putting a girl's Gallicisms into Russian iambics. And, finally, in XXXI both problems —matter and manner—merge, and the text of the letter is introduced by means of a pretty metaphor (great music and its expression by the stumbling fingers of a budding pianist).

"Tatiana's Letter" has seventy-nine lines. Its text is inserted between sts. XXXI and XXXII. Tatiana imitates stylistically the epistles of lovers in her favorite novels, and Pushkin renders this in Russian iambic tetrameters.

XXXII: A charming description of Tatiana's bare shoulder and of daybreak. The night has passed in terms of the love letter she wrote (in Chapter Five, another night, six months later, will pass in a dreadful prophetic dream).

XXXIII–XXXV: Another dialogue with the old nurse, whom Tatiana asks to have the letter transmitted to Onegin.

XXXVI: No answer. (This will be echoed in Chapter Eight, when it is Onegin who waits for an answer to his letter.) Next day Lenski arrives, and there is a brief dialogue between him and Mme Larin, who inquires about Onegin.

XXXVII: Evening tea. Tatiana, pensive at the window, traces the initials E O on the glass.

XXXVIII–XXXIX: Onegin arrives, and before he enters the house Tatiana, from another porch, dashes through garden and park and (in a remarkable enjambment from stanza to stanza) drops on a bench (XXXIX : 1). Slave girls are picking berries near by, and their song is given (eighteen trochaic trimeters with long terminals).

XL: Tatiana continues in a tremor of apprehension, but Onegin does not appear.

XLI: She finally sighs, leaves her bench, turns into the linden avenue—and there he is before her. The stanza and canto end in a professional remark, imitated from Western romances in verse: "I need a little jaunt, a little rest; some other time I'll tell the rest."

CHAPTER FOUR

If Chapter Three, with its eminently functional digressions and vigorous flow of events, constitutes a most harmoniously constructed entity with a streamlined body and symmetrical wings, Chapter Four, on the other hand, compares with Chapter Seven in weak structure and poorly balanced digressions. It consists of forty-three stanzas (of which one is incomplete): VII–XXXV, XXXVII (stopping at 5/8 of l. 13), and XXXIX–LI. Pushkin himself saw its hub in the theme of country life, continuing in a different key the Horatian *rus* themes of One : LII–LVI and Two : I–II. (It will be noted, incidentally, that now Onegin's indolent life in the country is just as pleasant as that evoked by Pushkin in One, for the express purpose of *differentiating* between himself and his hero!) But this rural theme comes only at the end of the canto (XXXVII–XLIV) and is preceded by an uncommonly bumpy succession of subthemes, among which the structurally important monologue of Onegin (XII–XVI), continuing the last theme of Three (his meeting with Tatiana), is precariously placed between philosophizings about women and philosophizings about friends, foes, kinsmen, women again, egotism, the consequences of the meeting (XXIII–XXIV), Lenski's love, albums, elegies, odes, and Pushkin's rather dreary life in the country (XXXV). The last, being followed by Onegin's enjoyment of country life, arbitrarily reverses the situation described so pointedly in One (Onegin, in fact, is now given Pushkin's manner of living at Mihaylovskoe!). The Lenski theme, which comes after the rural one, closes the canto with some fine stanzas (see especially the last two, L–LI) repeating the doomful notes to Two : XXXVI–XL.

Development of Themes in Four

VII–VIII: Pushkin judiciously dropped the first six stanzas of the semilyrical, semididactic, and on the whole mediocre discourse on women that opens Four. As a result, the two stanzas he preserved are somewhat redeemed, structurally speaking, by echoing the soliloquy note of One : I, especially since the next stanza here is introduced by means of a similar transition:

IX–X: "Exactly thus my Eugene thought" (cf. One : II, "Thus a young scapegrace thought"). Onegin's state of mind in regard to women, which culminated in his abandoning them in One : XLIII, is again given, with the belated information that his life of dissipation in St. Petersburg had lasted eight years (thus, from May, 1812, to May, 1820).

XI: The transition "But" introduces the little pang of sentimental recognition that he experienced upon receiving Tatiana's letter—and his decision not to give way to what he is to define in his letter of Chapter Eight as a "sweet habit." A rhetorical transition, "Now we'll flit over to the garden where Tatiana encountered him," leads to his monologue.

XII–XVIII : 3: He lectures poor Tatiana on youthful indiscretion and lack of self-control. They walk back to the house. A didactic transition ("You will agree, my reader, that very nicely acted our pal," etc.) leads to a digression.

XVIII : 11–XXII: The reference to Onegin's "foes" (from whom the author defends his hero by pointing out the nobility of his soul) brings about the easy transition, "Foes upon earth has everyone, but God preserve us from our friends!" (XVII : 11–13). In XIX our "friends" are taken to task for repeating slander about us, and the next transition is: your friend tells you, of course, that he loves you like a relative—well, let us look at relatives. These are passed in review in XX, and then the fickle fair are tackled (XXI). Finally, in XXII the rhetorical question, "*Whom*, then, to love?" is asked, and the answer is yourself; upon which this didactic digression of five stanzas ends.

XXIII–XXIV: The rhetorical question, "What was the interview's effect?" leads us back to Tatiana, and in XXIV : 8 comes a curious transition reminding us of Two : XXIII : 13–14, with its "let-me-turn-to-the-other-sister" device. There the switch was from the trite to the strange, from Olga to Tatiana; here it is from the sad to the gay, from Tatiana to Olga.

XXV–XXVII: So we take up Olga and Lenski, in a set of stanzas that describe their walks in the garden, their readings together, and their playing chess. The family novel Lenski reads out loud to Olga (XXVI) belongs to the heavily moralistic kind that, for instance, the German novelist August Lafontaine produced (in Russia he was read in French versions). The French writer of genius, Chateaubriand, is mentioned—somewhat irrelevantly— in XXVI : 4. In XXVII Lenski adorns Olga's album, whose description affords a natural transition to a digression on albums.

XXVIII–XXXI: Provincial albums are praised (XXIX), and the fashionable ones of society belles are disparaged (XXX). The painter Fyodor Tolstoy and the poet Baratïnski are mentioned by name (XXX : 6–7). A transition to the next theme is prepared by the reference to the "madrigals" that one is expected to turn out for the albums of modish belles.

XXXI: But Lenski writes not madrigals (see, however, Two : XXXVII) but elegies, and yet another contemporary poet, Yazïkov, is addressed. His elegies, like Lenski's, are documents of his destiny. Now the term "elegy" will lead to the next theme.

XXXII–XXXIII: But hush! A certain stern critic (identifiable as the poet Küchelbecker, Pushkin's schoolmate) advises one to abandon the elegy and turn to the ode. Pushkin does not wish to take sides, but reminds the critic, in a regular little dialogue (occupying XXXII : 5–14 and XXXIII : 1–12, with an elegant enjambment between these two stanzas), that the poet Dmitriev (the fourth contemporaneous poet mentioned or alluded to in the course of as many stanzas) had, in a famous satire, ridiculed the makers of odes. The word "ode" will now serve as a transition.

XXXIV: Lenski would have composed odes, perhaps, but Olga would not have read them. Happy is he who reads his verse to his mistress.

XXXV: The simple transition, "But I [read my verse] only to an old nurse," leads to an autobiographical picture of the countryside, amid which is inserted a professional allusion to the tragedy Pushkin was composing at the time (1825), *Boris Godunov*. With XXXV ends this long, complicated digression on literary matters triggered by the mention of Olga's album in XXVII—eight stanzas dealing with literary matters. A kind of general transition to Onegin's life in the country is now provided by the allusion to Pushkin's life in the country (XXXV and dropped XXXVI). Now comes a rhetorical transition.

XXXVII, XXXIX: "But what about Onegin?" In an account of Onegin's country life in the summer of 1820, Pushkin describes his own rural pleasures and habits in the summer of 1825. He canceled the very end of XXXVII and the whole of XXXVIII in the published text.

XL–XLIII: An easy transition ("But our Northern summer is a caricature of Southern winters") leads us to a description of autumn and winter. The professional note is represented by a facetious remark on expected rhymes (XLII : 3–4) and by the suggestion addressed to hibernators in the country to read the French political writer Pradt or the Waverley Novels (in French translation, naturally).

XLIV–XLIX: A description of the hero's usual dinner in the afternoon of his usual day in the winter sets the scene for Lenski's arrival. An autobiographic digression on wines (XLV–XLVI) marks Pushkin's mental participation in the dinner and the dusk. The rhetorical transition at the end of XLVII ("Now the two friends converse") introduces a dialogue between Onegin and Lenski (XLVIII–XLIX). The general idea of "winter in the country" is gradually to undergo a specific tapering to a definite day. Next week, on Saturday, is Tatiana's name day. St. Tatiana is honored January 12. The next chapter begins January 2–3. This places the dialogue not later than January 2. The gay chat over wine takes on a fateful shade: had Lenski forgotten to transmit to Onegin the Larins' invitation to the name-day party, or had Onegin refused to accept it, there would have been no discord in Chapter Five and no duel in Chapter Six.

L–LI: Lenski is merry. He thinks that only two weeks remain till his wedding. Actually, a little less than that remains till his death. The lyrical exclamation, "My poor Lenski," full of melancholy emphasis, resounds in L : 13, and will be repeated in the opening lines of two stanzas (x and xi) in Chapter Seven, when he is in the grave and Olga has married another. To be noted, too, is the contrast drawn between Lenski, the fond enthusiast, and the bored, blasé character (a shadow of Onegin, a stylization of Pushkin) who in these last two stanzas of Chapter Four is shown to be considering marriage in terms of the dreary didactic novels of Lafontaine (see xxvi) and to be incapable of any dizzy trance, any blissful oblivion.

CHAPTER FIVE

Chapter Five consists of forty-two stanzas: i–xxxvi, xxxix–xlii, xliv–xlv. It is beautifully shaped and is one of the two most colorful cantos (the other being One). Its two interrelated subjects are Tatiana's dream (eleven stanzas, xi–xxi) and the name-day party (eighteen stanzas, from xxv to the end of the chapter). The dream prophesies the party; the description of a dream book comes between the two sets of stanzas. The ten stanzas from i to x, which form a harmoniously graded preface to the dream, begin with a description of winter (i–iii) and then go through a series of images illustrating the custom of divination (*gadanie*) about New Year and culminating in the presageful fantasy of Tatiana's dream. A certain dreamlike quality is carried on to the name-day party and later to the duel. (Incidentally, it seems a rather odd waste of energy that some fifty guests were invited to celebrate Tatiana's Day on January 12, when the entire Larin household should have been preparing for the Lenski-Olga wedding scheduled for January 15 or 16.)

The theme of portents is a central one, both in significance and actual position, in *EO*. It is foreshadowed by the bloom-doom note running through Chapter Two (with Lenski's soliloquy on Larin's tomb preparing the

Translator's Introduction

intonations of his last elegy, *his* "gravestone madrigal," in Six), pervades Chapter Five at the middle of the novel, and is re-echoed in Eight : XXXVI–XXXVII, where Fancy faces Onegin at the faro table of fate.

Development of Themes in Five

I–III: In the preceding chapter winter had already come; November had been described in Four : XL, and the frosts of December had followed. The first snow mentioned at the end of Four : XLII had been a mere flurry. A blanketing snowfall occurs only now, in Five : I, on the night of January 2 (1821). Tatiana, upon rising on January 3, sees the blanched garden. St. II is a charming Flemish-schoollike picture of winter—a continuation of the November and December landscapes depicted in Chapter Four : XLI–XLII. St. III contains some professional matter. The two literary references in it are to Pushkin's friends, the poet Vyazemski (who will be alluded to again in Seven : XXXIV : 1 and mentioned in Seven : XLIX : 9–11) and the poet Baratïnski (mentioned earlier in Three : XXX and Four : XXX : 7).

IV–X: This set of seven stanzas concerns Twelfthnight divination games between Christmas and Epiphany (January 6) and is instrumental in leading up to Tatiana's presageful dream. A bit of didactic philosophizing about youth and old age marks the presence of the author in VII : 5–14, and so does the professional comparison in X : 5–8, in which Zhukovski's Svetlana (see Three : V and Five : Motto) is mentioned again. Tatiana places her little looking glass under her pillow and is ready for a dramatic dream. I should date it about January 5.

XI–XXI : 6: The dream. It contains several interesting structural elements. The turbulent torrent is a dream exaggeration of the idyllic brook near the bench upon which Tatiana dropped in her flight from Onegin in Three (XXXVIII : 13). Near a little stream of that idyllic brook Lenski will be buried in Six (XL : 8). This little river or brook symbolically separates Tatiana and Onegin. She crosses it in her dream with the assistance of a burly bear, who is Onegin's gossip, just as the burly general, Tatiana's husband in Chapter Eight, turns out to be Onegin's kinsman and chum. The ghouls of the dream, sitting at the table where Onegin presides, are thematically repeated in the guise of the grotesque guests at the name-day party. Lenski's quarrel with Onegin is predicted, and its horror causes Tatiana to awake.

XXI : 7–14: It is morning. Instead of the old nurse bringing tea (as in Chapter Three : XXXIII, on that summer morning after a night spent in writing the letter to Onegin), it is Olga who enters Tatiana's room, and asks: Well, what have you dreamed about? The transition to the next theme is: but she—Tatiana—is not listening.

XXII–XXIV: She is engrossed in the book of dream interpretations. While describing the way she acquired it from a book peddler, Pushkin refers in passing to yet another novel, *Malvina*, by Mme Cottin, to epic poems about Peter the Great, and to the French writer Marmontel, author of didactic tales.

XXV–XXXVI, XXXIX–XLII, XLIV–XLV: The rhetorical transition, *No vot*, "But lo," introduces the second main subject of the canto, the name-day party. The sunrise of January 12 is humorously described in a parody of an eighteenth-century ceremonial ode of Lomonosov. While this good-natured trumpet note seems to establish a deliberate contrast to the tragic intonations of Tatiana's nightmare, the jocularity is but an amiable mask, and at the end of XXV something about the very rhythm of the arrival of the guests reminds us ominously of the sequence of actions (barking, laughing, shouting, etc.) describing the behavior of the monsters of the fantastic feast in Tatiana's dream. A literary reference to Buya-

nov, the hero of a poem by Pushkin's uncle, occurs in
XXVI : 9–11. In XXIX the door flies open; Onegin and
Lenski arrive. This is Onegin's third visit to the Larins'
in the course of at least six months. He seems to be
touched by Tatiana's awful embarrassment, and he is
bitterly angry with Lenski, who spoke of a quiet family
dinner but instead brought him to a huge nightmare
feast with the grotesque neighbors Onegin had been
avoiding in Chapter Two. The caricatures of these guests
that Onegin now draws mentally may not have been un-
like the composite animals and the other ghouls of Ta-
tiana's dream. In XXXII, when the champagne appears,
there is an autobiographical metaphor referring to a girl
Pushkin courted, Zizi, diminutive of Evpraksia, whose
name day coincides with that of St. Tatiana. The festive
dinner lasts from the end of XXVIII to the beginning of
XXXV. There is some card playing after that, and then
tea, whereupon, in a professional aside (XXXVI : 9–14),
Pushkin remarks that he seems to talk about eating and
drinking as much as Homer does. The tone of the canto
at this point reminds us of Chapter One, with its sequence
of social pleasures, and the word "Bréguet," the faithful
timepiece twice used in the first chapter, now rings forth
a remindful chime (XXXVI : 8). The ball starts in XXXIX,
and in another professional aside in XL Pushkin refers
the reader to that passage in Chapter One in which One-
gin emerged from his dressing room to go to a ball,
which, as the author confesses, he never really described,
having been diverted by a digression about the little feet
of the ladies he had loved. The promise he makes here of
weeding out the digressive element (autobiographic,
professional, and philosophical) is not quite kept in Chap-
ter Five, but is reduced to a few brief interruptions (such
as the verses devoted to Zizi, for example, or the didactic
observations about fashion at the end of XLII). And what
is curious to note, there are in this canto practically none

of those abrupt, artificial, rhetorical transitions that occur in the other chapters: the narrative flow of this canto is remarkably natural. The whirl of the waltz and the gay crash of the mazurka, depicted in XLI and XLII, now come as a kind of compensation for the meagerness of the description of the ball in Chapter One : XXVIII, and the dramatic atmosphere of Tatiana's dream is suddenly felt with a shiver of recognition when Lenski, in jealous fury, sees Onegin flirting with Olga (XLIV) and leaves the house (XLV), resolved to challenge Onegin next day to a pistol duel.

CHAPTER SIX

Chapter Six consists of forty-three stanzas: I–XIV, XVII–XXXVII, XXXIX–XLVI. Its hub is the pistol duel between Lenski and Onegin. It takes place on January 14, two days after Tatiana's name-day party and (implicitly) on the eve of Lenski's projected wedding to Olga. The description of the fatal morning starts in XXIII (10–14), and by the end of XXXV Lenski's dead body is removed from the dueling ground—thus, a dozen stanzas of centralized action. The chapter opens with the continuation of the name-day-party theme for three stanzas, after which the preliminaries to the duel start with the appearance on the scene of Lenski's second (IV–XII), Lenski's last interview with Olga (XIII–XIX), and his last night of versemaking (XX–XXIII). The chapter ends, after Lenski's death, with a set of philosophical stanzas (XXXVI–XXXIX), a description of his grave (XL), the visit of a fair vacationist to it (XLI–XLII), and a set of four final stanzas dealing with autobiographical matters, both lyrical and professional.

Development of Themes in Six

I–III: Lenski has left, and after supper Onegin leaves, too. The remaining guests are bedded, from hallway to attic, in the Larins' house. Tatiana alone is awake at her favorite post, the moonlit window. Her reaction to Onegin's momentary glance of tenderness and to his odd behavior with Olga is described in III.

IV–VII: With the rhetorical apostrophe to his story, "Forward, forward," Pushkin summons a new character, the reformed rake Zaretski, whose turbulent past and peaceful present are depicted in these four stanzas.

VIII–IX: Onegin has little respect for him but likes his conversation and thus is not surprised when on the morning of January 13 Zaretski calls on him. This is the natural transition to the account of the challenge that Lenski has charged his second, Zaretski, to transmit to Onegin.

X–XII: Three stanzas describe Onegin's dissatisfaction with himself at accepting the challenge and Lenski's gleeful relief on learning from Zaretski that Onegin will fight.

XIII–XIX: The account of Lenski's last evening with Olga is interrupted by an authorial aside in XVIII, a fervid invocation of fate: if Tatiana had known that Onegin and Lenski . . . if Lenski had known that Tatiana . . . and so forth.

XX–XXIII : 8: This set of three and a half stanzas is devoted to Lenski's last night of inspiration. He reads his verses aloud just as Pushkin's friend, the poet Delvig, does when drunk. The text of Lenski's last poem to Olga (the epilogue, as it were, to the elegies he wrote in her album, with an appropriate gravestone in the margin) has been preserved by Pushkin, the third man in the novel, and its text, minus the first two lines, is quoted in XXI : 2–14 and XXII. Its position is a very preedy one, in even balance with the two epistles structurally equivalent to it: "Tatiana's Letter" in Three and "Onegin's Letter" in Eight. There follows a professional observation on "what we call romanticism" (XXIII : 2–4).

XXIII : 9–XXVII: This is the fateful morning of January 14. The duel is scheduled for about seven (see XXIII : 13–14). Onegin sets out for the dueling ground at least an hour and a half later than Lenski, who leaves at about 6:30 A.M. Onegin arrives in XXVI. "The two foes stand with lowered eyes."

XXVIII: "Foes!" This ejaculation serves as a conventional transition to another authorial invocation, similar in tone to XVIII. Is it long since they were intimate friends? Should they not make it up? This is clinched by means of a didactic criticism of false shame (XXVIII : 13–14).

XXIX–XXX: Of these two stanzas the first is devoted to the loading of the pistols and the measuring of the ground; the second, to the duel itself.

XXXI–XXXII: Two very interesting stanzas from a technical point of view. Pushkin defines Lenski's death in terms of a deliberate accumulation of classical and romantic metaphors: a mass of snow rolling downhill, the gust of a tempest, the withering of a flower at dawn, the extinguishing of fire on an altar, an abandoned house.

XXXIII–XXXIV: The reader is apostrophized in connection with dueling. This set of two didactic stanzas continues the theme of XXVIII.

XXXV: Lenski's body is removed from the dueling ground.

XXXVI–XXXVII, XXXIX: The rhetorical transition, "My friends, you're sorry for the poet," leads to a set of three stanzas (four in MS) in which various examples are given of what might have been Lenski's future had he lived.

XL: The rhetorical transition, "But, reader, be it as it may," leads to a description of Lenski's tomb—in Arcadia rather than in northwestern Russia.

XLI–XLII : 12: A herdsman plaits his wood-fiber shoe near the tomb, and a young townswoman, spending the summer in the country, stops her horse near the monument. In XLII : 5–12, Pushkin uses this Amazon to voice the rhetorical question: What has happened to Olga, Tatiana, and Onegin since Lenski's death? The question is rhetorically answered by Pushkin at the end of XLII: I shall tell you all in due time. The transitional remark, "But not now," opens the last set of stanzas.

XLIII–XLVI: In these final four stanzas several professional matters are mentioned: Pushkin confesses he now dallies more sluggishly with mistress rhyme and inclines toward prose (XLIII : 5–10). Elegiac conceits of the past are now gone (note here the XLIV : 5–6 echo of the "accepted-rhyme" theme that formed a little digression in Four : XLII : 3–4). The autobiographical strain, otherwise absent from the chapter, is now heard (chill dreams, stern cares, withering of youth, gratitude to past youth, hope for further inspiration). The poet takes leave of the quiet shelter of country life and closes the chapter with a didactic criticism of the vortex of the world.

CHAPTER SEVEN

Chapter Seven consists of fifty-two stanzas: I–VII, X–XXXVIII, XL–LV. Thus it is only two stanzas shorter than Chapter One (the longest). Pushkin saw the main part of the chapter in the theme of Moscow, which is first mentioned at the end of XXVI. This theme (if we include in it Tatiana's farewells addressed to the countryside and a description of the coming winter) occupies almost the entire second half of the chapter. The first half of the chapter consists of a description of spring (I–IV), an invitation to the countryside where Eugene had lived (V), a redescription of Lenski's grave (VI–VII), already known from Chapter Six, and an account of Olga's marriage to a dashing uhlan (X–XII), perhaps the Company Commander mentioned in Five : XXVIII. Then comes Tatiana's solitude (XIII–XIV), followed by ten stanzas (XV–XXIV)

that esthetically and psychologically form the real hub
of the chapter—the story of Tatiana's visit to Onegin's
abandoned castle during the summer of 1821. She and
her mother set out for Moscow not earlier than January,
1822, and the chapter ends with Tatiana having at-
tracted the notice of her future husband, at a Moscow
ball, in the spring of 1822. The time element dominates
this chapter rather obsessively, with rhetorical transi-
tions depending on the establishment of this or that
season or hour or of the passage of time.

Development of Themes in Seven

I–III: The canto opens with a pseudoclassical little pic-
ture of spring (I), followed by romantic meditations,
semilyrical, semiphilosophical, on the melancholy of
spring. Explanations of this vernal languish and dejec-
tion are listed in the form of questions. The "youth-is-
gone" theme of the four stanzas with which Chapter Six
ended is now continued in Seven : III.

IV: With the rhetorical transition, "Now is the time,"
various people (sage epicures, students of agriculture as
expounded by the writer Lyovshin, fathers of large fam-
ilies, and sentimental ladies) are urged to take advantage
of the spring and move to the country.

V: The same invitation is extended professionally by
Pushkin to his reader, and the country place is specified:
it is the region where Onegin has recently dwelt. This
establishes two important structural points: (1) that
Onegin has already left, and (2) that the spring described
in these stanzas is the spring of 1821, following the duel.
We also note that Pushkin's Muse, whom the reader ac-
companies to Krasnogorie, is a kind of substitute for the
Amazon of Six : XLI–XLII, whose curiosity will now be
satisfied.

VI–VII: Lenski's tomb is described in the same Arcadian
terms as it has been described in Six : XL–XLI. However,

the spring mentioned in Six : XLI is not the specific spring of Seven : VI, but a generalized and recurrent one. In other words, the description of Lenski's grave in Six is projected (through a series of seasons and years, with fields being tilled and harvested) beyond the specific spring of 1821. Pushkin wishes to combine two ideas: the idea of duration (Lenski's tomb is always there, in its permanent Arcadia) and the idea of fleeting time (Olga has forgotten him, the trail to the tomb is choked with weeds). Only a few months have passed, and the grass that came up in April is practically the same that overgrew the trail, after Olga's wedding and departure for some garrison town, less than five months or so after poor Lenski's death. In order to stress the idea of duration, Pushkin mentions (VII : 13–14) the herdsman as still sitting by Lenski's tomb. Actually, he begins to sit near it only now, in Seven. His appearance in Six, to which the "as before" refers, was really a series of appearances overlapping his appearance in Seven and projected into future seasons beyond the specific spring of 1821.

X–XI: Both these stanzas begin with the pathetic exclamation, "My poor Lenski!" Olga has married a cavalry officer (X). Is Lenski's shade aware of this? (XI). A didactic bit of philosophizing on oblivion and death, with ironic overtones, closes XI.

XII–XIV: Olga has gone. And for a long time through the mist Tatiana keeps looking after the receding carriage. (The intonation here, Seven : XIII : 1–2, echoes that of Six : XLII : 1–2, in which it is the mysterious Amazon who performs.) Tatiana is now left with her own thoughts—which she never shared with Olga, anyway, but the sharing of thoughts is now implied retrospectively in order to stress her loneliness—a none-too-honest device on the part of Pushkin (a deceiver as all artists are), who in this chapter stops at nothing to have his story move—and move the reader.

XV–XXV : 2: The temporal transition, " 'Twas eve-
ning," introduces the theme of Tatiana's visits to Onegin's
abandoned castle. Six stanzas (XV–XX) are devoted to her
first visit in early June, 1821, and four to the rest. St.
XXII contains a professional explanation of Eugene's
library, with a reference to his favorite books— *The
Giaour, Don Juan*, and two or three novels depicting the
man of the time (Pushkin lightly dismisses his earlier
statement in One about Onegin's denouncing and re-
nouncing books). The notes Onegin has left in the mar-
gins of his books tell Tatiana more about him than he
learned about her from her letter to him. From the
marks of his pencil and thumbnail she reconstructs
the man, and when three years later they meet again
she will know he is not a fascinating demon or angel
but an imitation of fashionable freaks—and still the
only love of her life.

XXV–XXVII: The temporal transition, "The hours run"
(XXV : 3), leads to a new theme. Tatiana's mother is
anxious to find a husband for her and is advised by
friends to take Tatiana to Moscow, the mart of brides.
Tatiana's horrified reaction is given in XXVII. Her meek
surrender to her mother's decision, despite the horror,
is inconsistent with the strongheadedness Pushkin has
explicitly bestowed on her (see, for example, Three :
XXIV), but on the other hand it does prepare us for her
submitting to her mother's choice of a husband, as ex-
plained retrospectively in Tatiana's sermon to Onegin
in Eight.

XXVIII–XXIX : 7: She bids farewell to her favorite
haunts in the country.

XXIX : 8–XXX: The temporal transition, "But the fast
summer flies," leads to a stylized picture of autumn, and
then winter and the "winter way" will lead to Moscow.

XXXI–XXXV: Five stanzas describe the departure for

Moscow and the week-long journey, covering some two hundred miles, in a sledded coach, with their own horses. Tatiana's final farewells to her fields at the end of XXXII, when she leaves the rustic shelter for the vanities of the city, not only conclude the elegiac theme of XXVIII and XXIX, but also echo the stylized autobiographical farewells voiced by Pushkin himself in Six : XLVI. A digression on roads occupies XXXIII–XXXV.

XXXVI–XXXVIII, XL: The transition, "But now 'tis near," brings us to the western gates of Moscow. An autobiographical strain permeates XXXVI : 5–14, in which Pushkin recollects his own arrival in Moscow from Mihaylovskoe on Sept. 8, 1826. The two-hour drive from the west gate to the east section of the city ends at the house of Princess Aline, surname withheld, Mme Larin's maiden cousin.

XLI–XLII: These two stanzas contain the dialogue between the two cousins, who have not seen each other for at least eighteen years.

XLIII: Tatiana, in unfamiliar surroundings, takes her usual position by the window.

XLIV–LV : 2: Eleven stanzas are now devoted to sad and indolent Tatiana's debut in Moscow society. A nice professional item is represented by a passage in XLIX in which, at a party given by one of Tatiana's numerous Moscow aunts, Pushkin delegates his friend, Prince Vyazemski, the poet responsible for the motto to Chapter One and already a participant in the novel (see the allusion to his winter scenes in Five : III : 6–12 and Pushkin's note to the description of roads in Seven : XXXIV), to entertain Tatiana. There is (in XLIX) a reference to fashionable youths with soft jobs in the Archives, and another to a writer of cheap elegies. There follow descriptions of the theater (L) and of the Club of the Nobility (LI–LIV). Autobiographical matters re-echo: in L, a theme from Chapter One (a parenthetical recollection

of Terpsichore; see One : XIX); and in LII, an apostrophe
to one of our author's numerous loves. In LIII Tatiana's
memories go back (as she sits near a marble column in
the ballroom) to the linden avenues where she had day-
dreamed of Onegin—it is then (in LIV) that two aunts
nudge her from either side. Her future husband, a fat
general, is looking at her.

LV: As if suddenly realizing that he had never written
a formal preface to his work, Pushkin leaves Tatiana to
her involuntary conquest and concludes the chapter with
an amusing exordium, a parody of classical introduc-
tions—leading back to Onegin, who will reappear in the
next chapter after three years of travel.

CHAPTER EIGHT

Chapter Eight consists of fifty-one stanzas, of which II
(1–4) and XXV (1–8) are incomplete, and a freely rhymed
epistle of sixty lines, "Onegin's Letter to Tatiana" (be-
tween XXXII and XXXIII). The structural hub of the canto
is felt by most readers to be Onegin's visit to Tatiana in
the spring of 1825, a set of ten stanzas occupying the en-
tire end of the chapter except for three stanzas formally
closing the novel with final farewells addressed by the
author to his characters and to his readers. Pushkin him-
self, however, saw the main part of the chapter in the
set of twenty-seven stanzas (VI–XXXII) devoted to a pic-
ture of high-life society in St. Petersburg (in the autumn
of 1824 by the calendar of the novel), interrupted by re-
flections on Onegin's arrival in St. Petersburg after three
years of travel and on Tatiana's metamorphosis from
provincial miss to fashionable lady: she has been mar-
ried to Prince N. since 1822 (we recall that she made his
acquaintance in Moscow at the end of Chapter Seven).
This set of beau-monde stanzas culminates in "Onegin's
Letter," which is followed by a description of Onegin's

solitary hibernation from the beginning of November, 1824, to sometime in April, 1825, when he dashes off to visit Tatiana. All this rather intricate pattern of situations and events is prefaced by a set of six stanzas (I–VI) in which Pushkin's Muse is the main character.

Development of Themes in Eight

I–V: The subject matter of these first stanzas is not so much biographical as bibliographical. Pushkin introduces a new female character, his Muse, and narrates his relations with her—his juvenile inspirations at school, Derzhavin's "blessing" (in 1817), and his young turbulent songs at feasts (1817–20). In 1820 she follows Pushkin to the Caucasus and the Crimea (the literary allusions in Eight : IV are to his romantic poems *The Caucasian Captive* and *The Fountain of Bahchisaray*, referred to earlier in One : LVII). In Eight : V she follows the poet to Moldavia, where the allusion (1–9) is to a third narrative poem, *The Gypsies*, and at the end of the stanza she appears as Tatiana's metaphysical cousin, the spirit of the present novel, a pensive provincial miss, in the poet's garden, in the province of Pskov. We recall that, very briefly, she guided us to Onegin's park and castle in Seven : V.

VI–VII: Finally, he brings her to a fashionable gathering in St. Petersburg, and this is the transition to a continuation of the novel. The rhetorical question, "But who's that in the chosen throng?" (VII : 5), leads to Onegin's reappearance in the novel.

VIII–XI: This is a set of didactic stanzas, of which VIII and IX continue the rhetorical-question intonations of VII : 5–14 and represent a kind of double-talk device: oblique and unspecified references to Onegin's oddities, feigned or otherwise. The technical purpose is to have Onegin win the reader's sympathy (jeopardized by the duel) and to lend additional interest to the drama that is going to develop in this chapter. Sts. x and xi shift to a series of philosophizings on the routine happiness of average natures (x) and the misery of disillusioned and nonconforming minds (xi).

xii–xiii: The transition to Onegin is complete. The rhetorical formula here is "let me take him up again" (xii : 8), following a professional remark about Pushkin's own *Demon*, a short poem treating of the spirit of cynicism and negation. These two stanzas inform us of Onegin's life between the day of the duel, Jan. 14, 1821, and the present time, autumn, 1824. We learn that he was twenty-six years of age in 1821, when, soon after the duel, he set out on a long journey. (This journey was to form a special chapter, but Pushkin published only a few fragments of it in an appendix to the novel. We learn from those fragments that Onegin, between 1821 and 1824, visited Moscow, Novgorod, the Volga region, the Caucasus, the Crimea, and, judging by additional MS stanzas, Odessa, where in 1823–24 he met his old friend Pushkin.) Now, in Eight : xiii, Onegin finds himself suddenly at a St. Petersburg ball.

xiv–xvi : 5: A rhetorical formula, "But lo!" leads to the next scene. Pushkin and his Muse see Princess N. as she enters the ballroom, followed by an imposing general, her husband (xiv : 1–4). Onegin, absorbed in bitter thought, does not see her enter. The subdued grace of her manner is described, and there are two professional asides: in the first aside (xiv : 13–14) Pushkin begs the pardon of Shishkov, champion of Slavisms, for employing the French term *comme il faut*, and in the second aside (xv : 14–xvi : 5) he humorously invokes his inability to translate the English term "vulgar" (and implies the possibility of playing on the name of a detested critic, Bulgarin-Vulgarin).

xvi: The rhetorical transition, "But to our lady let me turn," leads to the following situation: Tatiana has sat down next to a glamorous lady of fashion, who, however, cannot eclipse her. Her husband has gone over to the group where Onegin stands. Only now, from afar, does Onegin see the lady, and he notices her baffling resemblance to Tatiana.

XVII–XVIII: Onegin now turns to an old friend and kinsman, whom he has not seen since 1820, and inquires about the lady in the *framboise* beret now conversing with the Spanish ambassador. The friend is no other than the imposing general, Prince N., who had come in with Tatiana. In the course of a dialogue (XVII : 8– XVIII : 5) the identity of the lady, now Princess N., is settled, and Onegin meets her again.

XIX–XX: Her cold demeanor and her emotions are described.

XXI: Next morning he receives an invitation from Prince N. to a soiree and is perturbed.

XXII: Onegin can hardly wait till 10:00 P.M. The theme of her calm behavior and his perturbed mood is continued.

XXIII–XXVI: Here comes a set of four stanzas devoted to the high-life salon of Princess N. It is the weakest part of the chapter.

XXVII–XXXII: "But my Onegin"—the rhetorical formula leads to a sequence of reflections and actions that culminate in Onegin's writing Tatiana a love letter. Sts. XXVII–XXIX belong to the didactic philosophizing order, and the seasonal metaphors with which XXIX is crammed are repetitious and conventional. Sts. XXX–XXXI deal with Onegin's dogged but unsuccessful pursuit of Tatiana; and XXXII introduces his letter to her, with the formula "Here you have his letter word for word," reminding us of the introductions to Tatiana's letter and to Lenski's last elegy.

"Onegin's Letter": This epistle is based on French literary models. It is also a kind of mirror image of Tatiana's letter of four years before. The roles are reversed. Onegin's letter ends with a phrase similar to that with which her letter began. It is now he who must submit to her will.

XXXIII : 1–4: "There's no reply." This is a revengeful echo of Tatiana's former torments (Three : XXXVI : 1–4).

XXXIII : 5–XXXIV : 4: Yet another glimpse of Tatiana in the world of fashion is marked on Onegin's part by the wishful reflection (providing an interstrophic enjambment) that fear of exposure might be lurking behind the severity of her countenance.

XXXIV : 5–XXXVIII: This is the marvelous description of Onegin's seclusion during the winter of 1824. The theme of chondria, which we remember from One : XXXVIII and LIV; the theme of "locking oneself up and reading," which was dealt with in One : XLIV; and the theme of writing, which was treated in connection with verse in One : VII : 1–4 and in connection with prose in One : XLIII : 7–14—all these themes of Chapter One are now given new life and are modulated in a new key. A delightful autobiographical and professional aside follows the list of authors in XXXV, Pushkin recalling the compliments of critics in 1824–25 and contrasting that praise with the way they now (1830) disparage his writings. Sts. XXXVI–XXXVII depicting Onegin's hallucinations are the greatest in the entire novel.

XXXIX–XL : 1: "Days rushed." This temporal transition takes us to the April day in 1825 when Onegin, in a frenzy of bizarre haste, drives unbidden to the house of Princess N. The enjambment from stanza to stanza beautifully repeats the run-on in the passage of Three (XXXVIII–XXXIX), in which it was Tatiana who made the dash. That garden, those shadows of leaves, that avenue of limes, will presently arise again, in retrospective evocation.

XL–XLI: As in a fairy tale, door after door magically opens, and magically he finds Tatiana in her boudoir re-reading his letter of October, 1824.

XLII–XLVIII : 6: This last scene between them contains her monologue (XLII : 8–XLVII), which echoes his sermon in Four. Tatiana's emotion is artistically rendered by the spasmodic enjambments from verse to verse, with pauses within the lines. Tatiana concludes her speech with the words, "I love you . . . but to another I've been given away: to him I shall be faithful all my life." The first six lines of XLVIII represent the end of the story: Tatiana leaves the room, Onegin stands alone, and the clink of the husband's spurs is heard—upon which Pushkin abandons his hero forever.

In XLIX he bids his readers farewell, in L he takes leave of his book, and in LI he recalls old friends and concludes this epilogue with the rhetorical remark:

> Blest . . .
> who did not read life's novel to the end
> and all at once could part with it
> as I with my Onegin.

PUSHKIN'S NOTES AND "ONEGIN'S JOURNEY"

A set of forty-four authorial notes and passages from *Onegin's Journey*, in seventeen complete and four incomplete stanzas, with some brief comments to them, represent an additional small structure unattached compositionally to the main body of the novel. Editors are tempted to fill the gaps in the *Journey* with a number of MS stanzas that belong to it, but if this temptation is yielded to, then, naturally, all of the dropped stanzas must also be added to the text of the eight preceding chapters. I have collected and translated all the canceled material I could find in Russian editions, but I keep it strictly separate from the established text of the *editio optima* (1837). From many points of view, historical and human, psychological and philosophical, the omitted verses are of tremendous interest, and some of them rival, and perhaps surpass, the greatest passages in the established text. As Pushkin's historian, I gloat over them. As a fellow writer, I deplore the existence of many trivial scribblings, stillborn drafts, and vague variants that Pushkin should have destroyed. In a number of instances an omitted line, the place of which seems still warm and throbbing in the established text, explains or amplifies something of great artistic value, but I insist that these specious additions should be discounted in our judgment of *EO* as Pushkin published it. In a few instances we feel dreadfully certain that only the grotesque requirements of a despotic regime forced our poet to delete passages, to alter lines of development, to abolish whole sets of marvelous stanzas; but we are also aware that if today, in modern Russia, discarded stanzas such as the fragment of "Chapter Ten" are affixed by editors to the established text this is done under the pressure of an even more despotic and grotesque regime. We are acutely conscious of the fact that a living author's work may be published in a form he would have objected to under conditions of political freedom. And still the established text must stand. Indeed, there would be scarcely one masterpiece left untampered with and unchanged from beginning to end if we started to republish a dead author's works in the form we *think* he might have wished them to appear and endure.

The Genesis of "Eugene Onegin"

Without a direct personal study of the *EO* manuscripts, wherein Pushkin had the good habit of dating the stages of his work (besides leaving other invaluable marginalia), I cannot hope to describe the process of composition of *EO* in a way that would satisfy me. I have studied all the published photographs of the drafts; but these are few, and until reproductions of all Pushkin's manuscripts are printed (as advocated by Pushkinists fifty years ago) I have to rely on the writings of those who have glimpsed them. For the following rather vague account I have consulted G. Vinokur (*Works* 1936), B. Tomashevski (Acad 1937, 1949), and M. Tsyavlovski (*Letopis'*, 1951). The most careful and cautious work is Tomashevski's. I have ignored the hopelessly unreliable data published before 1936, as well as the worthless compilations (such as N. Brodski's, 1950, or D. Chizhevski's, 1953) that added their own blunders to those of their obsolete sources.

Pushkin's work on *EO* went on, with intermissions, for more than eight years: from May 9, 1823, to Oct. 5, 1831, in Kishinev (Bessarabia), Odessa, Mihaylovskoe (Nadezhda Pushkin's estate near Opochka, in the prov-

ince of Pskov), Moscow, Petersburg, Malinniki and Pav-
lovskoe (estates belonging to Praskovia Osipov and Pavel
Vulf, respectively, near Torzhok, in the province of
Tver), Boldino (Sergey Pushkin's estate near Lukoya-
nov, in the province of Nizhni Novgorod), and Tsarskoe
Selo (near Petersburg).

In a broad sense it can be said that Pushkin's pre-
occupation with *EO* lasted longer (1822–35) than the
span of life actually devoted to its composition (1823–31).
As early as 1822, Pushkin was contemplating a long
poem, *Tauris* (based on his Crimean impressions of
1820), in which, judging by the fragments that have
been preserved, certain lyrical themes were conceived
that he incorporated later in *EO*. As late as mid-Sep-
tember, 1835, in the last and least productive of his
Mihaylovskoe autumns, we find our poet toying with a
continuation of *EO* (see vol. 3, p. 376). And in summa-
tion of Onegiana we should ponder the following passage
from a letter our poet wrote on Nov. 10, 1836 (only
eighty days before his death), to Prince N. Golitsïn:
"Que je vous envie votre beau climat de Crimée. . . .
C'est le berceau de mon Onegin, et vous aurez sûrement
reconnu certains personnages." One wonders whom
Pushkin meant.

The first batch of stanzas was composed between May
9 and 28, 1823, in Kishinev. For his drafts Pushkin used
a large notebook bound in black morocco and stamped
with the letters *OV* within a Masonic triangle. This
ledger (now numbered 2369) was among a number of
other unused ones, originally designed for bookkeeping,
that Pushkin, a Mason since May 4, 1821, was given on
May 27, 1822, by one Nikolay Alekseev, treasurer of the
Kishinev lodge "Ovid," after it was disbanded, in com-
mon with other "secret associations," by governmental
decree on Dec. 9, 1821. The present numbers of the
cahiers, listed in the order of Pushkin's use of them, are

2369, 2370, 2368; they are full of these and other drafts, short and long poems, letters, pen drawings, and so forth. I cannot make out from published material whether the rest of Pushkin's notebooks containing *EO*'s drafts, Cahiers 2371 and 2382, also stemmed from the "Ovid" lodge storeroom. Vulf, in his diary (entry of Sept. 16, 1827), speaks of two black morocco cahiers: "On the larger one I noticed a half-effaced Masonic triangle." According to him, the smaller book (cover unmarked) contained the beginning of the historical novel about Pushkin's African ancestor (App. I, vol. 3, p. 396).

The first stanza in the draft of *EO* (2369) is headed "May 9," with the numeral portentously shaped. It was one of Pushkin's fatidic days, the anniversary of his expulsion from the province of St. Petersburg three years before (in a diary he kept in Kishinev the entry under May 9, 1821, reads: "It is now exactly one year since I left Petersburg"). It is curious that on the very day that our poet started to compose *EO* his lifelong friend and protector, Aleksandr Turgenev,* wrote from St. Petersburg to Vyazemski (see n. to Chapter One : Motto) that Count Vorontsov had just been made Governor General of New Russia and Bessarabia and that he (Turgenev) hoped Pushkin would be transferred to Vorontsov's headquarters in Odessa.

I have studied a reproduction of Pushkin's draft of the first stanza, and (as was conclusively shown in 1910 by P. Shchyogolev†) the initial date should be taken to be "May 9," not "May 28 [as written below it, with both words underscored] at night." Furthermore, Pushkin himself in his recapitulation (Sept. 26, 1830) noted that he had begun *EO* on May 9, 1823.

At least eight stanzas (probably more) were ready by

---

*Jurist and historian (1784–1845), Director of the Department of Foreign Faiths.
†In *P. i ego sovr.*, XIII, 165.

the time Pushkin moved to Odessa (at the beginning of July, 1823), where, by Sept. 5, he had written sts. I–XVII and XX–XXII. By the second week of September he had reached XXXI. Except for three stanzas, he finished Chapter One on Oct. 22, 1823 (and went on straight to Chapter Two). St. XXXIII was written (partly with the aid of the two-year-old draft of another composition) probably in the first half of June, 1824, in Odessa; he copied it out in the last days of September at Mihaylovskoe and added XVIII and XIX in the first week of October, 1824.

Chapter Two took him less than two months to compose. By Nov. 3, 1823, he had written seventeen stanzas, and by Dec. 1 ten more. The next batch, eleven stanzas, were composed in a week, and by Dec. 8, 1823, he had finished the chapter except for XL and XXXV, which he added sometime in the course of the next three months.

January, 1824, was marked by an intermission devoted to another poem (*The Gypsies*). Sts. I–XXXI (except XXV, added Sept. 25, 1824) of Chapter Three and, I think, "Tatiana's Letter" were composed in the spring of 1824, from Feb. 8 to May 31, in Odessa. On the back of a letter, dated June 13, we find the already-mentioned One : XXXIII (the complicated history of which is discussed in my notes to that stanza). Personal troubles and his official banishment to the familial estate in the province of Pskov (he left Odessa July 31 and arrived in Mihaylovskoe Aug. 9, 1824) were responsible for another interruption. He resumed the writing of *EO* (presumably at Three : XXXII) only on Sept. 5, 1824, in Mihaylovskoe (where he was to remain confined for two years), and finished the canto (with the exception of XXXVI, added later) on Oct. 2, 1824.

Sometime during that month he went on to Chapter Four. By the end of 1824 he had written twenty-three stanzas of it, and he reached XXVII by Jan. 5, 1825. Then, turning to his Odessa recollections, he composed the stanzas that much later were to become a part of *Onegin's Journey* (XX–XXIX). Other compositions (such as the drama *Boris Godunov*) intervened. By Sept. 12, 1825, he had given what he then thought was its final form to his first concept of Chapter Four, but then he rearranged it, omitting and adding stanzas, and had Chapter Four completely ready only by the first week of 1826.

He began Chapter Five on Jan. 4, 1826, and seems to have had at least twenty-four stanzas of Chapter Five ready when he set out for Moscow on Sept. 4, 1826, for his crucial conversation with the new tsar. Back at Mihaylovskoe by Nov. 2, he completed the chapter in a week's time (Nov. 15–22, 1826).

The MS of Chapter Six is lost; most of it seems to have been ready by the beginning of December, 1826, before he returned from Mihaylovskoe to Moscow (Dec. 19). He seems to have written a large part of it on Nov. 22–25, 1826. On Aug. 10, 1826 (or 1827), he composed sts. LIII–LV.

The composing and reshuffling of Chapter Seven (which was to include, tentatively, "Onegin's Album" and, still more tentatively, a description of Onegin's travels) gave Pushkin a lot of trouble. He began it during his next stay at Mihaylovskoe (July–October, 1827), after which he lived in Petersburg (from mid-October, 1827, to Oct. 19, 1828), where, by Feb. 19, 1828, he had a dozen stanzas ready and, by April 5, was working on the "Album" interpolation. In the small hours of Oct. 20, after a Lyceum reunion, he left for Malinniki and there completed Chapter Seven, making a fair copy of it (lost except for the two last stanzas; PD 157) on Nov. 4, 1828.

Upon returning to Moscow from a trip to the Caucasus in the summer of 1829, where he refreshed his impressions of 1820, he finished, on Oct. 2, 1829, five stanzas with which he intended to begin *Onegin's Journey* (i.e., "Chapter Eight"), but which later were either scrapped or assigned to the final Chapter Eight, becoming X, XI, and XII of the latter. He worked on it in mid-October, 1829, at Pavlovskoe and finished *Onegin's Journey* (which includes the Odessa stanzas composed more than five years earlier) at Boldino, the last batch of five being dated Sept. 18, 1830.

The chapter (now Eight) that at the time he regarded as "Nine" (to follow "Chapter Eight," i.e., *Onegin's Journey*) had been begun on Christmas Eve, 1829, in Petersburg. In August, 1830, he went to Boldino, where a God-sent epidemic of cholera kept him marooned for three months, during which he wrote a miraculous number of masterpieces. He finished copying out Eight (then "Chapter Nine") there on Sept. 25, 1830. Next day he summed up his work on *EO* in a celebrated page of jottings (PD 129; facsimile facing p. 248 in the collection *Rukoyu Pushkina*, 1935; deletions given in ⟨⟩; Pushkin underscored the deleted titles, here printed in italic):

Onegin

Part First	Foreword
I canto	⟨*Hypochondria*⟩* Kishinev, Odessa
II ——	⟨*The Poet*⟩ Odessa 1824
III ——	⟨*The Damsel*⟩† Odessa. Mih[aylovskoe]. 1824
Part Second	
IV canto	⟨*The Countryside*⟩ Mihaylov. 1825
V ——	⟨*The Name Day*⟩‡ Mih. 1825 1826
VI ——	⟨*The Duel*⟩ Mih. 1826
Part Third	
VII canto	⟨*Moscow*⟩ Mih. P[eters].B[urg]. Malinn-[iki]. 1827. [182]8

---

*The titles are struck out with a vertical slash from "Hypochondria," to "The Grand Monde."

†*Barīshnya*, the "young lady," the "miss," *la demoiselle.*

‡Before writing the word *Imenini*, "The Name Day," Pushkin began to write *Pra*, or *Pro*, which may have been meant as *Prazdnik*, "Fete," or *Prorochestvo*, "Prophecy."

VIII canto ⟨*The Wandering*⟩* Mosc[ow].
Pavl[ovskoe]. 1829 Bold[ino].
IX ——— ⟨*The Grand Monde*⟩ Bold[ino].

Notes
1823 9 May *Kishinev*—1830   25 Sep. *Boldino*

———

26 Sep. AP [A. Pushkin]
To live it hurries and to feel it hastes†
A. P.‡   P[rince]. V[yazemski].
7 ye[ars]. 4 mo[nths]. 17 d[ays].

Another set of autograph dates—those on the copy (PD 173) of the 1833 edition of *EO* presented by Pushkin to Baroness Evpraksia Vrevski on Sept. 22, 1833—reads:

Chapter   One: was written in Kishinev and Odessa, 1823

"   Two: Written in Odessa in 1823 and 24.

"   Three: Written in 1824 in Odessa and Mihaylovskoe

"   Four: In Mihayl. in 1825

"   Five: in Mih. in 1826

"   Six: in Mih. 1826

"   Seven: in Mih. and in P[eters]B[urg], 1827 and 1828

"   Eight: In Boldino, 1830

———

*I translate *Stranstvie* (the word here) as "Wandering" and *Puteshestvie* (the word used by Pushkin later for this chapter) as "Journey."

†*I zhit' toropitsya i chuvstvovat' speshit.* The first word is made out of a Russian capital *P.* I suggest that Pushkin started to write the preceding line, *Po zhizni,* "O'er life."

‡I further suggest that Pushkin wrote his initials here in order to mark the French motto (which became the master motto), of which he was the author. The initials under the Russian motto (which became the chapter motto) are "K[nyaz']. V[yazemskiy]" in the original.

In October, 1830, in Boldino, Pushkin composed at least eighteen stanzas of what was to be a tenth chapter, soon canceled. In Tsarskoe Selo, in the summer of 1831, he revised and completed Chapter Eight, and on Oct. 5, 1831, he composed "Onegin's Letter"; the remnants of *Onegin's Journey* were removed to an appendix.

Pushkin on "Eugene Onegin"

Pushkin's epistolary references to his work on *EO* are considerably more frequent in 1824–25 than in 1823 or 1826–31. Regarding the complete editions of 1833 and 1837 there reigns a rather eerie silence in his correspondence. In the following notes I have covered the ground prior to the publication of Chapter One fairly completely. Other excerpts will be found in the Commentary.

The first mention is in a letter from Odessa to the man who is alluded to or mentioned four times in the complete edition of *EO*, the poet and critic Prince Pyotr Vyazemski, who lived mainly in Moscow, near which he had a large estate (Ostafievo). The letter is dated Nov. 4, 1823. By that time (half a year after starting *EO*) Chapter One and at least seventeen stanzas of Two had been completed. The relevant passage reads: "As to my occupations, I am writing now—not a novel—but a novel in verse—a deuced difference [or "a devil of a difference," *d'yavol'skaya raznitsa, une diable de différence*]." Pushkin repeats the same expression in another connection, when writing to Vyazemski, on Dec. 13, 1825, from Mihaylovskoe, that his friends prevent him from com-

plaining about his banishment "not in verse but in prose
—a deuced difference." The passage continues:

It is in the genre of *Don Juan* [Byron's poem, the first five
cantos of which Pushkin had read in Pichot's French
prose]. Publication is unthinkable. I write without re-
straining myself [*spustya rukava*, an idiom that connotes
otherwise a careless manner]. Our censorship is so whimsi-
cal that it is impossible to shape a course of action—better
not to think about it at all.

(In the draft of the letter: "The first canto or chapter is
finished—I shall send it to you. I write it with rapture,
which has not happened to me in a long time.")

On Nov. 16 of the same year, 1823, he writes from
Odessa to St. Petersburg to the poet Baron Anton Delvig,
an old schoolmate of his, thus:

I am now writing a new *poema* ["long poem," "narrative
poem"], in which I permit myself to babble beyond all
limits. Biryukov [the censor] shall not see it because he is
a fie-baby, a capricious child. God knows when we shall
read it together.

On Dec. 1, 1823, from Odessa, to Aleksandr Turgenev
in St. Petersburg:

I, in my leisure hours, am writing a new *poema*, *Eugene
Onegin*, wherein I choke on my bile. Two cantos are now
ready.

From Odessa to St. Petersburg, in the second part of
January or the beginning of February, 1824, to his
brother Lev Pushkin:

Perhaps I shall send Delvig excerpts from *Onegin*—it is
my best work. Do not believe Nikolay Raevski, who be-
rates it: he expected Romanticism from me, found Satire
and Cynicism, and did not make out sufficiently [what
it was all about].

From Odessa to St. Petersburg, Feb. 8, 1824, to the
writer Aleksandr Bestuzhev-Marlinski:

As to [printing] my *poema*, no use thinking of it. [After
this in the draft of the letter: "Its stanzas are perhaps

even more licentious (*vol'nee*) than those of *Don Juan*.''] If it is to be published, this surely will be not in Moscow and not in St. Petersburg.

From Odessa to Moscow, at the beginning of April, 1824, to Vyazemski:

Slyonin [a publisher] offers me as much as I want for *Onegin*. What say you about Russia—verily she is in Europe, and I thought it was a mistake of the geographers. The obstacle is censorship, and this to me is no joking matter, for it is the question of my future fate, of the independence I need. In order to publish *Onegin* I am ready to . . . [my prudish Soviet sources expurgate an obscene phrase and a lewd proverb, which I cannot reconstruct exactly]. Anyway, I am ready to hang myself if necessary.

In a letter (intercepted by the police and known only from a fragment), written in Odessa, presumably in early May, 1824, and addressed, perhaps, to the poet Küchelbecker, a Lyceum schoolmate: "I am writing the motley strophes of a romantic poem" (*romanticheskoy poemï*, "poème romantique," as Pichot translated Byron's term "romaunt," in *Childe-Harold*, 1822; *Œuvres de Lord Byron*, 4th edn., vol. II).

From Odessa to Moscow, June 7, 1824, to Vyazemski:

I shall send you with your wife* the first canto of *Onegin*. Mayhap [*avos'*] the cabinet change† will lead to its getting published.

From Odessa to St. Petersburg, June 13, 1824, to Lev Pushkin:

I shall attempt to knock at the holy gate of the censorship with the first chapter or canto of *Onegin*. Mayhap we may wriggle through. You demand of me details anent *Onegin*. The matter bores me, my dear old fellow.

---

*Vera Vyazemski, who had arrived that day and was to spend three months in Odessa; actually, Pushkin left before she did.

†Admiral Aleksandr Shishkov, a man of letters, had replaced Prince A. Golitsïn as Minister of Public Education, which post he was to occupy till 1828.

Another time. I am not writing anything now—have worries of a different kind.

(Pushkin had quarreled with Count Vorontsov, the Governor of New Russia, to whose chancery he was attached.)

From Odessa to Moscow, June 29, 1824, to Bestuzhev-Marlinski:

My *Onegin* is growing;* yet the devil knows who will publish it; I thought censorship had become more intelligent under Shishkov but now I see that under the old [some kind of slip here] everything remains as of old.

From Odessa to St. Petersburg, July 14, 1824, to A. Turgenev:

Knowing your ancient affection for the pranks of my outcast Muse, I was about to send you several stanzas of my *Onegin* but was too lazy to do so. I do not know if they will let my poor *Onegin* into the Heavenly Kingdom of Publication; in any case I will try.

A fortnight later Pushkin was expelled from Odessa to his mother's country estate, Mihaylovskoe, in the province of Pskov. From there, in the autumn of 1824, he dispatched Chapter One of *EO* with Lev Pushkin to Pletnyov in St. Petersburg for publication. In my Commentary, I quote the accompanying letter as well as some other letters of that period.

On Jan. 25, 1825, from Mihaylovskoe, in a letter to the poet Kondratiy Rïleev in St. Petersburg, he complains about Bestuzhev-Marlinski's not understanding *EO*, of which he had seen the Chapter One transcript:

Bestuzhev writes me a lot about *Onegin*. Tell him he is wrong: does he really want to banish from the domain of poetry all that is light and gay? Whither then should satires and comedies go? In result, one would have to abolish *Orlando furioso* [by Ariosto] and *Gudibras* [*Hudibras*, by Samuel Butler], and the *Pucelle* [by Voltaire], and *Ver-ver* [*Vert-Vert*, by Gresset], and *Renike-*

---

*Which surely means that Pushkin had been continuing Chapter Three, after his gloomy letter of June 13.

fuks [*Reineke Fuchs*, by Goethe], and the best part of *Little Psyche* [by Bogdanovich] and the tales [*Contes*] of La Fontaine, and Krïlov's fables, etc., etc., etc., etc., etc. This is rather strict. Pictures of society life also enter the domain of poetry; but enough of *Onegin*.

To Bestuzhev in St. Petersburg he writes from Mihaylovskoe on Mar. 24, 1825:

Your letter is very clever, but still you are wrong, still you regard *Onegin* from the wrong point of view, still it is my best work. You compare the first chapter with *Don Juan*. None esteems *Don Juan* (its first five cantos [in Pichot's French]—I have not read the rest) more than I, but it has nothing in common with *Onegin*. You speak of a satire by an Englishman, Byron, and you compare it with mine, and demand one like it from me! No, my dear old fellow, you ask too much. Where do I have a satire? There is not the ghost of it in *Eugene Onegin*. With me, the embankment would crack [idiom for, say, "the earth would rumble"] if I touched satire. The very word "satirical" should not have occurred in my preface. Wait till you see the other cantos. Ah, if only I could lure you to Mihaylovskoe! You would see that if one really must compare *Onegin* with *Don Juan* it should be done in one respect only: who is more winsome and more charming, *gracieuse* [Fr.], Tatiana or Julia? Canto One is merely a rapid introduction, and I am pleased with it (which very seldom happens to me).

Vyazemski, as already mentioned, was Pushkin's first correspondent to learn of *EO* (Nov. 4, 1823). At the end of March, 1825, from Mihaylovskoe, our poet informs his old friend (whom by now he has not seen for more than five years) that he is doing something quite special for him—copying out Chapter Two:

I wish it might help to make you smile.* This is the first time a reader's smile *me sourit* (pardon this platitude:

*Vyazemski had just lost a child, little Nikolay, and had been seriously ill himself; it is curious to note that in a kind of poetical compensation Vyazemski cheers up Tatiana in the imaginary Moscow of Chapter Seven.

'tis in the blood).* Meantime, be grateful to me—never in my life have I copied out anything.

This is followed up by a letter of Apr. 7, "the anniversary of Byron's death," in which Pushkin, from Mihaylovskoe, informs Vyazemski that he has had the village pope sing a Requiem Mass for God's slave, *boyarin Georgiy*, complete with an apportioned piece of blessed bread, *prosvira*, which he sends Vyazemski, also a great admirer of Pichot's author. "I am transcribing *Onegin*. He too will soon reach you."

With Delvig, who visited him in Mihaylovskoe in mid-April, 1825, Pushkin sent this MS copy of Chapter Two to Vyazemski, "made for you and only for you" (letter to Vyazemski of c. Apr. 20). Delvig took it to Petersburg; Vyazemski was expected to come there from Moscow, but his arrival was postponed. Throughout May Chapter Two was eagerly read by Pushkin's and Delvig's literary friends, and the MS ("only for you") reached Vyazemski in Moscow only in the first week of June. To him Pushkin wrote from Mihaylovskoe a year later (May 27, 1826):

If the new tsar [Nicholas I] grants me my freedom, I will not stay [in Russia] another month. We live in a sorry era, but when I imagine London, railroads, steamships, the English reviews or the theaters and bordellos of Paris— then my Mihaylovskoe backwoods make me sick and mad. In Canto Four of *Onegin* I have depicted my life [at Mihaylovskoe].

In a letter to Vyazemski, dated Dec. 1, 1826, from an inn in Pskov, where he stopped for a few days on his way to Moscow, after a sojourn of three weeks at Mihaylovskoe, Pushkin says of this same Canto Four: "In Pskov, instead of writing Chapter Seven of *Onegin*, I go and lose Chapter Four at stuss—which is not funny."

_____
*Both Pushkin's father and uncle, Vasiliy Pushkin, were incorrigible punsters.

Note: The place of publication is St. Petersburg unless otherwise indicated. Except in the titles of separate printings, *Eugene Onegin* is abbreviated as *EO*, and Aleksandr Pushkin as AP.

(1) Mar. 3, (O.S.), 1824.

One : xx : 5–14, quoted by Fadey Bulgarin in the section "Literary News" in *Literaturnïe listki* (Literary Leaflets), no. 4 (Mar. 3, 1824), 148–49.

(2) Last week of December, 1824.

Two : vii : 1–8, viii : 1–9, ix–x : 1–12, published as "Passages from *EO*, a long poem by AP," in Baron Anton Delvig's annual anthology (*al'manah*), *Severnïe tsvetï* (Northern Flowers; 1825), pp. 280–81.

(3) Feb. 16, 1825; first separate edition of Chapter One.

Evgeniy Onegin . . . In the printing shop of the Department of Public Education, 1825.

12°. xxiv + 60 pp. Contents: i, half title; iii, title; iv, permission to print; v, dedication to Lev Pushkin; vii–viii, foreword; ix, divisional title of "Conversation of Bookseller with Poet"; xi–xxii, text of "Conversa-

74

tion . . . ," 192 ll. in iambic tetrameter and one eight-
word line of prose; xxiii, divisional title; xxiv, motto,
"Pétri de vanité . . ."; 1–49, text, sts. I–VIII, X–XII,
XV–XXXVIII, XLII–LX; 51–59, nn.; 60, erratum and note,
"NB. All the omissions in this work, marked by dots,
have been made by the author himself."

(4) Apr. 7, 1826.
　　Two : XXIV–XXIX : 1–12, XXXVII–XL; printed as "Pas-
sages from the Second Canto of *EO*, a long poem by
AP," in the poetry section of Delvig's *Northern Flowers*
(1826), pp. 56–62.

(5) C. Oct. 20, 1826; first separate edition of Chapter Two.
　　Evgeniy Onegin . . . Moscow: In the printing shop
of Avgust Semen, at the Imperial Medicochirurgical
Academy, 1826.
　　12°. 42 pp. Contents: 1, half title; 3, title; 4, per-
mission to print, "September 27, 1826. This book was
inspected by the associate [*ekstraordinarnïy*] professor,
civil servant of the 7th rank [*nadvornïy sovetnik*] and
knight [*kavaler*], Ivan Snegiryov";* 5, divisional title
with note, "Written in 1823"; 6, motto, "O rus! . . .
Hor."; 7–42, text, sts. I–VIII : 1–8, IX–XXXV : 1–4 and
12–14, XXXVI–XL.
　　On the paper wrapper is engraved a small stylized
nymphalid butterfly, with half-closed wings and over-
sized abdomen, in profile.

(6) Mar. 19, 1827.
　　Seven : XX–XXX : 1 ["Onegin's Journey"]; published
as "Odessa (From the Seventh Chapter of *EO*)"; un-
signed; in *Moskovskiy vestnik* (Moscow Herald), pt. 2,
no. 6 (Mar. 19, 1827), pp. 113–18.

(7a) C. Mar. 25, 1827.
　　"Tatiana's Letter (From the Third Canto of *EO*),"

---
*See n. to Two : XXXV : 10.

79 ll.; signed; in Delvig's *Northern Flowers* (1827), pp. 221–24.

(7b) Same as 7a.

Three : XVII–XX; printed as "A passage from the Third Chapter of *EO*. The night conversation between Tatiana and the nurse"; signed; in the same publication as 7a, pp. 282–84.

(8) C. Oct. 10, 1827; first separate edition of Chapter Three.

Evgeniy Onegin . . . In the printing shop of the Department of Public Education, 1827.

12°. 52 pp. Contents: 1, half title; 3, title; 4, "With the permission of the Government"; 5, "The first chapter of *EO*, written in 1823, came out in 1825. Two years later, the second was published. This slowness proceeded from extrinsic circumstances. Henceforth publication will follow an uninterrupted order, one chapter coming immediately after another"; 7, divisional title; 8, motto, Elle était fille . . ."; 9–51, text, sts. I–III : 1–8, IV–XXXI, "Tatiana's Letter to Onegin" (79 ll.), XXXII–XXXIX, "The Song of the Girls" (18 trochaic ll.), XL–XLI.

(9) Last week of October, 1827.

Four : I–IV, published as "Women. A passage from *EO*"; signed; in *Moskovskiy vestnik*, pt. 5, no. 20 (Oct., 1827), pp. 365–67.

(10) Jan. 9–18, 1828.

Seven : XXXV–LIII, published as "Moscow (From *EO*)"; signed; text preceded by the three mottoes to Seven (see no. 19 below); in *Moskovskiy vestnik*, pt. 7, no. 1 (Jan. 9–18, 1828), pp. 5–12.

(11) Jan. 31–Feb. 2, 1828; first separate edition of Chapters Four and Five.

Evgeniy Onegin . . . In the printing shop of the Department of Public Education, 1828.

12°. 94 pp. Contents: 1, half title; 3, title; 4, "With the permission of the Government"; 5, "Petru Aleksandrovichu Pletnyovu"; 7, dedication, "Not thinking to amuse . . . December 29, 1827"; 9, divisional title for Four; 10, motto, "La morale est . . ."; 11–50, text of Four : VII–XXXVII : 1–13, XXXIX–LI; 51, divisional title for Five; 52, motto, "Never know these frightful dreams . . ."; 53–92, text of Five : I–XLII, XLIII : 5–14, XLIV–XLV; 93, "Note. In the 13th verse of p. 48 [Four : L : 7] the misprinted *zaveti* [the precepts] should be *zevoti* [of yawning]."

(12) Feb. 1, 1828.

Four : XXVII–XXX, published as "Albums (From the Fourth Chapter of *EO*)"; signed; in *Moskovskiy vestnik*, pt. 7, no. 2 (Feb. 1, 1828), pp. 148–50.

(13) Feb. 9, 1828.

Seven: same stanzas as no. 10 above, prefaced by the three mottoes, published as "Moscow (From *EO*)"; in *Severnaya pchela* (Northern Bee), no. 17 (Feb. 9, 1828), pp. 3–4. Footnote to the title: "This fragment was printed in a magazine with unseemly mistakes. By the wish of the esteemed Author, we insert it in the *Northern Bee* with corrections. The iteration of A. S. Pushkin's verses (N.B. with his permission) can never be superfluous. Ed. [Fadey Bulgarin]."

(14) Mar. 23, 1828; first separate edition of Chapter Six.

Evgeniy Onegin . . . In the printing shop of the Department of Public Education, 1828.

12°. 48 pp. Contents: 1, half title; 3, title; 4, "With the permission of the Government"; 5, divisional title; 6, motto, "Là sotto giorni . . ."; 7–46, text, I–XIV, XVII–XXXVII, XXXIX–XLVII; 46–48, "Note. In the course of the publication of Part First of *EO* [at the time this meant Chapters One to Five] there have crept into it several serious mistakes. The most important of these are listed here. We have italicized the corrections . . ." [a list of these follows; six refer to the "Conversation . . ."; four are misprints in *EO*; the rest are given in my Commentary as follows : One : XXX : 12–14, XLII : 9–12, XLV : before 1; Two : added motto ("O Rus'!"), VII : 14, XI : 14, XXXII : 7, XXXVIII : 11; Three : V : 9, XX : 13–14, "Tatiana's Letter" : 5–7, XXXIV : 7–8; Four : XXIX : 13, XXX : 10, XXXII : 6; Five : IV : 14, V : 9, XV : vars. 9–10, XVII : 7, XXX : 6, XLIV : 3, XLV : 14]; 48, "End of first part."

(15) C. Jan. 20, 1829.

Passages from *EO* reprinted as legends to six engravings by Aleksandr Notbek, purporting to illustrate scenes from *EO*,* as follows: One : XLVIII : 5–12, Two : XII, Three : XXXII, Four : XLIV : 9–14, Five : IX : 1–8, and Six : XLI : 5–14; published by Egor Aladyin in *Nevskiy al'manah* (Nevski Almanac, 1829), pp. v–x.

(16) Mar. 27–28, 1829; second separate edition of Chapter One.

Evgeniy Onegin . . . In the printing shop of the Department of Public Education, 1829.

12°. xxiv + 60 pp. Contents as in no. 3 above, except that p. 60 is blank and its erratum and author's note do not appear.

(17) Last week of December, 1829.

Seven : I–IV, published as "A Passage from the Seventh Chapter of *EO*"; signed; in the poetry section of Delvig's *Northern Flowers* (1830), pp. 4–6.

(18) Jan. 1, 1830.

Eight : XVI–XIX : 1–10, published as "A Passage from the Eighth Chapter of *EO*" ["Onegin's Journey"]; signed; in Delvig's *Literaturnaya gazeta* (Literary Gazette), vol. I, no. 1 (Wednesday, Jan. 1, 1830), pp. 2–3.

---

*See n. to One : XLVIII : 2.

(19) Mar. 18–19, 1830; first separate edition of Chapter Seven.

Evgeniy Onegin . . . In the printing shop of the Department of Public Education, 1830.

12°. 58 pp. Contents: 1, half title; 3, title; 4, "By the permission of the Government"; 5, divisional title; 6, three mottoes, "Moscow . . . ," "How can one . . . ," "Antagonism to Moscow . . ."; 7–53, text, sts. I–VII, X–XXXVIII, XL–LV; 55–57, notes [to IV : 4, XXXIV : 1, and XXXV : 8; these are nn. 41, 42, and 43 of the 1837 edn.].

(20) May 7–8, 1830; second separate edition of Chapter Two.

Evgeniy Onegin . . . In the printing shop of the Department of Public Education, 1830.

12°. 42 pp. Contents: 1, half title; 3, title; 4, "By permission of the Government"; 5, divisional title; 6, two mottoes, "O rus! . . . *Hor.*" and "O Rus'!"; 7–42, text, stanzas I–VIII : 1–9, IX–XL.

(21) C. Jan. 10, 1832; first separate edition of Chapter Eight.

Evgeniy Onegin . . . In the printing shop of the Department of Public Education, 1832.

12°. viii + 52 pp. Contents: i, half title; iii, title; iv, permission to print, "Censor . . . Nov. 16, 1831"; v–vi, foreword, "The dropped stanzas . . . [quoting XLVIIIa : 1–5]"; vii, divisional title; viii, motto, "Fare thee well . . ."; 1–51, text, sts. I–II : 1–4, III–XXV : 1–8, XXVI–XXXII, "Onegin's Letter to Tatiana" (60 ll.), XXXIII–LI; 51, after the last line of text, "The end of the eighth and last chapter."

The paper wrapper bears the legend, "The last chapter of *EO*."

(22) Apr. 20, 1832.

Eight : XXXIX : 4–14, XL–XLVIII : 1–4, published as

"A Passage from the last chapter of *EO*, a novel in verse, composed by A. S. Pushkin"; in literary supplement to *Russkiy invalid* (Disabled Soldier), no. 32 (Apr. 20, 1832), pp. 253–54.

(23) C. Mar. 23, 1833; first complete edition.

Evgeniy Onegin . . . In the printing shop of Aleksandr Smirdin, 1833.

8°. vi + 288 pp. Contents: i, half title; iii, title; iv, "By the permission of the Government," "Edition of the bookseller Smirdin"; vi, master motto, "Pétri de vanité . . ."; 1–37, One, with motto, "To live it hurries . . . ," and text, sts. I–VIII, X–XII, XV–XXXVIII, XLII–LX; 39–66, Two, with mottoes, "O rus! *Hor.*" and "O Rus'!," and text, sts. I–VIII : 1–9, IX–XXXV : 1–4 and 12–14, XXXVI–XL; 67–99, Three, with motto, "Elle étoit fille . . . ," and text, sts. I–III : 1–8, IV–XXXI, "Tatiana's Letter to Onegin" (79 iambic ll.), XXXII–XXXIX, "The Song of the Girls" (18 trochaic ll.), XL–XLI; 101–30, Four, with motto, "La morale est . . . ," and text, sts. VII–XXXV, XXXVII : 1–13, XXXIX–LI; 131–59, Five, with motto, "Never know . . . ," and text, sts. I–XXXVI, XXXIX–XLII, XLIV–XLV; 161–90, Six, with motto, "Là sotto giorni . . . ," and text, sts. I–XIV, XVII–XXXVII, XXXIX–XLVI; 191–226, Seven, with three mottoes, "Moscow, of Russia . . . ," "How can one not . . . ," "Antagonism to Moscow . . . ," and text, sts. I–VII, X–XXXVIII, XL–LV; 227–64, Eight, with motto, "Fare thee well . . . ," and text, sts. I–II : 1–4, III–XXV : 1–8, XXVI–XXXII, "Onegin's Letter to Tatiana" (60 iambic ll.), XXXIII–LI; 265–72, "Notes to *EO*" [as follows: in Chapter One, n. 1, II : 14; n. 2, IV : 7; n. 3, XV : 10; n. 4, XVI : 5; n. 5, XXI : 14; n. 6, XXIV : 12; n. 7, XLII : 14; n. 8, XLVII : 3; n. 9, XLVIII : 4; n. 10, L : 3; n. 11, L : 11, "The author, on his mother's side, is of African descent"; in Chapter Two, n. 12, XII : 14; n. 13, XXIV : 1; n. 14, XXX : 4; n. 15,

XXXI : 14; n. 16, XXXVII : 6; in Chapter Three, n. 17,
IV : 2; n. 18, IX : 10; n. 19, XII : 11; n. 20, XXII : 10;
n. 21, XXVII : 4; n. 22, XXX : 1; in Chapter Four, n. 23,
"Chapters Four and Five came out with the following
dedication to P. A. Pletnyov: Not thinking to amuse the
haughty world . . ." (17 ll.); n. 24, XLI : 12; n. 25,
XLII : 7; n. 26, XLV : 5; n. 27, L : 12; in Chapter Five,
n. 28, III : 8; n. 29, III : 14; n. 30, VIII : 14; n. 31, IX : 13;
n. 32, XVII : 8; n. 33, XX : 5; n. 34, XXII : 12; n. 35, XXV :
1; n. 36, XXVI : 10; n. 37, XXVIII : 9; in Chapter Six, n.
38, V : 13; n. 39, XI : 12; n. 40, XXV : 12; n. 41, XLVI :
14; in Chapter Seven, n. 42, IV : 4; n. 43, XXXIV : 1; n.
44, XXXV : 8; in Chapter Eight, n. 45, VI : 2]; 273–87,
"Passages from Eugene Onegin's Journey" [containing
the following: 273, "The Last Chapter (Eight) of *EO*
was published separately with the following preface";
followed by text of pp. v–vi of no. 21 above; 274–87,
fragments of "Journey" with preface beginning "P. A.
Katenin . . ." and text, sts. IX : 2–14, X : 1, XII–XV : 9–
14, XVI–XXX : 1, with brief interpolations in prose].

Wrapper: "For sale at the bookshop of A. Smirdin.
Price 12 rubles."

(24) January (not later than 19), 1837; second complete
edition.*

Evgeniy Onegin . . . Third edition . . . In the print-
ing shop of the Office of Purveyance of State Papers,
1837.

16° in eights. viii+310 pp. Contents: iii, half title;
iv, permission to print, "November 27, 1836"; v, title;
vi, master motto, "Pétri de vanité . . ."; vii–viii, pref-
atory piece, "Not thinking to amuse . . ." (17 ll.);
1–280, mottoes and text as in no. 23 above [the chapters
paged as follows: 1–40, One; 41–69, Two; 71–105,
Three; 107–38, Four; 139–69, Five; 171–202, Six;

---

* For a photographic reproduction, see vol. 4 in 4-vol. edition.

203–40, Seven; 241–80, Eight]; 281–93, "Notes to *EO*" [the same as in no. 23 above, except that n. 11 (One : L : 11) has been changed to read, "See the first edition of *EO*," and the substance of n. 23 has been printed in the preliminaries as pp. vii–viii, so it is omitted and the following nn. originally numbered 24–45 are here numbered 23–44]; 295–310, "Passages from Onegin's Journey," same text as in no. 23 above.

Wrapper: (front) "Eugene Onegin" (back) "Published by Ilya Glazunov."

A copy of this edition has recently come to light (see the collection *Pushkin*, ed. A. Ergolin, I, 379) with a dedication by Pushkin to Lyudmila Shishkin (wife of the usurer who lent him money) dated Jan. 1, 1837.

It would take too much space to enumerate even the main editions of *EO* published after Pushkin's death. One can judge of the popularity of the novel in Russia by the avalanche of editions it went through between, say, 1911 and 1913. I borrow this information from A. Fomin's *Pushkiniana for 1911–1917* (published by the Academy of Sciences of the U.S.S.R., 1937). Fifty kopecks equaled twenty-five cents. You could buy a loaf of bread for a couple of cents and a copy of *EO* for ten cents.

Place	Year	Publisher	Price	Copies
St. Petersburg	1911	Stasyulevich	40 kop.	5000
Moscow	1912	Sïtin	20 kop.	10,000
St. Petersburg	1912	Suvorin	1.50 kop.	2000
Moscow	1912	Panafidin	20 kop.	10,000
Kiev	1912	Ioganson	35 kop.	5000
Warsaw	1913	Shkola	20 kop.	10,000

There were also several new editions in 1914–16, not to mention numerous editions of the complete works (as many as five in 1911).

The only satisfactory modern edition of *EO* is the one edited by B. Tomashevski and published as vol. VI (1937) of the sixteen-volume *Works* published by the Academy of Sciences of the U.S.S.R. This is referred to in the Commentary as "Acad 1937." A prefatory note in this edition describes the contents as follows:

The present volume contains the text of *EO* and all variants in MSS and in editions printed during the poet's lifetime. In the basic text of this volume the novel is given in the version that was decided upon by Pushkin himself in the editions of 1833 and 1837, with the censored passages restored. In the section entitled "Other Redactions and Variants" appears all that material which was not included in the final version of the novel, such as all that has been preserved of two chapters not included in the final text: namely, what was initially the eighth chapter, known as "Onegin's Journey," and the tenth chapter, preserved only in small fragments coded by Pushkin and saturated with political subject matter. The material pertaining to these chapters is in each case collected in one place, since the absence of a unifying final text did not allow for the distribution of the chapter variants in various subdivisions of the second section of the volume. The text of these chapters is reproduced in the first subdivision of the section "Other Redactions and Variants" ("Draft Variants in the MSS"), where the text of the MSS is presented in full. The present volume is edited by B. V. Tomashevski. Control recensionist, G. O. Vinokur.

The volume also contains a reproduction of the water-color portrait of Pushkin by P. F. Sokolov, 1830, and seven facsimiles of leaves of various autograph MSS.

For the discarded stanzas and MS variants pertaining to *EO*, I have relied mainly on the *only* satisfactory modern edition, that edited by B. Tomashevski in 1937, referred to as Acad 1937.

I have also had to consult vol. V (containing *EO* and dramatic works) of two much inferior (in fact, very poor) editions of Pushkin's works in ten volumes brought out by Akademiya nauk SSSR, Institut Literaturï (Pushkinskiy Dom), in Moscow, 1949 (621 pp.) and 1957 (639 pp.), where considerable pressure must have been exerted on the annotator (Tomashevski) by the governmental publishers, in the course of presenting deleted readings as noncanceled ones and leaving without any comment a number of new recensions. I refer to these editions as "*Works* 1949" and "*Works* 1957." * Some of Pushkin's autographs are described by L. B. Modzalevski and Tomashevski in *Rukopisi Pushkina hranyashchiesya v Pushkinskom dome* (Leningrad, 1937), but otherwise

---

*Vol. IV of Collected Works, yet another unscholarly production, published by Hudozhestvennaya Literatura, Moscow, 1960, has also been taken into account and appears as "*Works* 1960."

considerable ingenuity has to be exercised in tracking down references to the location of MSS and their description. Other works to which abbreviated reference is made in my Commentary are *P. i ego sovr.* (the series *Pushkin i ego sovremenniki* [Pushkin and His Contemporaries], nos. 1–39, 1903–30) and its continuation *Vremennik* (*Vremennik Pushkinskoy komissii* [Annals of the Pushkin Commission], vols. I–VI, 1936–41); and the collection *Lit. nasl.* (*Literaturnoe nasledstvo* [Literary Heritage], especially nos. 16–18, 1934).

When I started about 1950 on the present work, the autographs of Pushkin pertaining to *EO* were preserved (according to Acad 1937, p. 660) mainly in four places: (1) the Rumyantsov Museum (termed after the Revolution Publichnaya Biblioteka Soyuza SSR imeni V. I. Lenina or Leninskaya Biblioteka) in Moscow, which I refer to in my notes as "MB" (Moscow Biblioteka); (2) the Moscow Tsentrarhiv (Central Archives), referred to further as "MA"; (3) the St. Petersburg, later Leningrad, Public Library, also known as Publichnaya Biblioteka imeni Saltïkova-Shchedrina,* referred to further as "PB"; and (4) Pushkinskiy Dom (the Pushkin House), also known as Institut Literaturï Akademii nauk SSSR, in Leningrad, and referred to as "PD." By the time I had completed my work all these MSS had been concentrated in PD, but for purposes of co-ordination I have preserved the key ciphers in my references to them.

The main body of the *EO* drafts is found in Cahiers 2368, 2369, 2370, 2371, and 2382, with additional material numbered 1254, 2366, 2387, 3515, and 8318. All these were formerly preserved in MB. Most of the fair copies were preserved in PB (8, 9, 10, 14, 18, 21–26, 42, 43). PD had 46, 108, 155–73, collection (*fond*) 244, and

---

*Mihail Saltïkov, pen name Shchedrin (1826–89), a second-rate writer of politico-satirical fiction.

inventories (*opisi*) 1 and 5–45. MA had only 22 / 3366 and an unnumbered MS (the second fair copy of Chapter Two). The drafts are distributed as follows:

Chapter One

The drafts of the first chapter begun in May, 1823, in Kishinev, are in Cahier 2369 (ff. 4^v–22^v), excepting those of sts. XXXIII (1254, f. 24^v, 2366, ff. 13^v, 17^v, and 2370, f. 4^r) and XVIII–XIX (2370, f. 20^v). The fair copy (a transcript) is numbered 8 (PB).

Chapter Two

The drafts are in 2369 (ff. 23^r–43^v). There is a first fair copy numbered 9 (PB) and a second fair copy, unnumbered, preserved (according to Acad 1937) in MA.

Chapter Three

The drafts are in 2369 (f. 39^v, ff. 48^v–51^v, first six sts.) and 2370 (ff. 2^r–7^r, 11^v, 12^r, 17^v–20^r, 28), a cahier he began using in May, 1824, in Odessa. The fair copy is numbered 10 (PB), and there is an additional fair copy of four sts. (XVII, XVIII, XIX, XX : 1–12) in PD 154.

Chapter Four

The drafts are in 2370 (ff. 28^v–29^v, 31^r–34^r, 39, 41, 50^v–54^r, 58^r, 64^v, 70^r–79^r). The fair copy (with that of Five) is numbered 14 (PB). A fair copy of I–IV is in MB 3515 (pp. 415–17), which is a letter from Pushkin to Mihail Pogodin, Aug. 15, 1827.

Chapter Five

The drafts are in 2370 (ff. 70^v–84^r, I–XX; ff. 38^v–40, XXXII–XXXVIII; and ff. 64, 68, 50, XXI), and the rest in 2368 (ff. 3^r, 41^r–43^v, 49^v, 50^r), which he began in 1826. The fair copy is PB 14.

Chapter Six

Only very few autographs of this canto have come down to us. The drafts of XLIII–XLV are contained in 2368 (f. 24). Drafts of X–XXIV, a, b, and the first line of c, are in PD 155; and a final draft (or first fair copy) of XXXVI–XXXVII exists (or existed in 1937) in a private collection abroad. Excepting a fragment of XLVI in an album, no fair copies exist.

Chapter Seven

The drafts are in 2368 (ff. 21ʳ–23ᵛ, 27ʳ, 30ʳ–32ʳ, 35) and 2371 (ff. 2ʳ–10ʳ, 17ʳ, 68ʳ–69ʳ, 71ᵛ–75ʳ). The only fair copies are in PB 43 and consist of alt. XXI–XXII and "Onegin's Album." Drafts of VIII–IX are in MB 71 (f. 4).

Onegin's Journey (initially Chapter Eight)

The drafts of sts. XX–XXIX, composed immediately after Four (1825), are in 2370 (ff. 65ʳ–68ᵛ). The drafts of I–XIX, composed at the end of 1829, are in PD 161–62 (I–III); 2382 (ff. 90ʳ, 98ʳ, 111ʳ–112ʳ, 115ᵛ–119ʳ, V–XII, not in this order); PD 168 (XIIa, b); 2382 (f. 39ᵛ, XIIc; f. 116ʳ, XIII; ff. 111ᵛ and 115, XV; ff. 111ʳ and 112ʳ, XVI–XVII); PB 18 (XVIII); 2382 (f. 90ʳ, XIX); with a last batch, finished Sept. 18, 1830, in 2368 (f. 30ʳ, XXX; f. 17ᵛ, XXXII) and PB 18 (XXXI). The fair copies are in 2382 (f. 100ʳ, IV; ff. 119ʳ–120ʳ, I–III), PB 18 (V–XII, XIII–XXXIII), and PD 169 (XXXIV).

Chapter Eight (initially Chapter Nine)

Little is left of the drafts of this canto. In 2382 are found the drafts of Ia and Ib (f. 25ᵛ) and of XXVIa (f. 32ᵛ); other drafts are 2387A (f. 17ʳ, frags. of VI); PD 159 and 160 (frags. of IX); PD 163 (XVIII : 9–14, XIX); PD 164 (XXV); 2371 (f. 88ᵛ, XXVIIa, 1st alt.); PD 165 ("Onegin's Letter"); and PD 166 (XXXVII).The fair copy, PB 21–26, entitled *Evgeniy Onegin*, *Pes[nya]* *IX* (Canto Nine), and dated (st. LI) "Boldino, Sept. 25 [1830], 3¼," comprises sts. (numbered differently; see Commentary) Ia, Id, Ie, If, II–VIII, XVII–XXIV, XXVII, XXX–XXXVI (marked "XXXIII"), XXXVIII–LI (this last batch unnumbered).

Chapter Ten

The fragments of this canto are in PD 170 and 171 (see Commentary).

Pushkin's Notes to *EO*

A draft made in 1830 is in PD 172.

EUGENE ONEGIN

A Novel in Verse

by Aleksandr Pushkin

Pétri de vanité il avait encore plus de cette espèce
d'orgueil qui fait avouer avec la même indifférence les
bonnes comme les mauvaises actions, suite d'un senti-
ment de supériorité, peut-être imaginaire.

Tiré d'une lettre particulière

Not thinking to amuse the proud world,
having grown fond of friendship's attention,
I wish I could present you
4   with a gage worthier of you—
worthier of a fine soul
[full of a holy] dream,
of poetry, vivid and clear,
8   of high thoughts and simplicity.
But so be it. With partial hand
take this collection of variegated chapters:
half droll, half sad,
12   plain-folk, ideal,
the careless fruit of my amusements,
insomnias, light inspirations,
unripe and withered years,
16   the intellect's cold observations,
and the heart's sorrowful remarks.

CHAPTER ONE

To live it hurries and to feel it hastes.

Prince Vyazemski

Chapter One

_____

I

"My uncle has most honest principles:
when taken ill in earnest,
he has made one respect him
4   and nothing better could invent.
To others his example is a lesson;
but, good God, what a bore
to sit by a sick man both day and night,
8   without moving a step away!
What base perfidiousness
the half-alive one to amuse,
adjust for him the pillows,
12   sadly present the medicine,
sigh—and think inwardly
when *will* the devil take you?"

II

Thus a young scapegrace thought,
with posters flying in the dust,
by the most lofty will of Zeus
4   the heir of all his relatives.
Friends of Lyudmila and Ruslan!
The hero of my novel,
without preambles, forthwith,
8   I'd like to have you meet:
Onegin, a good pal of mine,
was born upon the Neva's banks,
where maybe you were born,
12   or used to shine, my reader!
There formerly I too promenaded—
but harmful is the North to me.[1]

[[1] For Pushkin's notes, see below, pp. 313–20]

III

Having served excellently, nobly,
his father lived by means of debts;
gave three balls yearly
4   and squandered everything at last.
Fate guarded Eugene:
at first, Madame looked after him;
later, Monsieur replaced her.
8   The child was boisterous but nice.
Monsieur l'Abbé, a poor wretch of a Frenchman,
not to wear out the infant,
would teach him everything in play,
12   bothered him not with stern moralization,
scolded him slightly for his pranks,
and to the Letniy Sad took him for walks.

IV

Then, when tumultuous youth's
season for Eugene came,
season of hopes and tender melancholy,
4   Monsieur was ousted from the place.
Now my Onegin is at large:
hair cut after the latest fashion,
dressed like a London Dandy—[2]
8   and finally he saw the World.
In French impeccably
he could express himself and write,
danced the mazurka lightly,
12   and bowed unconstrainedly—
what would you more? The World decided
he was clever and very nice.

V

All of us had a bit of schooling
in something and somehow:
hence education, God be praised,
4   is in our midst not hard to flaunt.
Onegin was, in the opinion of many
(judges resolute and stern),
a learned fellow but a pedant.
8   He had the happy talent,
without constraint, in conversation
slightly to touch on everything,
with an expert's learned air
12   keep silent in a grave discussion,
and provoke the smile of ladies
with the fire of unexpected epigrams.

VI

Latin has gone at present out of fashion;
still, to tell you the truth,
he had enough knowledge of Latin
4   to make out epigraphs,
descant on Juvenal,
put at the bottom of a letter *vale*,
and he remembered, though not without fault,
8   two lines from the *Aeneid*.
He had no urge to rummage
in the chronological dust
of the earth's historiography,
1 2   but anecdotes of days gone by,
from Romulus to our days,
he did keep in his memory.

VII

Lacking the lofty passion
not to spare life for the sake of sounds,
an iamb from a trochee he could not—
4   no matter how we strove—distinguish;
dispraised Homer, Theocritus,
but read, in compensation, Adam Smith,
and was a deep economist:
8   that is, he could assess the way
a state grows rich,
and what it lives upon, and why
it needs not gold
1 2   when it has got the simple product.
His father could not understand him,
and mortgaged his lands.

VIII

All Eugene knew besides
I have no leisure to recount;
but where he was a veritable genius,
4   what he more firmly knew than all the arts,
what since his prime had been to him
toil, anguish, joy,
what occupied the livelong day
8   his fretting indolence—
was the art of soft passion
which Naso sang,
wherefore a sufferer he ended
12   his brilliant and tumultuous span
in Moldavia, in the wild depth of steppes,
far from his Italy.

IX

.   .   .   .

X

How early he was able to dissemble,
conceal a hope, show jealousy,
shake one's belief, make one believe,
4   seem gloomy, pine away,
appear proud and obedient,
attentive or indifferent!
How languorously he was silent,
8   how flamingly eloquent,
in letters of the heart, how casual!
With one thing breathing, one thing loving,
how self-oblivious he could be!
12   How quick and tender was his gaze,
bashful and daring, while at times
it shone with an obedient tear!

99

XI

How he was able to seem new,
to amaze innocence in sport,
alarm with ready desperation,
4 amuse with pleasant flattery,
catch the minute of softheartedness;
the prejudices of innocent years
conquer by means of wits and passion,
8 wait for involuntary favors,
beg and demand avowals,
eavesdrop upon a heart's first sound,
pursue a love—and suddenly
12 obtain a secret assignation,
and afterward, alone with her,
in the quietness give her lessons!

XII

How early he already could disturb
the hearts of the professed coquettes!
Or when he wanted to annihilate
4 his rivals,
how bitingly he'd tattle!
What snares prepare for them!
But you, blest husbands,
8 you remained friends with him:
him petted the sly spouse,
Faublas' disciple of long standing,
and the distrustful oldster,
12 and the majestical cornuto,
always pleased with himself,
his dinner, and his wife.

XIII, XIV

. . . .

XV

It happened, he'd be still in bed
when little billets would be brought him.
What? Invitations? Yes, indeed,
4   to a soirée three houses bid him!
here, there will be a ball; elsewhere, a children's
So whither will my prankster scurry?   [fete.
Whom will he start with? Never mind:
8   no problem getting everywhere in time.
Meanwhile, in morning dress,
having donned a broad bolivar,[3]
Onegin drives to the boulevard
12   and there goes strolling unconfined
till vigilant Bréguet
to him chimes dinner.

XVI

It is already dark. He gets into a sleigh.
The cry "Way, way!" resounds.
With frostdust silvers
4   his beaver collar.
To Talon's[4] he has dashed off: he is certain
that there already waits for him [Kavérin];
has entered—and the cork goes ceilingward,
8   the flow of comet wine has spurted,
a bloody roast beef is before him,
and truffles, luxury of youthful years,
the best flower of French cookery,
12   and a decayless Strasbourg pie
between a living Limburg cheese
and a golden ananas.

XVII

Thirst clamors for more beakers
to drown the hot fat of the cutlets;
but Bréguet's chime reports to them
4   that a new ballet has begun.
The theater's unkind lawgiver,
inconstant worshipper
of the enchanting actresses,
8   honorary citizen of the coulisses,
Onegin has flown to the theater,
where everybody, breathing criticism,
is ready to applaud an *entrechat*,
1 2   hiss Phaedra, Cleopatra,
call out Moëna—for the purpose
merely of being heard.

XVIII

A magic region! There in olden years
the sovereign of courageous satire,
Fonvízin shone, the friend of freedom,
4   and adaptorial Knyazhnín;
there Ózerov involuntary tributes
of public tears, of plaudits
shared with the young Semyónova;
8   there our Katénin resurrected
Corneille's majestic genius;
there caustic Shahovskóy brought forth
the noisy swarm of his comedies;
1 2   there, too, Didelot with glory crowned himself;
there, there, beneath the shelter of coulisses,
my young days swept along.

XIX

My goddesses! What has become of you? Where
Hark my sad voice: [are you?
Are all of you the same? Have other maidens
4   taken your place without replacing you?
Am I to hear again your choruses?
Am I to see Russian Terpsichore's
flight, full of soul?
8   Or will the mournful gaze not find
familiar faces on the dreary stage,
and at an alien world having directed
a disenchanted lorgnette,
12   of gaiety indifferent spectator
shall I yawn wordlessly
and bygones recollect?

XX

The house is full already; boxes glitter,
parterre and stalls—all seethes;
in the top gallery impatiently they clap,
4   and, soaring up, the curtain swishes.
Resplendent, half ethereal,
obedient to the magic bow,
surrounded by a throng of nymphs,
8   Istómina stands: she,
while touching with one foot the floor,
gyrates the other slowly,
and suddenly a leap, and suddenly she flies,
12   she flies like fluff from Eol's lips
now twines and now untwines her waist
and beats one swift small foot against the other.

XXI

All clap as one. Onegin enters:
he walks—on people's toes—between the stalls;
askance, his double lorgnette trains
4 upon the loges of strange ladies;
he has scanned all the tiers;
he has seen everything; with faces, garb,
he's dreadfully displeased;
8 with men on every side
he has exchanged salutes; then at the stage
in great abstraction he has glanced,
has turned away, and yawned,
12 and uttered: "Time all were replaced;
ballets I've long endured,
but even of Didelot I've had enough."5

XXII

Still amors, devils, serpents
on the stage caper and make noise;
still the tired footmen
4 sleep on the pelisses at the carriage porch;
still people have not ceased to stamp,
blow noses, cough, hiss, clap;
still, outside and inside,
8 lanterns shine everywhere;
still, feeling chilled, the horses fidget,
bored with their harness,
and the coachmen around the fires
12 curse their masters and beat their palms
and yet Onegin has already left;   [together;
he's driving home to dress.

XXIII

Shall I present a faithful picture
of the secluded cabinet,
where the exemplary pupil of fashions
4   is dressed, undressed, and dressed again?
Whatever, for the copious whim,
London the trinkleter deals in
and o'er the Baltic waves
8   conveys to us for timber and for tallow;
whatever avid taste in Paris,
a useful trade having selected,
invents for pastimes,
12   for luxury, for modish mollitude;
all this adorned the cabinet
of a philosopher at eighteen years of age.

XXIV

Amber on Tsargrad's pipes,
porcelain and bronzes on a table,
and—of the pampered senses joy—
4   perfumes in crystal cut with facets;
combs, little files of steel,
straight scissors, curvate ones,
and brushes of thirty kinds—
8   these for the nails, those for the teeth.
Rousseau (I shall observe in passing)
could not understand how dignified Grimm
dared clean his nails in front of *him*,
12   the eloquent crackbrain.[6]
The advocate of liberty and rights
was in the present case not right at all.

XXV

One can be an efficient man—
and mind the beauty of one's nails:
why fruitlessly argue with the age?
4   Custom is despot among men.
My Eugene, a second [Chadáev],
being afraid of jealous censures,
was in his dress a pedant
8   and what we've called a fop.
He three hours, at the least,
in front of mirrors spent,
and from his dressing room came forth
12   akin to giddy Venus
when, having donned a masculine attire,
the goddess drives to a masquerade.

XXVI

With toilette in the latest taste
having engaged your curious glance,
I might before the learned world
4   describe here his attire;
this would, no doubt, be bold,
however, 'tis my business to describe;
but "pantaloons," "dress coat," "waistcoat"—
8   in Russian all these words are not;
whereas, I see (my guilt I lay before you)
that my poor style already as it is
might be much less variegated
12   with outland words,
though I did erstwhile dip
into the Academic Dictionary.

XXVII

Not this is our concern at present:
we'd better hurry to the ball
whither headlong in a hack coach
4 already my Onegin has sped off.
In front of darkened houses,
alongst the slumbering street in rows
the twin lamps of coupés
8 pour forth a merry light
and project rainbows on the snow.
Studded around with lampions,
glitters a splendid house;
12 across its whole-glassed windows shadows move:
there come and go the profiled heads
of ladies and of modish quizzes.

XXVIII

Up to the entrance hall our hero now has driven;
past the concierge he, like an arrow,
has flown up the marble stairs,
4 has run his fingers through his hair,
has entered. The ballroom is full of people;
the music has already tired of crashing;
the crowd is occupied with the mazurka;
8 there's all around both noise and crush;
there clink the cavalier guard's spurs;
the little feet of winsome ladies flit;
upon their captivating tracks
12 flit flaming glances,
and by the roar of violins is drowned
the jealous whispering of fashionable women.

XXIX

In days of gaieties and desires
I was mad about balls:
there is no safer spot for declarations
4   and for the handing of a letter.
O you, respected husbands!
I'll offer you my services;
pray, mark my speech:
8   I wish to forewarn you.
You too, mammas: most strictly
follow your daughters with your eyes;
hold up your lorgnettes straight!
12   Or else . . . else—God forbid!
If this I write it is because
already a long time I do not sin.

XXX

Alas, at various pastimes
I've ruined a lot of life!
But if morals did not suffer,
4   I'd like balls up to now.
I like furious youth,
the crush, the glitter, and the gladness,
and the considered dresses of the ladies;
8   I like their little feet; but then 'tis doubtful
that in all Russia you will find
three pairs of shapely feminine feet.
Ah me, I long could not forget
12   two little feet! . . . Doleful, grown cool,
I still remember them, and in my sleep
they disturb my heart.

XXXI

So when and where, in what reclusion,
will you forget them, crazy fool?
Ah, little feet, little feet! Where are you now?
4   Where do you trample vernant blooms?
Fostered in Oriental mollitude,
on the Northern sad snow
you left no prints:
8   you liked the yielding rugs'
luxurious contact.
Is it long since I would forget for you
the thirst for fame and praises,
12   the country of my fathers, and confinement?
The happiness of youthful years has vanished
as on the meadows your light trace.

XXXII

Diana's bosom, Flora's cheeks,
are charming, dear friends!
However, the little foot of Terpsichore
4   is for me in some way more charming.
By prophesying to the gaze
an unpriced recompense,
with token beauty it attracts
8   the willful swarm of longings.
I'm fond of it, my friend Elvina,
beneath the long napery of tables,
in springtime on the turf of meads,
12   in winter on the hearth's cast iron,
on mirrory parquet of halls,
by the sea on granite of rocks.

XXXIII

I recollect the sea before a tempest:
how I envied the waves
running in turbulent succession
4 with love to lie down at her feet!
How much I longed then with the waves
to touch the dear feet with my lips!
No, never midst the fiery days
8 of my ebullient youth
did I long with such torment
to kiss the lips of young Armidas,
or the roses of flaming cheeks,
12 or the breasts full of languishment—
no, never did the surge of passions
thus rive my soul!

XXXIV

I have remembrance of another time:
in chary fancies now and then
I hold the happy stirrup
4 and in my hands I feel a little foot.
Again imagination seethes,
again that touch
has fired the blood within my withered heart,
8 again the ache, again the love!
But 'tis enough extolling haughty ones
with my loquacious lyre:
they are not worth either the passions'
12 or songs by them inspired;
the words and gaze of these bewitchers
are as deceptive as their little feet.

XXXV

And my Onegin? Half asleep,
he drives from ball to bed,
while indefatigable Petersburg
4   is roused already by the drum.
The merchant's up, the hawker's on his way,
the cabby to the hack stand drags,
the Okhta girl hastes with her jug,
8   the morning snow creaks under her.
Morn's pleasant hubbub has awoken,
unclosed are shutters, chimney smoke
ascends in a blue column,
12   and the baker, a punctual German
in cotton cap, has more than once
already opened his *vasisdas*.

XXXVI

But by the ball's noise tired,
and having morn into midnight transformed,
sleeps peacefully in blissful shade
4   the child of pastimes and of luxury.
He will awake past midday, and again
till morn his life will be prepared,
monotonous and motley,
8   and next day same as yesterday.
But was my Eugene happy—
free, in the bloom of the best years,
amidst resplendent conquests,
12   amidst daily delights?
Was he, midst banquets, with impunity
reckless and hale?

111

XXXVII

No, feelings early cooled in him.
Tedious to him became the social hum.
The fair remained not long
4   the object of his customary thoughts.
Betrayals finally fatigued him.
Friends and friendship palled,
since plainly not always could he
8   beefsteaks and Strasbourg pie
sluice with a champagne bottle
and scatter piquant sayings
when his head ached;
12   and though he was a fiery scapegrace,
he lost at last his liking
for strife, saber and lead.

XXXVIII

A malady, the cause of which
'tis high time were discovered,
similar to the English "spleen"—
4   in short, the Russian "chondria"—
took hold of him little by little.
To shoot himself, thank God,
he did not care to try,
8   but toward life became quite cold.
Like Childe Harold, ill-humored, languid,
in drawing rooms he would appear;
neither the tattle of the *monde* nor boston,
12   neither a winsome glance nor an immodest sigh,
nothing moved him,
he noticed nothing.

XXXIX, XL, XLI

. . . .

XLII

Capricious belles of the *grand monde*!
Before all others you he left;
and it is true that in our years
4 the upper *ton* is rather tedious.
Although, perhaps, this or that dame
interprets Say and Bentham,
in general their conversation
8 is insupportable, though harmless twaddle.
On top of that they are so pure,
so stately, so intelligent,
so full of piety,
12 so circumspect, so scrupulous,
so inaccessible to men,
that the mere sight of them begets the spleen.[7]

XLIII

And you, young beauties,
whom at a late hour
fleet droshkies carry off
4 over the Petersburgan pavement,
you also were abandoned by my Eugene.
Apostate from the turbulent delights,
Onegin locked himself indoors;
8 yawning, took up a pen;
wanted to write; but persevering toil
to him was sickening: nothing
from his pen issued,
12 nor did he get into the cocky guild
of people, upon whom I pass no judgment—
since I belong to them.

XLIV

And once again to idleness consigned,
oppressed by emptiness of soul,
he settled down with the laudable aim
4   to make his own another's mind;
he put a troop of books upon a shelf,
read, read—and all without avail:
here there was dullness; there, deceit and raving;
8   this lacked conscience, that lacked sense;
on all of them were different fetters;
and the old had become old-fashioned,
and the new raved about the old.
1 2   As he'd left women, he left books
and, with its dusty tribe, the shelf
with funerary taffeta he curtained.

XLV

Having cast off the burden of the *monde*'s conven-
having, as he, from vain pursuits desisted, [tions,
with him I made friends at that time.
4   I liked his traits,
to dreams the involuntary addiction,
nonimitative oddity,
and sharp, chilled mind;
8   I was embittered, he was sullen;
the play of passions we knew both;
both, life oppressed;
in both, the heart's glow had gone out;
1 2   for both, there was in store the rancor
of blind Fortuna and of men
at the very morn of our days.

XLVI

He who has lived and thought can't help
despising people in his soul;
him who has felt disturbs
4   the ghost of irrecoverable days;
for him there are no more enchantments;
him does the snake of memories,
him does repentance bite.
8   All this often imparts
great charm to conversation.
At first, Onegin's language
would trouble me; but I grew used
12   to his sarcastic argument
and banter blent halfwise with bile
and virulence of gloomy epigrams.

XLVII

How oft in summertide,
when transparent and luminous
is the night sky above the Neva,[8]
4   and the gay glass of waters
does not reflect Diana's visage—
having recalled intrigues of former years,
having recalled a former love,
8   impressible, carefree again,
the breath of the benignant night
we silently drank in!
As to the greenwood from a prison
12   a slumbering clogged convict is transferred,
so we'd be borne off by a dream
to the beginning of young life.

XLVIII

With soul full of regrets,
and leaning on the granite,
Eugene stood pensive—
4   as his own self the Poet[9] has described.
'Twas stillness all; only the night
sentries to one another called,
and the far clip-clop of some droshky
8   from the Mil'onnaya resounded all at once;
only a boat, oars swinging,
swam on the dozing river,
and, in the distance, captivated us
12   a horn and a daredevil song.
But, sweeter 'mid the pastimes of the night
is the strain of Torquato's octaves.

XLIX

Adrian waves,
O Brenta! Nay, I'll see you
and, filled anew with inspiration,
4   I'll hear your magic voice!
'Tis sacred to Apollo's nephews;
through the proud lyre of Albion
to me 'tis known, to me 'tis kindred.
8   Of golden Italy's nights
the sensuousness I shall enjoy in freedom,
with a youthful Venetian,
now talkative, now mute,
12   swimming in a mysterious gondola;
with her my lips will find
the tongue of Petrarch and of love.

L

Will the hour of my freedom come?
'Tis time, 'tis time! To it I call;
I roam above the sea,[10] I wait for the right
4   I beckon to the sails of ships.   [weather,
Under the cope of storms, with waves disputing,
on the free crossway of the sea
when shall I start on my free course?
8   'Tis time to leave the dreary shore
of the element inimical to me,
and 'mid meridian ripples
beneath the sky of my Africa,[11]
12   to sigh for somber Russia,
where I suffered, where I loved,
where I buried my heart.

LI

Onegin was prepared with me
to see alien lands;
but soon we were to be by fate
4   sundered for a long time.
'Twas then his father died.
Before Onegin there assembled
a greedy host of creditors.
8   Each has a mind and notion of his own.
Eugene, detesting litigations,
contented with his lot,
relinquished the inheritance to them,
12   perceiving no great loss therein,
or precognizing from afar
the demise of his aged uncle.

LII

All of a sudden he received indeed
from the steward a report
that uncle was nigh death in bed
4   and would be glad to bid farewell to him.
The sad epistle having read,
Eugene incontinently to the rendez-vous
drove headlong, traveling post,
8   and yawned already in anticipation,
preparing, for the sake of money,
for sighs, boredom, and deceit
(and with this I began my novel);
12   but having winged his way to uncle's manor,
he found him laid already on the table
as a prepared tribute to earth.

LIII

He found the grounds full of attendants;
to the dead man from every side
came driving foes and friends,
4   the devotees of funerals.
The dead man was interred,
the priests and guests ate, drank,
and then gravely dispersed,
8   as though they had been sensibly engaged.
Now our Onegin is a rural dweller,
of workshops, waters, forests, lands,
absolute lord (while up to then
12   an enemy of order and a wastrel),
and very glad to have exchanged
his former course for something.

LIV

During two days seemed to him novel
the secluded fields,
the coolness of the somber park,
4   the bubbling of the quiet brook;
by the third day, grove, hill, and field
did not divert him any more;
then somnolence already they induced;
8   then plainly he perceived
that in the country, too, the boredom was the
                         [same,
although there were no streets, no palaces,
no cards, no balls, no verses.
12   The hyp was waiting for him on the watch,
and it kept running after him
like a shadow or faithful wife.

LV

I was born for the peaceful life,
for rural quiet:
the lyre's voice in the wild is more resounding,
4   creative dreams are more alive.
To harmless leisures consecrated,
I wander by a wasteful lake
and *far niente* is my rule.
8   By every morn I am awakened
unto sweet mollitude and freedom;
little I read, a lot I sleep,
fugitive fame do not pursue.
12   Was it not thus in former years,
that I spent in inaction, in the [shade],
my happiest days?

LVI

Flowers, love, the country, idleness,
ye fields! my soul is vowed to you.
I'm always glad to mark the difference
4   between Onegin and myself,
lest an ironic reader
or else some publisher
of complicated calumny,
8   collating here my traits,
repeat thereafter shamelessly
that I have scrawled my portrait
like Byron, the poet of pride
—as if for us it were no longer possible
to write long poems about anything
than just about ourselves!

LVII

In this connection I'll observe: all poets
are friends of fancifying love.
It used to happen that dear objects
4   I'd dream of, and my soul
preserved their secret image;
the Muse revived them later:
thus I, carefree, would sing
8   a maiden of the mountains, my ideal,
as well as captives of the Salgir's banks.
From you, my friends, at present
not seldom do I hear the question:
12   "For whom does your lyre sigh?
To whom, in the throng of jealous maids,
have you dedicated its strain?

LVIII

"Whose gaze, exciting inspiration,
with a touching caress rewarded
your pensive singing?
4   Whom did your verse idolatrize?"
Faith, nobody, my friends, I swear!
Love's mad anxiety
I joylessly went through.
8   Happy who blent with it
the ague of rhymes: thereby he doubled
poetry's sacred raving,
striding in Petrarch's tracks;
12   as to the heart's pangs, he allayed them,
caught also fame meanwhile—
but I, in love, was dense and mute.

LIX

Love passed, the Muse appeared,
and the dark mind cleared up.
Once free, I seek again the concord
4   of magic sounds, feelings, and thoughts;
I write, and the heart does not fret;
the pen, lost in a trance, does not delineate
next to unfinished lines,
8   feminine feet or heads;
extinguished ashes will no more flare up;
I'm melancholy still; but there are no more tears,
and soon, soon the storm's trace
12   will hush completely in my soul:
then I shall start to write
a poem in twenty-five cantos or so.

LX

Of the plan's form I've thought already
and what my hero I shall call.
Meantime, my novel's
4   first chapter I have finished;
all this I have looked over closely;
the inconsistencies are very many,
but to correct them I don't wish.
8   I shall pay censorship its due
and to the reviewers for devourment
give away the fruits of my labors.
Be off, then, to the Neva's banks,
1 2   newborn production!
And deserve for me fame's tribute,
false interpretations, noise, and abuse!

CHAPTER TWO

O rus!
> *Horace*

O Rus'!

Chapter Two

I

The country place where Eugene moped
was a charming nook;
there a friend of innocent delights
might have blessed heaven.
The manor house, secluded,
screened by a hill from the winds,
stood above a river; in the distance,
before it were, variegated and in bloom,
meadows and golden grainfields;
one could glimpse hamlets here and there;
herds roamed the meadows;
and its thick coverts spread
a huge neglected garden,
retreat of pensive dryads.

4

8

1 2

II

The venerable castle was built
as castles should be built:
excellent strong and comfortable
4   in the taste of sensible ancientry.
Tall chambers everywhere,
damask hangings in the drawing room,
portraits of grandsires on the walls,
8   and stoves with varicolored tiles.
All this today is antiquated,
I really don't know why;
and anyway my friend
12   bothered about it very little,
since he yawned equally
midst modish and ancient halls.

III

He settled in that chamber
where the rural old-timer
with his housekeeper forty years had squabbled,
4   looked through the window, and squashed flies.
It all was simple: floor of oak,
two cupboards, table, a divan of down,
and not an ink speck anywhere.
8   Onegin opened the cupboards;
found in one a notebook of expenses,
in the other a whole array of fruit liqueurs,
pitchers of *eau-de-pomme*,
12   and the calendar for eighteen-eight:
the old man, having much to do,
did not look into other books.

IV

Alone midst his possessions,
merely to while away the time,
our Eugene, first, conceived the plan
4   of instituting a new system.
In his backwoods an eremitic sage,
the ancient *corvée*'s yoke
by the light quitrent he replaced;
8   the muzhik blessed fate,
while in his corner went into a huff,
therein perceiving dreadful harm,
his thrifty neighbor.
12   Another slyly smiled,
and with one voice so all resolved
that he was a most dangerous eccentric.

V

At first they all would call on him,
but since to the back porch
there was habitually brought
4   a Don stallion for him
the moment that along the highway
one heard their homely shandrydans—
outraged by such behavior,
8   they all ceased to be friends with him.
"Our neighbor is a boor; acts like a crackbrain;
he's a Freemason; he drinks only
by the tumbler red wine;
12   he does not kiss a lady's hand;
it is all 'yes' and 'no'—he'll not say 'yes, sir,'
or 'no, sir.'" This was the general voice.

VI

To his estate at that same time
a new landowner had driven down
and for the same strict scrutiny
4   was to the neighbors giving cause.
By name Vladimir Lenski,
with a soul really Göttingenian,
a handsome chap, in the full bloom of years,
8   Kant's votary, and a poet.
He out of misty Germany
had brought the fruits of learning:
liberty-loving dreams,
12   a spirit impetuous and rather strange,
an always enthusiastic speech
and shoulder-length black curls.

VII

From the world's cold depravity
not having yet had time to wither,
his soul was warmed
4   by a friend's hail, by the caress of maidens.
In matters of the heart he was a winsome dunce.
Hope nursed him,
and the globe's new glitter and noise
8   still captivated his young mind.
He would amuse with a sweet dream
his heart's incertitudes.
The purpose of our life to him
12   was an alluring riddle;
he racked his brains over it
and suspected marvels.

VIII

He believed that a kindred soul
to him must be united;
that, joylessly pining away,
4   it daily kept awaiting him;
he believed that his friends were ready
to accept fetters to defend his honor
and that their hand would never falter
8   to smash the vessel of the slanderer;
that there were some chosen by fate

. . . .
. . . .
. . . .
. . . .
. . . .

IX

Indignation, compassion,
pure love of Good,
and fame's delicious torment
4   early had roused his blood.
He wandered with a lyre on earth.
Under the sky of Schiller and of Goethe,
with their poetic fire
8   his soul had kindled;
and the exalted Muses of the art
he, happy one, did not disgrace:
he proudly in his songs retained
12   always exalted sentiments,
the surgings of a virgin fancy,
and the charm of grave simplicity.

X

He sang love, to love submissive,
and his song was as clear
as a naïve maid's thoughts,
4   as the sleep of an infant, as the moon,
in the untroubled wildernesses of the sky,
goddess of mysteries and tender sighs.
He sang parting and sadness,
8   and *something*, and the misty distance,
and the romantic roses.
He sang those distant lands
where long into the bosom of the stillness
12   flowed his live tears.
He sang life's faded bloom
at not quite eighteen years of age.

XI

In the wilderness where Eugene alone
was able to appreciate his gifts,
the neighboring village owners'
4   feasts did not please him;
he fled their noisy concourse.
Their reasonable conversation
of haymaking, of liquor,
8   of kennel, of their kin,
to be sure did not shine with feeling,
or with poetic fire,
or sharp wit, or intelligence,
12   or with the art of sociability;
but the conversation of their dear wives
was much less intelligent.

XII

Wealthy, good-looking, Lenski
was as a suitor everywhere received:
such is the country custom;
4   all for their daughters planned a match
with the half-Russian neighbor.
Whenever he drops in, at once the converse
broaches a word, obliquely,
8   about the tedium of bachelor life;
the neighbor is invited to the samovar,
and who but Dunya pours the tea;
they whisper to her: "Dunya, mark!"
12   Then the guitar (that, too) is brought,
and she will start to squeak (my God!):
"Come to me in my golden castle! . . ."[12]

XIII

But Lenski, not having, of course,
the urge to bear the bonds of marriage,
wished cordially with Onegin
4   a close acquaintanceship to form.
They got together; wave and stone,
verse and prose, ice and flame,
were not so different from one another.
8   At first, because of mutual disparity,
they found each other dull;
then liked each other; then
met riding every day on horseback,
12   and soon became inseparable.
Thus people—I'm the first to own it—
out of do-nothingness are friends.

XIV

But in our midst there's even no such friendship:
having destroyed all prejudices,
we deem all people naughts
4   and ourselves units.
We all expect to be Napoleons;
the millions of two-legged creatures
for us are only tools;
8   feeling to us is weird and ludicrous.
More tolerant than many was Eugene,
though he, of course, knew men
and on the whole despised them;
12   but no rules are without exceptions:
some people he distinguished greatly
and, though estranged from it, respected feeling.

XV

He listened with a smile to Lenski:
the poet's fiery conversation,
and mind still vacillant in judgments,
4   and gaze eternally inspired—
all this was novel to Onegin;
the chilling word
he tried to hold back on his lips,
8   and thought: foolish of me to interfere
with his brief rapture;
without me just as well that time will come;
let him live in the meanwhile
12   and believe in the world's perfection;
let us forgive the fever of young years
both its young glow and young delirium.

XVI

Between them everything brought forth dis-
and to reflection led: [cussions
the pacts of gone-by races,
4   the fruits of learning, Good and Evil,
and centuried prejudices,
and the grave's fateful mysteries,
destiny and life in their turn—
8   all was subjected to their judgment.
The poet in the heat of his contentions
recited, in a trance, the whilst,
fragments of Nordic poems;
12   and lenient Eugene,
although he did not understand them much,
assiduously hearkened to the youth.

XVII

But passions occupied more often
the minds of my two eremites.
Having escaped from their tumultuous power,
4   Onegin spoke of them
with an involuntary sigh of regret.
Happy who knew their agitations
and finally detached himself from them;
8   still happier who did not know them,
who cooled with separation love,
with tattle, enmity; at times
yawned with his friends and wife,
12   by jealous anguish undisturbed,
and the safe capital of forefathers
did not entrust to a perfidious deuce!

XVIII

When we have flocked under the banner
of sage tranquillity,
when the flame of the passions has gone out
4   and laughable become to us
their willfulness, [their] surgings
and tardy repercussions,
not without difficulty tamed,
8   sometimes we like to listen
to the tumultuous language of another's passions,
and it excites our heart;
exactly thus an old disabled soldier
12   does willingly bend an assiduous ear
to the yarns of young mustached braves,
forgotten in his shack.

XIX

Now as to flaming youth,
it can't hide anything:
enmity, love, sadness, and gladness
4   'tis ready to blab out.
Deemed invalided in love matters,
with a grave air Onegin listened
as, loving the confession of the heart,
8   the poet his whole self expressed.
His trustful conscience
naïvely he laid bare.
Eugene learned without difficulty
12   the youthful story of his love—
a tale abounding in emotions
long since not new to us.

XX

Ah, he loved as in our years
one loves no more; as only
the mad soul of a poet
4   is still condemned to love:
always, everywhere, one reverie,
one customary wish,
one customary woe!
8   Neither the cooling distance,
nor the long years of separation,
nor hours given to the Muses,
nor foreign beauties,
12   nor noise of merriments, nor studies,
had changed in him a soul
warmed by a virgin fire.

XXI

When scarce a boy, by Olga captivated,
heart pangs not knowing yet,
he'd been a tender witness
4   of her infant amusements.
He, in the shade of a protective park,
shared her amusements,
and for these children destined wedding crowns
8   their fathers, who were friends and neighbors.
In the backwoods, beneath a humble roof,
full of innocent charm,
under the eyes of her parents, she
12   bloomed like a hidden lily of the valley
which is unknown in the dense grass
either to butterflies or bee.

XXII

To the poet she awarded
the first dream of young transports,
and thought of her inspirited
4   the first moan of his Panpipes.
Farewell, golden games!
He grew fond of thick groves,
seclusion, stillness,
8   and night, and stars, and moon—
the moon, celestial lamp,
to which we dedicated
walks midst the evening darkness,
1 2   and tears, of secret pangs the joyance . . .
But now we only see in her
a substitute for bleary lanterns.

XXIII

Always modest, always obedient,
always as merry as the morn,
as naïve as a poet's life,
4   as winsome as love's kiss;
eyes, azure as the sky,
smile, flaxen locks,
movements, voice, light waist—
8   everything in Olga . . . but any novel
take, and you'll surely find
her portrait; it is very winsome;
I liked it once myself,
1 2   but it has palled me beyond measure.
Let me, my reader,
take up the elder sister.

XXIV

Her sister was called Tatiana.[13]
For the first time with such a name
the tender pages of a novel
4   we'll whimsically grace.
And why not? It is pleasing, sonorous,
but from it, I know, is inseparable
the memory of ancientry
8   or housemaids' quarters. We must all
admit that very little taste
we have even in our names
(to say nothing of verse);
12   enlightenment does not suit us,
and what we have derived from it
is affectation—nothing more.

XXV

So she was called Tatiana.
Neither with her sister's beauty
nor with the latter's rosy freshness
4   would she attract one's eyes.
Sauvage, sad, silent,
as timid as the sylvan doe,
in her own family
8   she seemed a strangeling.
She was not apt to snuggle up
to her father or mother;
a child herself, among a crowd of children,
12   wished not to play and skip,
and often all day long, alone,
sat silent by the window.

XXVI

Pensiveness, her companion,
even from cradle days,
the course of rural leisure
4   with daydreams beautified for her.
Her delicate fingers
knew needles not; inclined upon the tambour,
with a silk pattern she
8   did not enliven linen.
Sign of the urge to domineer:
with her obedient doll, the child
prepares in play
12   for etiquette, law of the *monde*,
and gravely to her doll repeats
her mamma's lessons;

XXVII

but even in those years a doll
Tatiana took not in her hands;
about town news, about the fashions,
4   did not converse with it;
and childish pranks
to her were foreign; [grisly] tales
in winter, in the dark of nights,
8   captivated more her heart.
And when the nurse assembled
for Olga, on the spacious meadow,
all her small girl companions,
12   she did not play at barleybreaks,
dull were to her both ringing laughter
and the noise of their giddy pleasures.

138

XXVIII

On the balcony she liked
to prevene Aurora's rise,
when on the pale sky
4   disappears the choral dance of stars,
and earth's rim softly lightens,
and, morning's herald, the wind whiffs,
and rises by degrees the day.
8   In winter, when night's shade
possesses longer half the world,
and longer in the idle stillness,
by the bemisted moon,
12   the lazy orient sleeps,
awakened at her customary hour
she would get up by candles.

XXIX

She early had been fond of novels;
for her they replaced all;
she grew enamored with the fictions
4   of Richardson and of Rousseau.
Her father was a kindly fellow
who lagged in the precedent age
but saw no harm in books;
8   he, never reading,
deemed them an empty toy,
nor did he care
what secret tome his daughter had
12   dozing till morn under her pillow.
As to his wife, she was herself
mad upon Richardson.

XXX

The reason she loved Richardson
was not that she had read him,
and not that Grandison
4   to Lovelace she preferred,[14]
but anciently, Princess Alina,
her Moscow maiden cousin,
would often talk to her about them.
8   At that time still affianced was
her husband, but against her will.
She sighed after another
whose heart and mind
12   were much more to her liking;
that Grandison was a great dandy,
a gamester, and an Ensign in the Guards.

XXXI

Like him, she was dressed always
according to the fashion and becomingly;
but without asking her advice
4   they took the maiden to the altar;
and to dispel her grief
the sensible husband drove off soon
to his countryseat, where she,
8   God knows by whom surrounded,
tossed and wept at first,
almost divorced her husband,
then got engaged in household matters,
12   became habituated, and content.
Habit to us is given from above:
it is a substitute for happiness.[15]

XXXII

Habit allayed the grief
that nothing else could ward;
a big discovery soon
4   fully consoled her.
Between the dally and the do
a secret she discovered: how her spouse
to govern monocratically,
8   and forthwith everything went right.
She would drive out to tour the farming,
she pickled mushrooms for the winter,
she kept the books, "shaved foreheads,"
12   to the bathhouse would go on Saturdays,
walloped her maids when angered—
all this without asking her husband's leave.

XXXIII

Time was, she used to write in blood
in tender maidens' albums,
would call Praskóvia "Polína,"
4   and speak in singsong tones;
a very tight corset she wore,
and Russian *Nash* as a French *N*
knew how to nasalize;
8   but soon all this ceased to exist;
corset, albums, Princess [Alina],
cahier of sentimental rhymes,
she forgot, started to call
12   "Akúl'ka" the one-time "Selína,"
and finally inaugurated
the quilted chamber robe and mobcap.

XXXIV

But dearly did her husband love her,
into her projects did not enter;
on every score, carefree, he trusted her
4 whilst in his dressing gown he ate and drank.
His life rolled comfortably on;
at evenfall sometimes assembled
a kindly group of neighbors,
8 unceremonious friends,
to rue, to tattle,
to chuckle over this or that.
Time passes; meanwhile
12 Olga they'd tell to get tea ready;
then supper comes, then, lo, 'tis bedtime,
and the guests drive away.

XXXV

They in their peaceful life preserved
the customs of dear ancientry:
with them, during fat Butterweek
4 Russian pancakes were wont to be.
 . . . .
 . . . .
 . . . .
 . . . .
 . . . .
 . . . .
 . . . .
12 kvas was as requisite to them as air,
and at their table to the guests
by rank the dishes were presented.

XXXVI

And thus they both declined,
and opened finally
before the husband the grave's portals,
4   and a new crown upon him was bestowed.
He died at the preprandial hour,
bewailed by neighbor,
children, and faithful wife,
8   more candidly than some.
He was a simple and kind squire,
and there where lies his dust
the monument above the grave proclaims:
12   "The humble sinner Dmitri Larin,
slave of our Lord, and Brigadier,
beneath this stone enjoyeth peace."

XXXVII

To his penates restored,
Vladimir Lenski visited
his neighbor's humble monument,
4   and dedicated a sigh to his dust,
and long his heart was doleful.
"Poor Yorick!"[16] mournfully he uttered,
"in his arms he hath borne me.
8   How oft I played in childhood
with his Ochákov medal!
For me he destined Olga;
he said: 'Shall I be there to see the day?'"
12   And full of sincere sadness,
Vladimir there and then set down
a gravestone madrigal for him.

XXXVIII

And there, too, with a sad inscription,
in tears, his father's and mother's
patriarchal dust he honored.
4   Alas! Upon life's furrows,
in a brief harvest, generations
by Providence's secret will
rise, ripen, and must fall;
8   others come in their wake . . .
Thus our frivolous race
waxes, is in commotion, seethes,
and tombward crowds its ancestors.
12   Our time likewise will come, will come,
and one fine day our grandsons
out of the world will crowd us too.

XXXIX

In the meanwhile imbibe your fill of it
—of this light life, friends!
Its insignificance I realize
4   and little am attached to it;
to phantoms I have closed my eyelids;
but distant hopes
sometimes disturb my heart:
8   without an imperceptible trace,
to leave the world I would be sad.
I live, I write not for the sake of praise;
but I'd have liked, meseems,
12   to glorify my woeful lot,
so that, like a true friend, remindful
of me would be, at least, one sound.

XL

And somebody's heart it will move;
and kept by fate,
perhaps in Lethe will not drown
4   the strophe I compose;
perhaps—flattering hope!—
a future dunce will point
at my famed portrait
8   and utter: "*That* now was a poet!"
So do accept my thanks,
admirer of the mild Aonian maids,
O you whose memory will preserve
12   my fugitive creations,
whose benevolent hand
will pat the old man's laurels!

XLI

. . . .

CHAPTER THREE

Elle était fille; elle était amoureuse.

Malfilâtre

Chapter Three

I

"Whither? Ah me, those poets!"
"Good-by, Onegin. Time for me to leave."
"I do not hold you, but where do you
4   spend your evenings?"
"At the Larins'." "Now, that is marvelous.
Mercy—and you don't find it difficult
thus every evening to kill time?"
8 "Not in the least." "I cannot understand.
From here I see what it is like
first—listen, am I right?—
a simple, truly Russian family,
12 a great solicitude for guests,
jam, never-ending talk
of rain, of flax, of cattle yard."

II

"So far I do not see what's bad about it."
"Ah, but the boredom—that is bad, my friend."
"Your fashionable world I hate;
4   dearer to me is the domestic circle
in which I can . . ." "Again an eclogue!
Ah, that will do, old boy, for goodness' sake.
Well, so you're off; it's a great pity.
8   Oh, Lenski, listen—is there any way
for me to see this Phyllis,
subject of thoughts, and pen,
and tears, and rhymes, et cetera?
1 2   Present me." "You are joking." "No."
"I'm glad." "So when?" "Now, if you like.
They will be eager to receive us.

III

Let's go." And off the two friends drove;
they have appeared; upon them are bestowed
the sometimes onerous attentions
4   of hospitable ancientry.
The ritual of the treat is known:
in little dishes jams are brought,
on an oilcloth'd small table there is set
8   a jug of lingonberry water.

. . . .
. . . .
. . . .
. . . .
. . . .
. . . .

IV

They by the shortest road
fly home at full career.[17]
Now let us eavesdrop furtively
4 upon our heroes' conversation.
"Well now, Onegin, you are yawning?"
"A habit, Lenski." "But you're bored
somehow more." "No, the same.
8 I say, it's dark already in the field;
faster! get on, get on, Andryushka!
What silly country!
Ah, apropos: Dame Larin's on the simple side
12 but she's a very nice old lady;
I fear that lingonberry water
may not unlikely do me harm.

V

Tell me, which was Tatiana?"
"Oh, she's the one who, melancholy
and silent like Svetlana,
4 entered and sat down by the window."
"How come you're with the younger one in love?"
"Why, what's the matter?" "I'd have chosen the
if I had been like you a poet.   [other,
8 In Olga's features there's no life,
just as in a Vandyke Madonna:
she's round and fair of face
as is that silly moon
12 up in that silly sky."
Vladimir answered curtly
and thenceforth the whole way was silent.

VI

Meanwhile Onegin's apparition
at the Larins' produced
on everyone a great impression
4   and entertained all the neighbors.
Conjecture on conjecture followed.
All started furtively to reason,
to joke, to judge not without malice,
8   a suitor for Tatiana to assign.
Some folks even asserted
the wedding was arranged completely,
but had been stayed because
12   of fashionable rings' not being got.
Concerning Lenski's wedding, long ago
they had already settled things.

VII

Tatiana listened with vexation
to gossip of that sort; but secretly
with joy ineffable
4   she could not help thinking about it;
and the thought sank into her heart;
the time had come—she fell in love.
Thus, dropped into the earth, a seed
8   is quickened by the fire of spring.
Long since had her imagination,
consumed with mollitude and yearning,
craved for the fatal food;
12   long since had the heart's languishment
constrained her youthful bosom;
her soul waited—for somebody.

VIII

And its wait was rewarded. Her eyes opened;
she said: "'Tis he!"
Alas! now both the days and nights,
4   and hot, lone sleep,
all's full of him; to the dear girl
unceasingly with magic force
all speaks of him. To her are bothersome
8   alike the sounds of friendly speeches
and the gaze of solicitous domestics.
Plunged in dejection,
to visitors she does not listen,
12   and imprecates their leisures,
their unexpected arrival
and protracted sit-down.

IX

With what attention she now
reads a delicious novel,
with what vivid enchantment
4   drinks the seductive fiction!
By the happy power of reverie
animated creations,
the lover of Julie Wolmar,
8   Malek-Adhel, and de Linar,
and Werther, restless martyr,
and the inimitable Grandison,[18]
who brings upon *us* somnolence—
12   all for the tender dreamer
have been invested with a single image,
have in Onegin merged alone.

X

Imagining herself the heroine
of her beloved authors—
Clarissa, Julie, Delphine—
4   Tatiana in the stillness of the woods
alone roams with a dangerous book;
in it she seeks and finds
her secret glow, her daydreams,
8   the fruits of the heart's fullness;
she sighs, and having made her own
another's ecstasy, another's melancholy,
she whispers in a trance, by heart,
12   a letter to the amiable hero.
But our hero, whoever he might be,
quite surely was no Grandison.

XI

His style to a grave mood having attuned,
time was, a flaming author
used to present to us his hero
4   as a model of perfection.
He'd furnish the loved object—
always iniquitously persecuted—
with a sensitive soul, intelligence,
8   and an attractive face.
Nourishing the glow of the purest passion,
always the enthusiastic hero
was ready to sacrifice himself
12   and by the end of the last part,
always vice got punished,
virtue got a worthy crown.

XII

But nowadays all minds are in a fog,
a moral brings upon us somnolence,
vice is attractive also in a novel,
4   there also it already triumphs.
The British Muse's never-haps
disturb the young girl's sleep,
and now her idol has become
8   either the pensive Vampyre,
or Melmoth, gloomy vagabond,
or the Wandering Jew, or the Corsair,
or the mysterious Sbogar.[19]
12   Lord Byron, by an opportune caprice,
has draped in glum romanticism
even hopeless egotism.

XIII

My friends, what sense is there in this?
Perhaps, by heaven's will,
I'll cease to be a poet;
4   a new fiend will inhabit me;
and having scorned the threats of Phoebus,
I shall descend to humble prose:
a novel in the old mood then
8   will occupy my gay decline.
Not secret pangs of villainy
shall I grimly depict in it,
but simply shall detail to you
12   traditions of a Russian family,
love's captivating dreams,
and manners of our ancientry.

XIV

I shall detail the simple speeches
of a father or aged uncle,
the children's assigned meetings
4   by the old limes, by the small brook;
torments of hapless jealousy,
parting, reconciliation's tears;
once more I'll have them quarrel, and at last
8   conduct them to the altar.
I shall recall the accents of impassioned
the words of aching love,   [sensuousness,
which in bygone days
12   at the feet of a fair mistress
came to my tongue;
from which I now have grown disused.

XV

Tatiana, dear Tatiana!
I now shed tears with you.
Into a fashionable tyrant's hands
4   your fate already you've relinquished.
Dear, you shall perish; but before,
in dazzling hope,
you summon obscure bliss,
8   you learn the sensuousness of life,
you quaff the magic poison of desires,
daydreams pursue you:
you fancy everywhere
12   retreats for happy trysts;
everywhere, everywhere before you,
is your fateful tempter.

XVI

The ache of love chases Tatiana,
and to the garden she repairs to brood,
and all at once her moveless eyes she lowers
4   and is too indolent farther to step;
her bosom has risen, her cheeks
are covered with an instant flame,
her breath has died upon her lips,
8   and in her ears there's noise, before her eyes a
Night comes; the moon tours   [flashing.
on patrol the far vault of heaven,
and in the murk of trees the nightingale
12 intones sonorous strains.
Tatiana in the darkness does not sleep
and in low tones talks with her nurse.

XVII

"I can't sleep, nurse: 'tis here so stuffy!
Open the window and sit down by me."
"Why, Tanya, what ails you?" "I'm dull.
4   Let's talk about old days."
"Well, what about them, Tanya? Time was, I
kept in my memory no dearth
of ancient haps and never-haps
8   about dire sprites and about maidens;
but all to me is dark now, Tanya:
What I knew I've forgotten. Yes,
things have come to a sorry pass!
12 My mind is fuddled." "Tell me, nurse,
about your years of old.
Were you in love then?"

XVIII

"Oh, come, come, Tanya! In those years
we never heard of love;
elsewise my late mother-in-law
4   would have chased me right off the earth."
"But how, then, were you wedded, nurse?"
"It looks as if God willed it so. My Vanya
was younger than myself, my sweet,
8   and I was thirteen years of age.
For some two weeks came a matchmaking woman
to see my kinsfolk, and at last
my father blessed me.
12   Bitterly I cried for fear;
crying, my braid they unplaited
and, chanting, churchward led me.

XIX

"And so they made me enter a strange family. . . .
But you're not listening to me."
"Oh, nurse, nurse, I feel dismal,
4   I'm sick at heart, my dear,
I'm on the point of crying, sobbing!"
"My child, you are not well;
the Lord have mercy upon us and save us!
8   What would you like, do ask.
Here, let me sprinkle you with holy water,
you're all a-burning." "I'm not ill;
I'm . . . do you know, nurse . . . I'm in love."
12   "My child, the Lord be with you!"
And the nurse, with a prayer, the maiden
crossed with decrepit hand.

XX

"I am in love," whispered anew
  to the old crone with sorrow she.
"Friend of my heart, you are not well."
4 "Leave me. I am in love."
  And meantime the moon beamed
  and with dark light irradiated
  the pale charms of Tatiana
8 and her loose hair,
  and drops of tears, and, on a benchlet,
  before the youthful heroine,
  a kerchief on her hoary head,
12 the little crone in a long "body warmer";
  and in the stillness everything
  dozed by the inspirative moon.

XXI

And far away her heart was ranging
  as Tatiana looked at the moon . . .
  All at once in her mind a thought was born . . .
4 "Go, let me be alone.
  Give me, nurse, a pen, paper,
  and move up the table; I'll soon go to bed;
  good night." Now she's alone,
8 all's still. The moon gives light to her.
  Tatiana, leaning on her elbow, writes,
  and Eugene's ever present in her mind,
  and in an unconsidered letter
12 an innocent maid's love breathes forth.
  The letter's ready, folded.
  Tatiana! Whom, then, is it for?

XXII

I've known belles inaccessible,
cold, winter-chaste;
inexorable, incorruptible,
4   unfathomable to the mind;
I marveled at their modish morgue,
at their natural virtue,
and, to be frank, I fled from them,
8   and I, meseems, with terror read
above their eyebrows Hell's inscription:
"Abandon hope for evermore!"[20]
To inspire love is bale for them,
12   to frighten folks for them is joy.
Perhaps, on the banks of the Neva
similar ladies you have seen.

XXIII

Amidst obedient admirers,
other odd females I have seen,
conceitedly indifferent
4   to sighs impassioned and eloges:
And what, to my amazement, did I find?
They, by austere demeanor,
frightening timid love,
8   had the knack of attracting it again,
at least by their compassion;
at least the sound of spoken words
sometimes would seem more [tender],
12   and with credulous blindness
again the youthful lover
pursued dear vanity.

XXIV

Why is Tatiana, then, more guilty?
Is it because in dear simplicity
she does not know deceit
4   and in her chosen dream believes?
Is it because she loves without art,
obedient to the bent of feeling?
Because she is so trustful,
8   because by heaven is endowed
with a restless imagination,
intelligence, and a live will,
and headstrongness,
12   and a flaming and tender heart?
Can it be that you won't forgive her
the thoughtlessness of passions?

XXV

The coquette reasons coolly;
Tatiana in dead earnest loves
and unconditionally yields
4   to love like a dear child.
She does not say: Let us defer;
thereby we shall augment love's value,
inveigle into toils more surely;
8   let us first prick vainglory
with hope; then with perplexity
harass a heart, and then
revive it with a jealous fire,
12   for otherwise, cloyed with delight,
the cunning captive from his shackles
hourly is ready to escape.

XXVI

Another hindrance I foresee:
saving the honor of my native land,
undoubtedly I'll be obliged
4   Tatiana's letter to translate.
She knew Russian badly,
did not read our reviews,
and expressed herself with difficulty
8   in her native tongue;
hence wrote in French.
What's to be done about it! I repeat again;
as yet a lady's love
12   has not expressed itself in Russian,
as yet our proud tongue has
to postal prose not got accustomed.

XXVII

I know: some would make ladies
read Russian. Horrible indeed!
Can I imagine them
4   with *The Well-Meaner*[21] in their hands?
My poets, I appeal to [you]!
Is it not true that the amiable objects
for whom, to expiate your sins,
8   in secret you wrote verses,
to whom your heart you dedicated—
did not they all, the Russian tongue
wielding poorly, and with difficulty,
12   so amiably garble it,
and on their lips a foreign tongue
did not it turn into a native one?

XXVIII

The Lord forbid my meeting at a ball
or at its breakup, on the porch,
a seminarian in a yellow shawl
4   or an Academician in a bonnet!
As vermeil lips without a smile,
with no grammatical mistake
I don't like Russian speech.
8   Perchance (it would be my undoing!)
a generation of new belles,
the pleading voice of journals having heeded,
to Grammar will inure us;
12   verses will be brought into use.
Yet I . . . what do I care?
I shall be true to ancientry.

XXIX

An incorrect, negligent patter,
an inexact delivery of words,
as heretofore a flutter of the heart
4   will in my breast produce;
in me there's no force to repent;
to me will Gallicisms remain as dear
as the sins of past youth,
8   as Bogdanovich's verse.
But that will do. 'Tis time to occupy myself
with my fair damsel's letter;
my word I've given—and what now? Yea, yea!
12   I'm now quite ready to back out.
I know: tender Parny's
pen in our days is out of fashion.

XXX

Bard of *The Feasts* and languorous melancholy,[22]
if you were still with me,
I would have with an indiscreet request,
4   my dear fellow, importuned you:
that into magic strains
you would transpose a passionate maid's
outlandish words.
8   Where are you? Come! My rights
I with a bow transfer to you . . .
But in the midst of woeful rocks,
his heart disused from praise,
12   alone, under the Finnish sky
he wanders, and his soul
hears not my worry.

XXXI

Tatiana's letter is before me;
religiously I keep it;
I read it with a secret heartache
4   and cannot get my fill of reading it.
Who taught her both this tenderness
and amiable carelessness of words?
Who taught her all that touching [tosh],
8   mad conversation of the heart
both fascinating and injurious?
I cannot understand. But here's
an incomplete, feeble translation,
12   the pallid copy of a vivid picture,
or *Freischütz* executed
by timid female learners' fingers.

TATIANA'S LETTER TO ONEGIN
I write to you—what would one more?
What else is there that I could say?
'Tis now, I know, within your will
4 *to punish me with scorn.*
But you, for my unhappy lot
keeping at least one drop of pity,
you'll not abandon me.
8 *At first, I wanted to be silent;*
believe me: of my shame
you never would have known
if I had had the hope,
12 *even seldom, even once a week,*
to see you at our country place,
only to hear your speeches,
to say a word to you, and then
16 *to think and think about one thing,*
both day and night, till a new meeting.
But, they say, you're unsociable;
in backwoods, in the country, all bores you,
20 *while we . . . with nothing do we glitter,*
though simpleheartedly we welcome you.

Why did you visit us?
In the backwoods of a forgotten village,
24 *I would have never known you*
nor have known bitter torment.
The tumult of an inexperienced soul
having subdued with time (who knows?),
28 *I would have found a friend after my heart,*
have been a faithful wife
and a virtuous mother.

Another! . . . No, to nobody on earth
32 *would I have given my heart away!*
That has been destined in a higher council,
that is the will of heaven: I am thine;
my entire life has been the gage
36 *of a sure tryst with you;*
I know, you're sent to me by God,
you are my guardian to the tomb. . . .
You had appeared to me in dreams,
40 *unseen, you were already dear to me,*
your wondrous glance pervaded me with languor,
your voice resounded in my soul
long since . . . No, it was not a dream!

44 *Scarce had you entered, instantly I knew you,*
I felt all faint, I felt aflame,
and in my thoughts I uttered: It is he!
Is it not true that it was you I heard:
48 *you in the stillness spoke to me*
when I would help the poor
or assuage with a prayer
the yearning of my agitated soul?

52 *And at this very moment*
was it not you, dear vision,
that slipped through the transparent darkness,
softly bent close to my bed head?
56 *Was it not you that with [joy] and love*
words of hope whispered to me?
Who are you? My guardian angel
or a perfidious tempter?

60   *Resolve my doubts.*
         Perhaps, 'tis nonsense all,
         an inexperienced soul's delusion,
         and some quite different thing is destined . . .

64   *But so be it! My fate*
         henceforth I place into your hands,
         before you I shed tears,
         for your defense I plead.
68   *Imagine: I am here alone,*
         none understands me,
         my reason is breaking down,
         and, silent, I must perish.
72   *I'm waiting for you: with a single look*
         revive my heart's hopes,
         or interrupt the heavy dream
         alas, with a deserved rebuke!

76   *I close! I dread to read this over.*
         I'm faint with shame and fear . . .
         But to me your honor is a pledge,
         and boldly I entrust myself to it.

XXXII

By turns Tatiana sighs and ohs.
The letter trembles in her hand;
the pink wafer dries
4   on her fevered tongue.
Her poor head shoulderward she has inclined;
her light chemise has slid
down from her charming shoulder.
8   But now already the moonbeam's
radiance fades. Anon the valley
grows through the vapor clear. Anon the stream
starts silvering. Anon the horn
12   of the herdsman wakes up the villager.
Here's morning; all have risen long ago:
to my Tatiana it is all the same.

XXXIII

She takes no notice of the sunrise;
she sits with lowered head
and on the letter does not
4   impress her graven seal.
But, softly opening the door,
now gray Filatievna for her
brings tea upon a tray.
8   "'Tis time, my child, get up;
why, pretty one, you're ready!
Oh, my early birdie!
I was indeed so anxious yesternight—
12   but glory be to God, you're well!
No trace at all of the night's fret!
Your face is like a poppy flower."

XXXIV

"Oh, nurse, do me a favor."
"Willingly, darling, order me."
"Don't think . . . Really . . . Suspicion . . .
4   But you see . . . Oh, do not refuse!"
"My friend, here's God to you for pledge."
"Well, send your grandson quietly
with this note to O . . . to that . . .
8   to the neighbor. And let him be told
that he ought not to say a word,
that he ought not to name me."
"To *whom*, my dear?
12   I'm getting muddled nowadays.
There's lots of neighbors all around
even to count them over is beyond me."

XXXV

"Oh, nurse, how slow-witted you are!"
"Friend of my heart, I am already old,
old; blunted grows the reason, Tanya;
4   but time was, I used to be sharp:
time was, one word of master's wish . . ."
"Oh, nurse, nurse, is this relevant?
What matters your intelligence to me?
8   You see, it is about a letter,
to Onegin." "Well, this makes sense.
Do not be angry, my dear soul;
I am, you know, not comprehensive . . .
12   But why have you turned pale again?"
"Never mind, nurse, 'tis really nothing.
Send, then, your grandson."

169

XXXVI

But the day lapsed, and no reply.
Another came up; nothing yet.
Pale as a shade, since morning dressed,
4 Tatiana waits: when is it coming, the reply?
Olga's adorer drove up.
"Tell me, where's your companion?"
was the chatelaine's question to him;
8 "He seems to have forgotten us entirely."
Tatiana, flushing, quivered.
"He promised he would be today,"
Lenski replied to the old dame,
12 "but evidently the mail has detained him."
Tatiana dropped her gaze
as if hearing an unkind rebuke.

XXXVII

'Twas growing dark; upon the table, shining,
there hissed the evening samovar,
warming the Chinese teapot;
4 light vapor undulated under it.
Poured out by Olga's hand,
into the cups, in a dark stream,
the fragrant tea already ran,
8 and a footboy served the cream;
Tatiana stood before the window;
breathing on the cold panes,
lost in thought, the dear soul
12 wrote with her charming finger
on the bemisted glass
the cherished monogram: an O and E.

XXXVIII

And meantime her soul pined,
and full of tears was her dolorous gaze.
Suddenly, hoof thuds! Her blood froze.
4 Now nearer! Coming fast . . . and in the yard
is Eugene! "Ach!"—and lighter than a shade
Tatiana skips into another hallway,
from porch outdoors, and straight into the
8 She flies, flies—glance back   [garden;
dares not; has traversed in a trice
platbands, footbridges, lawn,
the avenue to the lake, the bosquet;
12 has broken bushes [,] lilac,
flying across the flower plots to the brook,
and, panting, on a bench

XXXIX

has dropped. "He's here! Eugene is here!
Good God, what did he think!"
Her heart, full of torments,
4 retains an obscure dream of hope;
she trembles, and glows hotly,
and waits: does he not come? But hears not.
Girl servants, in the garden, on the beds,
8 were picking berries in the bushes
and singing by decree in chorus
(a decree based on that
in secret the seignioral berry
12 sly mouths would not eat
and would be busy singing;
device of rural wit!):

THE SONG OF THE GIRLS
Maidens, pretty maidens,
darling ones, companions,
romp unhindered, maidens,
4   *have your fling, dear ones!*
Start to sing a ditty,
sing our private ditty,
and allure a fellow
8   *to our choral dance.*

When we've lured a fellow,
when afar we see him,
we shall scatter, dear ones,
12   *pelter him with cherries,*
with cherries, with raspberries,
with red currants.

"Do not come eavesdropping
16   *on our private ditties,*
do not come a-spying
on our girlish games!"

XL

They sing; and with neglection
harking their ringing voice,
Tatiana waited with impatience
4   for the heart's tremor to subside in her,
for her cheeks to cease flaming;
but in her breasts there's the same quivering,
nor ceases the glow of her cheeks:
8   yet brighter, brighter do they burn.
Thus a poor butterfly both flashes
and beats an iridescent wing,
captured by a mischievous schoolboy;
12   thus in the winter corn a small hare quivers
upon suddenly seeing from afar
the shotman in the bushes crouch.

XLI

But finally she sighed
and from her bench arose;
started to go; but hardly had she turned
4   into the avenue when straight before her,
eyes blazing, Eugene
stood, similar to some dread shade,
and as one seared by fire
8   she stopped.
But the effects of the unlooked-for meeting
today, dear friends,
I have not the strength to detail;
12   after this long discourse I need
a little jaunt, a little rest;
some other time I'll tell the rest.

CHAPTER FOUR

La morale est dans la nature des choses.

Necker

Chapter Four

_____

.   .   .   .

VII

The less we love a woman
the easier 'tis to be liked by her,
and thus more surely we undo her
4   amid seductive toils.
Time was when cool debauch
was lauded as the art of love,
trumpeting everywhere about itself,
8   and taking pleasure without loving.
But that grand pastime
is worthy of old sapajous
of our forefathers' vaunted times;
12   the fame of Lovelaces has faded
with the fame of red heels
and of majestic periwigs.

VIII

Who does not find it tedious to dissemble;
diversely to repeat the same;
try gravely to convince one
4   of what all have been long convinced;
to hear the same objections,
annihilate the prejudices
which never had and hasn't
8   a little girl of thirteen years!
Who will not grow weary of threats,
entreaties, vows, feigned fear,
notes running to six pages,
12   deceptions, gossiping, rings, tears,
surveillances of aunts, of mothers,
and onerous friendship of husbands!

IX

Exactly thus my Eugene thought.
In his first youth he had
been victim of tempestuous errings
4   and of unbridled passions.
Spoiled by a habitude of life,
with one thing for a while enchanted,
disenchanted with another,
8   irked slowly by desire,
irked, too, by volatile success,
harking, in hum and hush,
the everlasting mutter of his soul,
12   smothering yawns with laughter:
this was the way he killed eight years,
having lost life's best bloom.

X

With belles no longer did he fall in love,
but dangled after them just anyhow;
when they refused, he solaced in a twinkle;
4   when they betrayed, was glad to rest.
He would seek them without intoxication,
while he left them without regret,
hardly remembering their love and spite.
8   Exactly thus does an indifferent guest
drive up for evening whist:
sits down; then, once the game is over,
he drives off from the place,
12   at home falls peacefully asleep,
and in the morning does not know himself
where he will drive to in the evening.

XI

But on receiving Tanya's missive,
Onegin was intensely moved:
the language of a maiden's dreamings
4   in him roused up thoughts in a swarm;
and he recalled winsome Tatiana's
both pallid hue and mournful air;
and in a dream, delicious, sinless,
8   his soul became absorbed.
Maybe an ancient fervidness of feelings
possessed him for a minute;
but he did not wish to deceive
12   an innocent soul's trustfulness.
Now we'll flit over to the garden
where Tatiana encountered him.

XII

For a few seconds they were silent;
but up to her Onegin went
and quoth: "You wrote to me.
4 Do not disown it. I have read
a trustful soul's avowals,
an innocent love's outpourings;
your candidness is dear to me,
8 in me it has excited
emotions long grown silent.
But I don't want to praise you—
I will repay you for it
12 with an avowal likewise void of art;
hear my confession;
unto your judgment I commit myself.

XIII

"If life by the domestic circle
I'd want to limit;
if to be father, husband,
4 a pleasant lot had ordered me;
if with the familistic picture
I were but for one moment captivated;
then, doubtlessly, save you alone
8 no other bride I'd seek.
I'll say without madrigal spangles:
my past ideal having found,
I'd doubtlessly have chosen you alone
12 for mate of my sad days,
in gage of all that's beautiful,
and been happy—as far as able!

XIV

"But I'm not made for bliss;
  my soul is strange to it;
  in vain are your perfections:
4   I'm not at all worthy of them.
  Believe me (conscience is thereof the pledge),
  wedlock would be anguish to us.
  However much I loved you, I,
8   having grown used, would cease to love at once;
  you would begin to weep; your tears
  would fail to move my heart—
  and would only enrage it.
12   Judge, then, what roses
  Hymen would lay in store for us—
  and, possibly, for many days!

XV

"What in the world can be worse
  than a family where the poor wife
  broods over an unworthy husband
4   and day and evening is alone;
  where the dull husband, conscious of her merit
  (yet cursing fate),
  is always scowling, silent,
8   cross, and coldly jealous?
  Thus I. And it is *this* you sought
  with a pure flaming soul
  when with so much simplicity,
  so much intelligence, to me you wrote?
12   Can it be true that such a portion
  is by stern fate assigned to you?

XVI

"For dreams and years there's no return;
I shall not renovate my soul.
I love you with a brother's love
4   and maybe still more tenderly.
So listen to me without wrath:
a youthful maid more than once will exchange
for dreams light dreams;
8   a sapling thus its leaves
changes with every spring.
By heaven thus 'tis evidently destined.
Again you will love; but . . .
12   learn to control yourself;
not everyone as I will understand you;
to trouble inexperience leads."

XVII

Thus Eugene preached.
Nought seeing through her tears,
scarcely breathing, without objections,
4   Tatiana listened to him.
His arm to her he offered. Sadly
(as it is said: "mechanically"),
Tatiana leaned on it in silence,
8   bending her dolent little head;
homeward [they went] around the kitchen gar-
together they arrived, and none   [den;
dreamt of reproving them for this:
12   Country freedom possesses
its happy rights
just as does haughty Moscow.

XVIII

You will agree, my reader,
that very nicely acted
our pal toward sad Tanya;
4   not for the first time here did he reveal
a genuine nobility of soul,
though people's ill will
spared nothing in him:
8   his foes, his friends
(which is the same thing, maybe)
vilified him this way and that.
Foes upon earth has everyone,
12   but God preserve us from our friends!
Ah me, those friends, those friends!
Not without cause have I recalled them.

XIX

What's that? Oh, nothing. I am lulling
empty black dreams;
I only in parenthesis observe
4   that there's no despicable slander
spawned in a garret by a babbler
and by the rabble of the *monde* encouraged,
that there's no such absurdity,
8   nor an ignoble epigram,
that with a smile your friend
in a circle of decent people
without the slightest rancor or designs
12   will not repeat a hundred times in error;
yet he professes to stand up for you:
he loves you so! . . . Oh, like a kinsman!

XX

Hm, hm, gent reader,
is your entire kin well?
Allow me; you might want, perhaps,
4   to learn now from me
what "kinsfolks" means exactly?
Well, here's what kinsfolks are:
we are required to pet them,
8   love them, esteem them cordially,
and, following popular custom,
come Christmas, visit them,
or else congratulate them postally,
12   so that for the rest of the year
they will not think about us.
So grant them, God, long life!

XXI

As to the love of tender beauties,
'tis surer than friendship or kinship.
Over it even mid tumultuous storms
4   rights you retain.
No doubt, so. But there's fashion's whirl,
there's nature's waywardness,
there's the stream of the *monde*'s opinion—
8   while the amiable sex is light as fluff.
Moreover, the opinions of her spouse
should by a virtuous wife
be always honored;
12   your faithful mistress thus
may in a trice be bundled off:
with love jokes Satan.

XXII

Whom, then, to love? Whom to believe?
Who is the only one that won't betray us?
Who measures all deeds, all speeches
4   obligingly by our own foot rule?
Who does not sow slander about us?
Who coddles us with care?
To whom our vice is not so bad?
8   Who never bores us?
Unlike a futile phantom-seeker
who wastes efforts in vain—
love your own self,
12   my honorworthy reader.
A worthy object! Nothing
more amiable surely exists.

XXIII

What was the interview's effect?
Alas, it is not hard to guess!
Love's frenzied sufferings
4   did not stop agitating
the youthful soul avid of sadness;
nay, more intensely with a joyless passion
poor Tatiana burns;
8   sleep shuns her bed;
health, life's bloom and its sweetness,
smile, virginal peace—
all, like an empty sound, has ceased to be,
12   and darkening is dear Tanya's youth:
thus a storm's shadow clothes
the scarce-born day.

XXIV

Alas, Tatiana fades away,
grows pale, is wasting, and is silent!
Nothing interests her
4   or stirs her soul.
Shaking gravely their heads,
among themselves the neighbors whisper:
Time, time she married! . . .
8   But that will do. I must make haste
to cheer up the imagination
with the picture of happy love.
Involuntarily, my dears,
12   pity constrains me;
forgive me: I do love so much
my dear Tatiana!

XXV

From hour to hour more captivated
by the charms of young Olga,
Vladimir to delicious thralldom
4   fully gave up his soul.
He's ever with her. In her chamber
they sit together in the dark;
or in the garden, arm in arm,
8   promenade at morningtide;
and what of it? With love intoxicated,
in the confusion of a tender shame,
he only dares sometimes,
12   by Olga's smile encouraged,
play with an unwound curl
or kiss the border of her dress.

XXVI

Sometimes he reads to Olya
a moralistic novel—
in which the author has more knowledge
4   of nature than Chateaubriand—
and meanwhile, two-three pages
(the empty divagations, never-haps,
for hearts of maidens dangerous)
8   he leaves out with a blush.
Secluded far from everybody,
over the chessboard they,
their elbows on the table, sometimes
12   sit deep in thought,
and Lenski with a pawn
takes in abstraction his own rook.

XXVII

When he drives home, at home he also
is with his Olga occupied,
the fugitive leaves of an album
4   assiduously adorns for her:
now draws therein agrestic views,
a gravestone, the temple of Cypris,
or a dove on a lyre
8   (using a pen and, slightly, colors);
anon on the leaves of remembrance,
beneath the signatures of others,
he leaves a tender verse—
12   a silent monument of reverie,
an instant thought's light trace,
still, after many years, the same.

XXVIII

You have, of course, seen more than once
the album of a provincial miss,
in which all her girl friends have scribbled
4 from the end, the beginning, and all over.
Here, in defiance of orthography,
lines without meter, by tradition,
in sign of friendship faithfully are entered,
8 diminished, lengthened.
On the first leaf you are confronted with:
Qu'écrirez-vous sur ces tablettes?
signed: *toute à vous Annette*;
12 and on the last one you will read:
"Whoever more than I loves you,
let him write farther than I do."

XXIX

Here you are sure to find
two hearts, a torch, and flowerets;
here you will read no doubt the vows
4 of love "Unto the tomb slab";
some military "poet"
here has dashed off a roguish rhyme.
In such an album, my friends,
8 frankly, I too am glad to write,
at heart being convinced
that any zealous trash of mine
will merit an indulgent glance
12 and that thereafter, with an unkind smile,
none will gravely examine
if I could babble wittily or not.

XXX

But you, odd volumes
out of the devils' library,
the magnificent albums,
4 the torment of modish rhymesters;
you, nimbly ornamented
by Tolstoy's wonder-working brush,
or Baratïnski's pen,
8 let the Lord's levin burn you!
Whenever a resplendent lady
offers me her in quarto,
a trembling and a waspishness possess me,
12 and an epigram stirs
in the depth of my soul—
but madrigals you have to write for them!

XXXI

Not madrigals does Lenski write
in the album of young Olga;
his pen breathes love—
4 it does not glitter frigidly with wit.
Whatever he notes, whatever he hears
concerning Olga, this he writes about;
and full of vivid truth
8 flow, riverlike, his elegies.
Thus you, inspired Yazïkov,
in the impulsions of your heart,
sing God knows whom,
12 and the precious code of elegies
will represent for you someday
the entire story of your fate.

XXXII

But soft! You hear? A critic stern
commands us to throw off
elegy's wretched wreath;
4   and to our brotherhood of rhymesters
cries: "Do stop whimpering
and croaking always the same thing,
regretting 'the foregone, the past';
8   enough! Sing about something else!"
You're right, and surely you'll point out to us
the trumpet, mask, and dagger,
and a dead stock of thoughts
12   bid us revive from everywhere.
Thus, friend? Nowise! Far from it!
"Write odes, gentlemen,

XXXIII

"as in the mighty years one wrote them,
as was in times of yore established."
Nothing but solemn odes!
4   Oh, come, friend; what's the difference?
Recall what said the satirist!
Can the shrewd lyrist in "As Others See It"
be more endurable to you
8   than our dejected rhymesters?—
"But in the elegy all is so null;
its empty aim is pitiful;
whilst the aim of the ode is lofty
12   and noble." Here I might
argue with you, but I keep still:
I do not want to set two ages by the ears.

XXXIV

A votary of fame and freedom,
in the excitement of his stormy thoughts,
Vladimir might indeed have written odes,
4 only that Olga did not read them.
Have the larmoyant poets ever chanced
to read before the eyes of loved ones
their works? 'Tis said
8 that in the world there are no higher rewards.
And, verily, blest is the modest lover
reading his daydreams
to the object of songs and love,
12 a pleasantly languorous beauty!
Blest—although, maybe, she
by quite another matter is diverted.

XXXV

But I the products of my reveries
and of harmonious device
read only to an old nurse,
4 companion of my youth;
or after a dull dinner,
the neighbor who has strayed my way
catching abruptly by a coat skirt,
8 I choke him in a corner with a tragedy,
or else (but that's apart from jokes),
by yearnings and by rhymes oppressed,
roaming along my lake,
12 I scare a flock of wild ducks:
on harking to the chant of sweet-toned strophes,
they fly off from the banks.

191

XXXVI

. . . .

XXXVII

But what about Onegin? By the way, brothers!
I beg your patience:
his daily occupations
4   in detail I'll describe to you.
Onegin anchoretically lived;
he rose in summer between six and seven
and, lightly clad, proceeded
8   to the river that ran below the hill;
the songster of Gulnare imitating,
across this Hellespont he swam,
then drank his coffee,
12   flipping through some worthless review,
and dressed. . . . .
. . . .

XXXVIII

. . . .

XXXIX

Rambles, reading, sound sleep,
the sylvan shade, the purl of streams,
sometimes a white-skinned, dark-eyed girl's
4   young and fresh kiss,
a horse of mettle, bridle-true,
a rather fancy dinner,
a bottle of bright wine,
8   seclusion, quiet—
this was Onegin's saintly life;
and he unconsciously to it
surrendered, the fair summer days
12   in carefree mollitude not counting,
oblivious of both town and friends
and of the boredom of festive devices.

XL

But our Northern summer
is a caricature of Southern winters;
it will glance by and vanish: this is known,
4   though to admit it we don't wish.
The sky already breathed of autumn,
the sun already shone more seldom,
the day was growing shorter,
8   the woods' mysterious canopy
with a sad murmur bared itself,
mist settled on the fields,
the caravan of cronking geese
12   was tending southward; there drew near
a rather tedious period;
November stood already at the door.

XLI

Dawn rises in cold murk;
stilled in the grainfields is the noise of labors;
with his hungry female,
4   the wolf comes out upon the road;
the road horse, upon sensing him,
snorts, and the wary traveler
sweeps uphill at top speed;
8   the herdsman at sunrise
no longer drives the cows out of the shippon,
and at the hour of midday in a circle
his horn does not call them together;
12   in her small hut singing, the maiden[23]
spins and, the friend of winter nights,
in front of her the splintlight crackles.

XLII

And there the frosts already crackle
and silver midst the fields
(the reader now expects the rhyme "froze-
4   here you are, take it quick!).   [rose"—
Neater than modish parquetry,
the ice-clad river shines.
The gladsome crew of boys[24]
8   cut with their skates resoundingly the ice;
a heavy goose with red feet,
planning to swim upon the bosom of the waters,
steps carefully onto the ice,
12   slidders, and falls. The gay
first snow flicks, swirls,
falling in stars upon the bank.

XLIII

What do then in the backwoods at this season?
Promenade? The country in that season
is an involuntary eyesore
4   in its unbroken nakedness.
Go galloping in the harsh prairie?
But with a blunted shoe the steed
catching the treacherous ice,
8   is likely any moment to come down.
Stay under your desolate roof,
read; here is Pradt, here's Walter Scott!
Don't want to? Verify expenses,
12   grumble or drink, and the long evening
somehow will pass; and next day the same thing,
and famously you'll spend the winter.

XLIV

Onegin like a regular Childe Harold
lapsed into pensive indolence:
right after sleep he takes a bath with ice,
4   and then, all day at home,
alone, absorbed in calculations,
armed with a blunt cue,
using two balls, at billiards
8   ever since morning plays.
The country evening comes:
billiards is left, the cue's forgot.
Before the fireplace the table is laid;
12   Eugene waits; here Lenski is arriving,
borne by a troika of roan horses;
quick, let's have dinner!

XLV

Of Veuve Clicquot or of Moët
the blesséd wine
in a befrosted bottle for the poet
4   is brought at once upon the table.
It sparkles Hippocrenelike;[25]
with its briskness and froth
(a simile of this and that)
8   it used to captivate me: for its sake
my last poor lepton I was wont
to give away—remember, friends?
Its magic stream
12   no dearth of foolishness engendered,
but also what a lot of jokes, and verse,
and arguments, and merry dreams!

XLVI

But it betrays with noisy froth
my stomach,
and I sedate Bordeaux
4   have actually now preferred to it.
For Ay I'm no longer fit,
Ay is like a mistress
glittering, volatile, vivacious,
8   and wayward, and shallow.
But you, Bordeaux, are like a friend
who is, in grief and in calamity,
at all times, everywhere, a comrade,
12   ready to render us a service
or share our quiet leisure.
Long live Bordeaux, our friend!

XLVII

The fire is out; barely with ashes
is filmed the golden coal;
in a barely distinguishable stream
4   weaves vapor, and with warmth
scarce breathes the grate. The smoke from pipes
goes up the chimney. The bright goblet
amid the table fizzes yet.
8   The evening murk comes on
(I'm fond of friendly prate
and of a friendly bowl of wine
at that time which is called
12   time between wolf and dog—
though why, I do not see).
Now the two friends converse.

XLVIII

"Well, how are the fair neighbors? How's Tatiana?
How's your spry Olga?"
"Pour me half a glass more. . . .
4   That'll do, dear chap. . . . The entire family
is well; they send you salutations. . . .
Ah, my dear chap, how beautiful have grown
Olga's shoulders! What a bosom!
8   What a soul! . . . Someday
let's visit them; they will appreciate it;
or else, my friend, judge for yourself—
you dropped in twice, and after that
12   you thenceforth did not even show your nose.
In fact—what a blockhead I am!—
you are invited there next week."

XLIX

"I?" "Yes, Tatiana's name day
is Saturday. Ólinka and the mother
bade me ask you, and there's no reason
4   you should not come in answer to their call."
"But there will be a mass of people
and all kinds of such scum . . ."
"Oh, nobody, I am quite certain.
8   Who might be there? The family only.
Let's go, do me the favor.
Well?" "I consent." "How nice you are!"
He emptied with these words
12   his glass, a toast to the fair neighbor—
then waxed voluble again,
talking of Olga. Such is love!

L

Merry he was. A fortnight hence
the happy date was set,
and the nuptial bed's mystery
4   and love's sweet crown
awaited his transports.
Hymen's chores, woes,
yawnings' chill train,
8   he never dreamed of.
Whereas we, enemies of Hymen,
perceive in home life nothing but
a series of wearisome images,
12   a novel in the genre of Lafontaine.[26]
My poor Lenski! He at heart
was for the said life born.

LI

He was loved—or at least
he thought so—and was happy.
Blest hundredfold who is to faith devoted;
4   who, having curbed cold intellect,
in the heart's mollitude reposes
as, bedded for the night, a drunken traveler,
or (more tenderly) as a butterfly
8   absorbed in a spring flower;
but pitiful is he who foresees all,
who's never dizzy,
who all movements, all words
12   in their translation hates,
whose heart experience has chilled
and has forbidden to be lost in dreams!

CHAPTER FIVE

Never know these frightful dreams,
   You, O my Svetlana!

Zhukovski

Chapter Five

———————————————

I

That year autumnal weather
was a long time abroad;
nature kept waiting and waiting for winter.
4   Snow only fell in January,
on the night of the second. Waking early,
Tatiana from the window saw
at morn the whitened yard,
8   flower beds, roofs, and fence;
delicate patterns on the panes;
the trees in winter silver,
gay magpies outside,
12   and the hills mellowly spread over
with the resplendent rug of winter.
All's brilliant, all is white around.

II

Winter! The peasant, celebrating,
in a flat sledge inaugurates the track;
his naggy, having sensed the snow,
4   shambles at something like a trot.
Plowing up fluffy furrows,
a fleet kibitka flies:
the driver sits upon his box
8   in sheepskin coat, red-sashed.
Here runs about a household lad,
a small "pooch" on a hand sled having seated,
having transformed himself into the steed;
12   the scamp already has frozen a finger.
He finds it both painful and funny—
while mother, from the window, threatens
                         [him. . . .

III

But, possibly, of such a kind
pictures will not attract you;
all this is lowly nature;
4   there is not much refinement here.
Warmed by the god of inspiration,
in a luxurious style another poet
for us has painted the first snow
8   and all the shades of winter's delectations.[27]
He'll captivate you, I am sure of it,
drawing in flaming verses
secret promenades in sleigh;
12   but I have no intention of contending
either with him for the time being or with you,
singer of the young Finnish Maid![28]

IV

Tatiana (being Russian, in her soul,
herself not knowing why)
with its cold beauty
4   loved Russian winter:
rime in the sun upon a frosty day,
and sleighs, and, at late dawn,
the radiance of pink snows, ·
8   and murk of Twelfthtide eves.
They celebrated in the ancient fashion
those evenings in their house:
the servant girls from the whole stead
12   told their young ladies' fortunes
and every year made prophecies to them
of military husbands and the march.

V

Tatiana believed in the lore
of plain-folk ancientry,
dreams, cartomancy,
4   and the predictions of the moon.
Portents disturbed her:
mysteriously all objects
foretold her something,
8   presentiments constrained her breast.
The mannered tomcat sitting on the stove,
purring, might wash his muzzlet with his paw:
to her 'twas an indubitable sign
12   that guests were coming. Seeing all at once
the young two-horned moon's visage
in the sky on her left,

VI

she trembled and grew pale.
Or when a falling star
along the dark sky flew
4 and dissipated, then
Tanya would hasten in confusion
while the star still was rolling
her heart's desire to whisper to it.
8 When anywhere she happened
a black monk to encounter,
or 'mongst the fields a rapid hare
would run across her path,
12 so scared she knew not what to undertake,
with sorrowful forebodings filled,
directly she expected some mishap.

VII

And yet—a secret charm she found
even in the terror itself:
thus nature has created us,
4 being inclined to contradictions.
Yuletide is here. Now that is gladness!
Frivolous youth divines—
who nought has to regret,
8 in front of whom the faraway of life
lies luminous, unlimited;
old age divines, through spectacles,
at its sepulchral slab,
12 all having irrecoverably lost;
nor does it matter: hope to them
lies with its childish lisp.

VIII

Tatiana with a curious gaze
looks at the submerged wax:
with a wondrous cast pattern it
4   proclaims to her a wondrous something.
From a dish full of water
rings come out in succession;
and when *her* little ring turned up,
8   'twas to a ditty of the ancient days:
"There all the countrymen are rich;
they heap up silver by the spadeful!
To those we sing to will come Good
12   and Glory!" But portends bereavements
the pitiful strain of this dit:
to maidens' hearts dearer is "Kit."[29]

IX

The night is frosty; the whole sky is clear;
the sublime choir of heavenly luminaries
so gently, so unisonally flows. . . .
4   Tatiana into the wide yard
in low-cut frock comes out;
she trains a mirror on the moon;
but in the dark glass only
8   the sad moon trembles. . . .
Hark! . . . the snow creaks . . . a passer-by; the
flits up to him on tiptoe—   [maiden
and her little voice sounds
12   more tender than a reed pipe's strain:
"What is your name?"[30] He looks,
and answers: "Agafón."

X

On the nurse's advice, Tatiana,
planning that night to conjure,
has on the quiet ordered in the bathhouse
4   a table to be laid for two.
But suddenly Tatiana is afraid. . . .
And I—at the thought of Svetlana—
I am afraid; so let it be . . .
8   we're not to conjure with Tatiana.
Her little silken sash Tatiana
has taken off, undressed, and to bed
has gone. Lel hovers over her,
1 2   while under her pillow of down
there lies a maiden's looking glass.
All has grown still. Tatiana sleeps.

XI

And dreams a wondrous dream Tatiana.
She dreams that she
over a snowy plain is walking,
4   surrounded by sad murk.
Before her, in the snowdrifts,
dins, undulates its wave
a churning, dark, and hoary
8   torrent, not chained by winter;
two thin poles, glued together by a piece of ice
(a shaky, perilous footbridge),
are laid across the torrent;
1 2   and in front of the dinning deep,
full of perplexity,
she stopped.

XII

As at a vexing separation,
Tatiana murmurs at the brook:
sees nobody who might a hand
4   offer her from the other side.
But suddenly a snowdrift stirred,
and who appeared from under it?
A large bear with a ruffled coat;
8   Tatiana uttered "Ach!" and he went roaring
and a paw with sharp claws
stretched out to her. Nerving herself,
she leaned on it with trembling hand
12   and with apprehensive steps
worked her way across the brook;
walked on—and what then? The bear followed
                      [her.

XIII

She, to look back not daring,
accelerates her hasty step;
but from the shaggy footman
4   can in no way escape;
grunting, lumbers the odious bear.
A wood before them; stirless are the pines
in their frowning beauty;
8   all their boughs are weighed down
by snow in clusters; through the summits
of aspens, birches, lindens bare
the ray of the night luminaries beams;
12   there is no path; bushes, precipices,
all are o'er-drifted by the blizzard,
plunged deep in snow.

XIV

Tatiana enters wood; bear follows;
up to her knee comes porous snow;
now by the neck a long branch
4   suddenly catches her, or out of her ears
tears by force their golden pendants;
now in the crumbly snow, off her winsome small
sticks fast a small wet shoe;   [foot,
8   now she lets fall her handkerchief—
she has no time to pick it up, is scared,
can hear the bear behind her,
and even, with a tremulous hand,
1 2   is shy to raise the border of her dress;
she runs; he keeps behind her;
and then she has no force to run.

XV

Into the snow she's fallen; the bear deftly
snatches her up and carries her;
she is insensibly submissive;
4   stirs not, breathes not;
he rushes her along a forest road;
sudden, 'mongst trees, there is a humble hut;
dense woods all round; from every quarter it
8   is drifted over with desolate snow,
and brightly throws its light a window;
and in the hut there are both cries and noise;
the bear commented: "Here's my gossip,
1 2   do warm yourself a little in his home!"
and straight he goes into the hallway
and on the threshold lays her down.

XVI

Tatiana comes to, looks:
no bear; she's in a hallway;
behind the door are cries and glass clink
4   as if at some big funeral.
Perceiving not a drop of sense in this,
she stealthily looks through the chink
—and what then? She sees . . . at a table
8   there sit monsters around:
one horned, with a dog's face,
another with a cock's head;
here is a witch with a goat's beard;
1 2   here, prim and proud, a skeleton;
yonder, a dwarf with a small tail; and there,
a half crane and half cat.

XVII

Still more frightening, still more wondrous:
there is a crab astride a spider;
there on a goose's neck a skull
4   in a red calpack twirls;
there a windmill the squat-jig dances
and with its vane-wings rasps and waves.
Barks, laughs, singing, whistling and claps,
8   parle of man and stamp of steed![31]
But what did Tatiana think
when 'mongst the guests she recognized
him who was dear to her and awesome—
1 2   the hero of our novel!
Onegin at the table sits
and through the door furtively gazes.

XVIII

He gives the signal—and all bustle;
he drinks—all drink and all cry out;
he laughs—all burst out laughing;
4   knits his brows—all are silent;
he is the master there, 'tis plain;
and Tanya is no longer quite so awestruck,
and being curious now
8   opened the door a little. . . .
Sudden the wind blew, putting out
the light of the nocturnal flambeaux;
the gang of goblins flinched;
12   Onegin, his eyes sparkling,
rises from table with a clatter;
all have risen; doorward he goes.

XIX

And she's afraid; and hastily
Tatiana does her utmost to escape:
not possible; impatiently
4   tossing about, she wants to scream—
cannot; Eugene has pushed the door,
and to the gaze of the infernal specters
the girl appeared; ferocious laughter
8   wildly broke out; the eyes of all,
hooves, curved proboscises,
tufted tails, tusks,
mustaches, bloody tongues,
12   horns, and fingers of bone—
all point as one at her,
and everybody cries: "Mine! Mine!"

XX

"Mine!" Eugene fiercely said,
and in a trice the whole gang vanished;
remained in frosty darkness
4   the youthful maid with him *à deux*.
Onegin gently draws [32]
Tatiana in a corner and deposits
her on a shaky bench
8   and lets his head sink
on her shoulder; abruptly Olga enters,
followed by Lenski; light has gleamed,
Onegin has swung back his lifted arm
12   and wildly his eyes roam,
and he berates the unbidden guests;
Tatiana lies barely alive.

XXI

The brawl grows louder, louder; suddenly
snatches a long knife, and forthwith   [Eugene
Lenski is felled; the shadows awesomely
4   have thickened; an excruciating cry
has broken forth . . . the cabin lurched . . .
and Tanya has woke up in terror. . . .
She looks—'tis light already in the room;
8   in the window through the befrosted pane
there scintillates dawn's crimson ray;
the door has opened. To her, Olga,
rosier than Northern Aurora
12   and lighter than a swallow, flits in;
"Well," she says, "now do tell me,
whom did you see in dream?"

XXII

But she, not noticing her sister,
lies with a book in bed,
turning over page after page,
4 and says nothing.
Although that book displayed
neither a poet's sweet conceits,
nor sapient truths, nor pictures,
8 yet neither Virgil, nor Racine,
nor Scott, nor Byron, nor Seneca,
nor even the Magazine of Ladies' Fashions
ever engrossed anybody so much:
12 it was, friends, Martin Zadeck,[33]
head of Chaldean sages,
divinistre, interpreter of dreams.

XXIII

This profound work
a wandering trader had peddled
one day into their solitude,
4 and for Tatiana finally,
with a broken set of *Malvina*, it
he'd ceded for three rubles fifty,
into the bargain taking also for them
8 a collection of common fables,
a grammar, two "Petriads,"
plus Marmontel, tome three.
Martin Zadeck later became
12 Tanya's favorite. He joys
in all her woes awards her,
and sleeps with her inseparably.

XXIV

The dream disturbs her.
Not knowing what to make of it,
the import of the dread chimera
4   Tatiana wishes to discover.
Tatiana in the brief index
looks up in alphabetic order
the words: forest, storm, raven, fir,
8   hedgehog, gloom, footbridge, bear, snowstorm,
et cetera. Her doubts
Martin Zadeck will not resolve;
but the ominous dream portends to her
12   a multitude of sad adventures.
For several days thereafter she
kept worrying about it.

XXV

But lo, with crimson hand[34]
Aurora from the morning dales
leads forth, with the sun, after her
4   the merry name-day festival.
Since morn Dame Larin's house with guests
is filled completely; in whole families
the neighbors have converged, in winter coaches,
8   kibitkas, britskas, and sleighs.
In vestibule there's jostling, turmoil;
in drawing room, the meeting of new people,
the bark of pugs, girls' smacking kisses,
12   noise, laughter, a crush at the threshold,
the bows, the scraping of the guests,
wet nurses' shouts, and children's cry.

XXVI

With his portly spouse
there came fat Pustyakóv;
Gvozdín, an admirable landlord,
4   owner of destitute muzhiks;
a gray-haired couple, the Skotínins,
with children of all ages, counting
from thirty years to two;
8   the district fopling, Petushkóv;
Buyánov, my first cousin,
covered with fluff, in a peaked cap[35]
(as he, of course, is known to you);
12   and the retired counselor Flyánov,
a heavy scandalmonger, an old rogue,
glutton, bribetaker, and buffoon.

XXVII

With the family of Panfíl Harlikóv
there also came Monsieur Triquet,
a wit, late from Tambov,
4   bespectacled and russet-wigged.
As a true Frenchman, in his pocket
Triquet has brought a stanza for Tatiana
fitting an air to children known:
8   "Réveillez-vous, belle endormie."
'Mongst the time-worn songs of an almanac
this stanza had been printed;
Triquet—resourceful poet—
12   out of the dust brought it to light
and boldly in the place of "belle Niná"
put "belle Tatianá."

XXVIII

And now from the near borough,
idol of ripened misses,
joyance of district mothers,
4   a Company Commander has arrived;
has entered. . . . Ah, news—and what news!
there will be regimental music:
"the Colonel himself has sent it."
8   What glee! There is to be a ball!
The young things skip beforehand.[36]
But dinner's served. In pairs,
they go to table, arm in arm.
12   The misses cluster near Tatiana;
the men face her; and, as all cross themselves,
the crowd buzzes, to table sitting down.

XXIX

Talks for a moment have subsided;
mouths chew. Upon all sides
the plates and covers clatter
4   and there resounds the clink of glasses.
But soon the guests gradually
raise a general hullabaloo.
None listens; they cry out,
8   laugh, dispute, and squeal.
The door leaves suddenly fly open: Lenski enters,
and with him Onegin. "Oh, my Maker!"
cries out the lady of the house. "At last!"
12   The guests make room, each shifts
covers, chairs quick;
they call, they seat the pair of friends

XXX

—seat them directly facing Tanya,
and paler than the morning moon,
and more aquiver than the hunted doe,
4   she darkening eyes
does not raise. Stormily there breathes
in her a passionate glow; she suffocates, feels
the two friends' greetings she   [faint;
8   does not hear; the tears from her eyes
are on the point of trickling; she is on the point,
poor thing, of swooning;
but will and reason's power
1 2   prevailed. A word or two
she uttered through her teeth in a low voice
and managed to remain at table.

XXXI

Tragiconervous scenes,
the fainting fits of maidens, tears,
long since Eugene could not abide:
4   enough of them he had endured.
The odd chap, on finding himself at a huge feast,
was cross already. But the dolent girl's
quivering impulse having noticed,
8   out of vexation lowering his gaze,
he went into a huff and, fuming,
swore he would enrage Lenski,
and thoroughly, in fact, avenge himself.
1 2   Now, triumphing beforehand,
he inwardly began to sketch
caricatures of all the guests.

XXXII

Of course, not only Eugene
Tanya's confusion might have seen;
but the target of looks and comments
4   was at the time a rich pie
(unfortunately, oversalted);
and here, in bottle sealed with pitch,
between meat course and blancmangér,
8   Tsimlyanski wine is brought already,
followed by an array of glasses, narrow, long,
similar to your waist,
Zizi, the crystal of my soul,
12   the subject of my innocent verse,
enluring vial of love,
you, of whom drunk I used to be!

XXXIII

Having got rid of its damp cork,
the bottle popped; the wine
fizzes; and now with an important mien,
4   long since tormented by his stanza,
Triquet stands up; before him the assembly
maintains deep silence.
Tatiana's scarce alive; Triquet,
8   addressing her, a slip of paper in his hand,
proceeds to sing, off key. Claps, acclamations,
salute him. She
must drop the bard a curtsy;
12   whereat the poet, modest although great,
is first to drink her health
and hands to her the stanza.

XXXIV

Greetings, congratulations follow;
Tatiana thanks everybody.
Then, when the turn of Eugene
4 arrived, the maiden's dolorous air,
her embarrassment, lassitude,
engendered pity in his soul:
he bowed to her in silence,
8 but somehow the look of his eyes
was wondrous tender. Whether
because he verily was touched
or he was being mischievous, coquetting,
12 whether unwillfully or by free will,
but tenderness that look expressed:
it revived Tanya's heart.

XXXV

The chairs, as they are pushed back, clatter;
the crowd presses into the drawing room:
thus bees out of the luscious hive
4 fly meadward in a noisy swarm.
Pleased with the festive dinner,
neighbor in front of neighbor wheezes;
the ladies by the hearth have settled;
8 the maidens whisper in a corner;
the green-baized tables are unfolded:
to mettlesome cardplayers call
boston and omber of the old,
12 and whist, up to the present famous:
monotonous family,
all sons of avid boredom.

XXXVI

Eight rubbers have already played
whist's heroes; eight times they
have changed their seats—
4   and tea is brought. I like the hour
to fix by dinner, tea,
and supper. We know time
in the country without great fuss:
8   the stomach is our accurate Bréguet;
and, apropos, I'll parenthetically note
that in my strophes I discourse
as frequently on feasts,
12   on various dishes and corks,
as you, divine Homer,
you, the idol of thirty centuries!

XXXVII, XXXVIII

. . . .

XXXIX

But tea is brought: the damsels primly
have scarcely taken hold of their saucers
than sudden from behind the door of the long
4   bassoon and flute resound.   [hall
By music's thunder gladdened,
leaving his cup of tea with rum,
the Paris of surrounding townlets,
8   Petushkov goes up to Olga,
Lenski, to Tatiana; Miss Harlikov,
a marriageable maid of overripe years
is secured by my Tambovan poet;
12   Buyanov has whirled off Dame Pustyakov;
and all have spilled into the hall,
and in full glory the ball glitters.

XL

At the beginning of my novel
(see the first fascicle)
I wanted in Albano's manner
4 a Petersburg ball to describe;
but, by an empty reverie diverted,
I got engrossed in recollecting
the little feet of ladies known to me.
8 Upon your narrow little tracks,
O little feet, enough roving astray!
With the betrayal of my youth
'tis time I grew more sensible,
1 2 improved in doings and in diction,
and this fifth fascicle
cleansed from digressions.

XLI

Monotonous and mad
like young life's whirl,
the waltz's noisy whirl revolves,
4 pair after pair flicks by.
Nearing the minute of revenge,
Onegin, chuckling secretly,
goes up to Olga, rapidly with her
8 twirls near the guests,
then seats her on a chair,
proceeds to speak of this and that;
a minute or two having lapsed, then
1 2 again with her he goes on waltzing;
all in amazement are. Lenski himself
does not believe his proper eyes.

XLII

The mazurka has resounded. Time was,
when the mazurka's thunder crashed,
in a huge ballroom everything vibrated,
4   the parquetry cracked under heel,
the window frames shook, rattled;
now 'tis not thus: we, too, like ladies,
glide o'er the lacquered boards.
8   But in [small] towns, in country places,
still the mazurka has retained
its pristine charms:
saltos, heel-play, mustachios
12 remain the same; them has not altered
highhanded fashion, our tyrant
the sickness of the latest Russians.

XLIII

· · · · · · · · · · · · · ·

XLIV

Buyanov, my mettlesome cousin,
has to our hero led
Tatiana with Olga; deft
4   Onegin with Olga has gone.
He steers her, gliding nonchalantly,
and, bending, whispers tenderly to her
some banal madrigal,
8   and her hand presses, and has flamed
in her conceited face
brighter the rose. My Lenski
has seen it all; flared up, beside himself;
12 in jealous indignation,
the poet waits for the end of the mazurka
and invites her for the cotillion.

XLV

But no, she cannot. Cannot? But what is it?
Why, Olga has given her word already
to Onegin. Ah, good God, good God!
4   What does he hear? She could . . .
How is it possible? Scarce out of swaddling
and a coquette, a giddy child!   [clothes—
Already she is versed in guile,
8   already to be faithless has been taught!
Lenski has not the strength to bear the blow;
cursing the pranks of women,
he leaves, demands a horse,
12   and gallops off. A brace of pistols,
two bullets—nothing else—
shall in a trice decide his fate.

CHAPTER SIX

Là, sotto i giorni nubilosi e brevi,
Nasce una gente a cui 'l morir non dole.

Petr.

Chapter Six

———————————————

I

On noticing that Vladimir had vanished,
Onegin, by boredom again beset,
by Olga's side sank into meditation,
4 pleased with his vengeance.
After him Olinka yawned too,
sought Lenski with her eyes,
and the endless cotillion
8 oppressed her like a grievous dream.
But it has ended.   They go in to supper.
The beds are made. For guests
night lodgings are assigned—from the entrance
                                                    [hall
12 even to the maids' quarters. By all is needed
restful sleep. My Onegin
alone has driven home to sleep.

II

All has become calm. In the drawing room
snores heavy Pustyakov
with his heavy better half.
4 Gvozdin, Buyanov, Petushkov,
and Flyanov (who is not quite well)
have bedded in the dining room on chairs,
and, on the floor, Monsieur Triquet
8 in underwaistcoat and old nightcap.
The maidens, in the chambers of Tatiana
and Olga, all are wrapped in sleep.
Alone, sadly at the window
12 illumined by Diana's ray,
poor Tatiana does not sleep
and gazes out on the dark field.

III

With his unlooked-for apparition,
the momentary softness of his eyes,
and odd conduct with Olga,
4 to the depth of her soul
she's penetrated; is unable
to understand him utterly. Disturbs
her the ache of jealousy,
8 as if a cold hand
compressed her heart; as if an abyss
blackened and dinned beneath her. . . .
"I'll perish," Tanya says,
12 "but perishing from him is lovely.
I murmur not: why murmur?
He cannot give me happiness."

IV

Forward, forward, my story!
A new persona summons us.
Five versts from Krasnogorie,
4 Lenski's estate, there lives
and thrives up to the present time
in philosophical reclusion
Zarétski, formerly a brawler,
8 the hetman of a gaming gang,
chieftain of rakehells, pothouse tribune,
but now a kind and simple
bachelor paterfamilias,
12 a steadfast friend, a peaceable landowner,
and even an honorable man:
thus does our age correct itself!

V

Time was, the *monde*'s obsequious voice
used to extol his wicked pluck:
an ace, 'tis true, he from a pistol
4 at twelve yards hit,
and, furthermore, in battle too
once, in genuine intoxication,
he distinguished himself, boldly in the mud
8 toppling from his Kalmuk steed,
swine drunk, and to the French
fell prisoner (prized hostage!)—
a modern Regulus, the god of honor,
12 ready to yield anew to bonds
in order every morning at Véry's[37]
to drain on credit some three bottles.

VI

Time was, he would chaff drolly,
knew how to gull a fool
and capitally fool a clever man,
4 either for all to see or on the sly;
though some tricks of his, too,
did not remain unchastised;
though sometimes, too, into a trap himself
8 he blundered like a simpleton.
He knew how gaily to dispute,
wittily or obtusely to reply,
now craftily to hold his tongue,
12 now craftily to raise a rumpus,
set young friends by the ears,
and place them on the marked-out ground,

VII

or have them make it up
so as to lunch all three,
and later secretly defame them
4 with a gay quip, with babble. . . .
Sed alia tempora! Daredevilry
(like love's dream, yet another caper)
passes with lively youth.
8 As I've said, my Zaretski,
beneath the racemosas and the pea trees
from storms having at last found shelter,
lives like a true sage,
12 plants cabbages like Horace,
breeds ducks and geese,
and teaches his children the A B C.

VIII

He was not stupid; and my Eugene,
while rating low the heart in him,
liked both the spirit of his judgments
4   and his sane talk of this and that.
He used with pleasure
to see him, and therefore not in the least
was he surprised at morn
8   when he saw him;
the latter, after the first greeting,
the started conversation interrupting,
with gaze atwinkle, to Onegin
12   handed a billet from the poet.
Onegin went up to the window
and read it to himself.

IX

It was a pleasant, gentlemanly,
brief challenge or cartel:
politely, with cold clearness,
4   to fight a duel Lenski called his friend.
Onegin, in a first reaction,
to the envoy of such an errand
turning, without superfluous words
8   said he was "always ready."
Zaretski got up without explanations—
did not want to stay longer,
having at home at lot of things to do—
12   and forthwith left; but Eugene,
alone remaining with his soul,
felt ill-contented with himself.

X

And serve him right: on strict examination,
he, having called his own self to a secret court,
accused himself of much:
4　First, on his part it had been wrong enough
at timid, tender love
so casually to poke fun yesternight;
and secondly: why, let a poet
8　indulge in foolery! At eighteen
'tis pardonable. Eugene,
loving the youth with all his heart,
ought to have shown himself to be
1 2　no bandyball of prejudices,
no fiery boy, no scrapper,
but a man of honor and sense.

XI

He might have manifested feelings
instead of bristling like a beast;
he ought to have disarmed
4　the youthful heart. "But now
too late; the time has flown away. . . .
Moreover," he reflects, "in this affair
an old duelist has intervened;
8　he's malicious, he's a gossiper, he's glib. . . .
Of course, contempt should be
the price of his droll sallies;
but the whisper, the snickering of fools . . ."
1 2　And here it is—public opinion! 38
Honor's mainspring, our idol!
And here is what the world twirls on!

XII

Boiling with an impatient enmity,
at home the poet for the answer waits.
And here the grandiloquent neighbor
4   has brought the answer solemnly.
Now, what a boon 'tis for the jealous one!
He had kept fearing that the prankster
might joke his way out somehow,
8   a dodge devising and his breast
averting from the pistol.
The doubts are now resolved:
down to the mill they must
12   tomorrow drive before daybreak,
at one another raise the cock,
and at the thigh or at the temple aim.

XIII

Having resolved to hate the flirt,
boiling Lenski did not wish
to see Olga before the duel.
4   The sun, his watch he kept consulting;
gave up at length—
and found himself at the fair neighbors'.
He thought he would embarrass Olinka,
8   confound her by his coming;
but nothing of the sort: just as before
to meet the poor bard
Olinka skipped down from the porch,
12   akin to giddy hope,
spry, carefree, gay—
well, just the same as she had been.

XIV

"Why did you vanish yesternight so early?"
was Olinka's first question.
In Lenski all the senses clouded,
4   and silently he hung his head.
Jealousy and vexation disappeared
before this clarity of glance,
before this soft simplicity,
8   before this sprightly soul! . . .
He gazes with sweet tender-heartedness;
he sees: he is still loved!
Already, by remorse oppressed,
1 2   he is prepared to beg her pardon,
he quivers, can't find words:
he's happy, he is almost well. . . .

XV, XVI

.   .   .   .

XVII

And once again pensive, dejected
before his winsome Olga,
Vladimir does not have the force
4   to remind her of yesterday;
"I" he reflects, "shall be her savior.
I shall not suffer a depraver
with the fire of both sighs and compliments
8   to tempt a youthful heart,
nor let a despicable, venomous worm
a lily's stalklet gnaw,
nor have a flower two morns old
1 2   wither while yet half blown."
All this, friends, meant:
I have a pistol duel with a pal.

XVIII

If he had known what wound
burned my Tatiana's heart!
If Tatiana had been aware,
4   if she could have known
that Lenski and Eugene tomorrow
were to compete for the tomb's shelter,
ah, possibly her love
8   might have conjoined the friends again!
But even by chance that passion
no one had yet discovered.
Onegin about everything was silent;
12   Tatiana pined away in secret;
alone the nurse might have known—
but then she was slow-witted.

XIX

All evening Lenski was abstracted,
now taciturn, now gay again;
but he who has been fostered by the Muse
4   is always thus; with knitted brow
he'd sit down at the clavichord
and play but chords on it;
or else, his gaze directing toward Olga,
8   he'd whisper, "I am happy, am I not?"
But it is late; time to depart. Contracted
in him the heart, full of its ache;
as he took leave of the young maiden,
12   it seemed to break asunder.
She looks him in the face.
"What ails you?" "Nothing." And makes for the
                                          [porch.

XX

On coming home his pistols
he inspected, then inserted
them back into the case, and, undressed,
4   by candle opened Schiller;
but there's one thought infolding him;
his melancholy heart does not drowse:
in loveliness ineffable
8   Olga he sees before him.
Vladimir shuts the book,
takes up his pen; his verses—
full of love's nonsense—
12   sound and flow. He reads them
aloud, in lyric fever,
like drunken D[elvig] at a feast.

XXI

The verses chanced to be preserved;
I have them; here they are:
"Whither, ah! whither are ye fled,
4   my springtime's golden days?
What has the coming day in store for me?
In vain my gaze attempts to grasp it;
In deep murk it lies hidden.
8   It matters not; fate's law is just.
Whether I fall, pierced by the arrow,
or whether it flies by,
all's right: of waking and of sleep
12   comes the determined hour;
blest is the day of cares,
blest, too, is the advent of darkness!

XXII

"'Tomorn will gleam the ray of daydawn,
and brilliant day will scintillate;
whilst I, perhaps—I to the tomb's
4   mysterious shelter shall descend,
and the young poet's memory
slow Lethe will engulf;
the world will forget me; but thou,
8   wilt thou come, maid of beauty,
to shed a tear over the early urn
and to reflect: he loved me,
to me alone he consecrated
12   the woeful daybreak of a stormy life! . . .
Friend of my heart, wished-for friend,
come! Come: I am thy spouse!"

XXIII

Thus did he write, "obscurely" and "limply"
(what we call romanticism—
though no romanticism here in the least
4   do I see; but what's that to us?),
and, before dawn, at last
sinking his weary head,
at the fashionable word "ideal",
8   Lenski dozed off gently;
but scarcely in the spell of sleep
has he been lost than the neighbor already
enters the silent study
12   and wakens Lenski with the proclamation,
"Time to get up; past six already.
Onegin's sure to be already waiting for us."

XXIV

But he was wrong: Eugene
was at the time in a dead sleep.
The shadows of the night now thin,
4   and Vesper by the cock is greeted;
Onegin soundly sleeps away.
By now the sun rides high,
and shifting flurries
8   glitter and swirl; but his bed
still Onegin has not left,
still sleep hovers over him.
Here finally he has awoken
12   and drawn apart the curtain's flaps;
looks—and sees that 'tis time
long since already to drive off.

XXV

Quickly he rings. Runs in
to him his French valet, Guillot,
offers him dressing gown and slippers,
4   and hands him linen.
Onegin hastes to dress,
orders his valet to prepare
to drive together with him and take also
8   the combat case along.
The racing sleigh is ready.
He has got in, flies to the mill.
They've come apace. He bids his valet
12   Lepage's[39] fell tubes
bear after him and has the horses
moved off into a field toward two oaklings.

XXVI

On the dam leaning, Lenski
long had impatiently been waiting;
meanwhile, rural mechanic,
4   Zaretski criticized the millstone.
Onegin with apologies comes up.
"But where," quoth with amazement
Zaretski, "where's your second?"
8   In duels classicist and pedant,
he liked method out of feeling,
and to stretch one's man
he allowed not anyhow
12   but by the strict rules of the art
according to all the traditions of old times
(which we must praise in him).

XXVII

"My second?" Eugene said.
"Here's he: my friend, Monsieur Guillot.
I don't foresee any objections
4   to my presentation:
although he is an unknown man,
quite surely he's an honest chap."
Zaretski bit his lip.
8   Onegin asked Lenski:
"Well, do we start?" "Let's start if you are
Vladimir said. And they repaired   [willing,"
behind the mill. While at a distance
12   our good Zaretski and the "honest chap"
enter into a solemn compact,
the two foes stand with lowered gaze.

XXVIII

Foes! Is it long since from each other
bloodthirst turned them away?
Is it long since their hours of leisure,
4   meals, thoughts, and doings
they shared in friendliness? Malevolently now,
similar to hereditary foes,
as in a frightful, enigmatic dream,
8   they for each other, in the stillness,
prepare destruction coolly. . . .
Should they not burst out laughing while
their hand is not encrimsoned?
12   Should they not amicably part? . . .
But wildly beau-monde enmity
is of false shame afraid.

XXIX

The pistols have already gleamed.
The mallet clanks against the ramrod.
Into the polyhedral barrel go the balls,
4   and the first time the cock has clicked.
Now powder in a grayish streamlet
is poured into the pan. The jagged,
securely screwed-in flint
8   is raised anew. Behind a near stump
perturbed Guillot places himself.
The two foes shed their cloaks.
Thirty-two steps Zaretski
12   with eminent exactness has paced off,
has placed his friends apart at the utmost points,
and each has taken his pistol.

XXX

"Now march toward each other." Coolly,
  not aiming yet, the two foes
  with firm tread, slowly, evenly
4 traversed four paces,
  four deadly stairs.
  His pistol Eugene then,
  not ceasing to advance,
8 gently the first began to raise.
  Now they have stepped five paces more,
  and Lenski, closing his left eye,
  started to level also—but right then
12 Onegin fired. . . . Struck have
  the appointed hours: the poet
  in silence drops his pistol.

XXXI

Gently he lays his hand upon his breast
  and falls. His misty gaze
  expresses death, not anguish.
4 Thus, slowly, down the slope of hills,
  in the sun with sparks shining,
  a lump of snow descends.
  Deluged with instant cold,
8 Onegin hastens to the youth,
  looks, calls him . . . vainly:
  he is no more. The youthful bard
  has met with an untimely end!
12 The storm has blown; the beauteous bloom
  has withered at sunrise;
  the fire upon the altar has gone out! . . .

XXXII

Stirless he lay, and strange
was his brow's languid peace.
Under the breast he had been shot clean through;
4   steaming, the blood flowed from the wound.
One moment earlier
in *this* heart had throbbed inspiration,
enmity, hope, and love,
8   life effervesced, blood boiled;
now, as in a deserted house,
all in it is both still and dark,
it has become forever silent.
12   The window boards are shut. The panes with
                        [chalk
are whitened over. The chatelaine is gone.
But where, God wot. All trace is lost.

XXXIII

'Tis pleasant with an insolent epigram
to madden a bungling foe;
pleasant to see how, stubbornly
4   bending his buttsome horns,
he can't help looking in the mirror
and is ashamed to recognize himself;
more pleasant, friends, if he
8   like a fool howls out: It is I!
Still pleasanter—in silence
for him an honorable grave to prepare
and quietly to aim at his pale forehead
12   at a gentlemanly distance;
but to dispatch him to his fathers
will hardly pleasant be for you.

XXXIV

What, then, if by your pistol
be smitten a young pal
who with a saucy glance or repartee
4   or any other bagatelle
insulted you over the bottle,
or even himself, in fiery vexation,
to combat proudly challenged you?
8   Say: your soul
with what feeling would be possessed
when, stirless on the ground,
in front of you, with death upon his brow,
12   he by degrees would stiffen,
when he'd be deaf and silent
to your desperate appeal?

XXXV

In the ache of the heart's remorse,
his hand squeezing the pistol,
at Lenski Eugene looks.
4 "Well, what—he's dead," pronounced the neigh-
Dead! . . . With this dreadful interjection   [bor.
smitten, Onegin with a shudder
walks hence and calls his men.
8   With care Zaretski lays
upon the sleigh the frozen corpse;
home he is driving the dread lading.
On sensing the corpse, snort
and jib the horses; with white foam
wet the steel bit;
and like an arrow off they fly.

XXXVI

My friends, you're sorry for the poet:
in the bloom of glad hopes,
not having yet fulfilled them for the world,
4 scarce out of infant clothes,
has withered! Where is the hot agitation,
where is the noble aspiration
both of young feelings and young thoughts,
8 high, tender, dashing?
Where are love's turbulent desires,
the thirst for knowledges and work,
and fear of vice and shame,
12 and you, fond musings,
you, [token] of unearthly life,
you, dreams of sacred poetry!

XXXVII

Perhaps, for the world's good
or, at the least, for glory he was born;
his silenced lyre
4 a resonant, uninterrupted ringing
in centuries might have aroused. The poet,
perhaps, upon the stairway of the world,
had a high stair awaiting him.
8 His martyred shade,
perhaps, had borne away with it
a sacred mystery, and for us
a life-creating voice has perished,
12 and past the tomb's confines
will not rush up to it the hymn of races,
the benediction of the times.

XXXVIII

. . . .

XXXIX

And then again: perhaps, the poet
had a habitual lot awaiting him.
The years of youth would have elapsed:
4   the fervor of the soul cooled down in him.
He would have changed in many ways,
have parted with the Muses, married,
up in the country, happy and cornute,
8   have worn a quilted dressing gown;
learned life in its reality,
at forty, had the gout,
drunk, eaten, moped, got fat, decayed,
12 and in his bed, at last,
died in the midst of children,
weepy females, and medicos.

XL

But, reader, be it as it may,
alas, the young lover,
the poet, the pensive dreamer,
4   is killed by a pal's hand!
There is a spot: left of the village
where inspiration's nursling dwelt,
two pines have grown together at the roots;
8   beneath them have meandered streamlets
of the neighboring valley's brook.
'Tis there the plowman likes to rest,
and women reapers to dip in the waves
12 their ringing pitchers come;
there, by the brook, in the dense shade
a simple monument is set.

XLI

Beneath it (as begins to drip
spring rain upon the herb of fields)
the herdsman, plaiting his pied shoe of bast,
4   sings of the Volga fishermen;
and the young townswoman
spending the summer in the country,
when she on horseback headlong
8   ranges, alone, over the fields,
before it halts her steed,
tightening the leathern rein;
and, turning up the gauze veil of her hat,
1 2   with skimming eyes reads
the simple scripture—and a tear
dims her soft eyes.

XLII

And at a walk in open champaign rides,
sunk in a reverie, she;
her soul a long time, willy-nilly,
4   is full of Lenski's fate;
and she reflects: "What has become of Olga?
Did her heart suffer long?
Or did the season of her tears soon pass?
8   And where's her sister now?
and where's the fleer from mankind and the
of modish belles the modish foe,   [world,
where's that clouded eccentric,
1 2   the slayer of the youthful poet?"
In due time an account to you
in detail about everything I'll give.

XLIII

But not now. Though with all my heart
I love my hero;
though I'll return to him, of course;
4   but now I cannot be concerned with him.
The years to austere prose incline,
the years chase rhyme, the romp, away,
and I—with a sigh I confess—
8   more indolently dangle after her.
My pen has not its ancient disposition
to scrawl fugitive leaves;
other, chill, dreams,
12   other, stern, cares,
both in the social hum and in the hush
disturb my soul's sleep.

XLIV

I have learned the voice of other desires,
I've come to know new sadness;
I have no expectations for the first,
4   and the old sadness I regret.
Dreams, dreams! Where is your dulcitude?
Where is (its stock rhyme) juventude?
Can it be really true that finally
8   its garland's withered, withered?
Can it be true that really and indeed,
without elegiac devices,
the springtime of my days is fled
12   (as I in jest kept saying hitherto),
and can it be that it has no return?
Can it be true that I'll be thirty soon?

XLV

So! My noontide is come, and I must
acknowledge this, I see.
But, anyway, as friends let's part,
4 O my light youth!
My thanks for the delights,
the melancholy, the dear torments,
the hum, the storms, the feasts,
8 for all, for all your gifts
my thanks to you. In you
amidst turmoils and in the stillness
I have delighted . . . and in full.
1 2 Enough! With a clear soul
I now set out on a new course
to rest from my old life.

XLVI

Let me glance back. Farewell now, coverts
where in the backwoods flowed my days,
fulfilled with passions and indolence
4 and the dreams of a pensive soul.
And you, young inspiration,
excite my fancy,
the slumber of the heart enliven,
8 into my nook more often fly,
let not a poet's soul grow cold,
callous, crust-dry,
and finally be turned to stone
1 2 in the World's deadening intoxication
in that slough where with you
I bathe, dear friends!⁴⁰

CHAPTER SEVEN

Moscow! Russia's favorite daughter!
Where is your equal to be found? -

Dmitriev

How not to love one's native Moscow?

Baratïnski

"Attacking Moscow! This is what
comes from seeing the world! Where is it better,
"Where we are not."   [then?"

Griboedov

Chapter Seven

_____

I

Chased by the vernal beams,
down the surrounding hills the snows already
have run in turbid streams
4   onto the inundated fields.
With a serene smile, nature
greets through her sleep the morning of the year.
Bluing, the heavens glisten.
8   The yet transparent woods
as if with down are greening.
The bee after the tribute of the field
flies from her waxen cell.
12   The dales grow dry and varicolored.
The herds are noisy, and the nightingale
has sung already in the silence of the nights.

II

How sad your coming is to me,
spring, spring, season of love!
What a dark agitation
4   in my soul, in my blood!
With what a heavy tender feeling
I revel in the whiff
of spring fanning my face
8   in the lap of the rural stillness!
Or is enjoyment strange to me,
and all that gladdens, animates,
all that exults and glitters,
1 2   casts tedium and irksomeness
upon a soul long dead,
and all looks dark to it?

III

Or not rejoiced by the return
of leaves that perished in the autumn,
a bitter loss we recollect,
4   harking the new sough of the woods;
or with reanimated nature we
compare in troubled meditation
the withering of our years,
8   for which there is no renovation?
Perhaps there comes into our thoughts,
midst a poetic daydream,
some other, ancient, spring,
1 2   and sets our heart aquiver
with the dream of a distant clime,
a marvelous night, a moon. . . .

IV

Now is the time: good lazybones,
epicurean sages,
you, even-minded fortunates;
4   you, fledglings of the Lyóvshin[41] school;
you, country Priams;
and sentimental ladies, you;
spring calls you to the country,
8   season of warmth, of flowers, of labors,
season of inspired rambles,
and of seductive nights.
Friends! to the fields, quick, quick;
12   in heavy loaden chariots;
with your own horses or with posters;
out of the towngates start to trek!

V

And you, indulgent reader,
in your imported calash,
forsake the indefatigable city
4   where in the winter you made merry;
with my wayward Muse
let's go to hear the murmur of a park
above a nameless river,
8   in the country place where my Eugene,
a hermit, idle and dejected,
still recently dwelt in the winter,
in the vicinity of youthful Tanya,
12   of my dear dreamer;
but where he is no longer now . . .
where he has left a melancholy trace.

VI

'Mongst hills disposed in a half circle,
let us go thither where a rill,
winding, by way of a green meadow, runs
4   through a lime bosquet to the river.
The nightingale, spring's lover, there
sings all night; the cinnamon rose blooms,
and the gurgle of the fount is heard.
8   There a tombstone is seen
in the shade of two old-aged pines.
The scripture to the stranger says:
"Here lies Vladimir Lenski,
12   who early died the death of the courageous,
in such a year, at such an age.
Repose, boy poet!"

VII

On the inclined bough of a pine,
time was, the early breeze
above that humble urn
4   swayed a mysterious wreath;
time was, during late leisures,
two girl companions hither used to come;
and, by the moon, upon the grave,
8   embraced, they wept;
but now . . . the drear memorial is
forgot. The wonted trail to it,
weed-choked. No wreath is on the bough.
12   Alone, beneath it, gray and debile,
the herdsman as before keeps singing
and plaiting his poor footgear.

VIII, IX

. . . .

X

My poor Lenski! Pining away,
she did not weep for long.
Alas! The young fiancée
4 is to her woe untrue.
Another fascinated her attention,
another her suffering managed
to lull with love's flattery:
8 an uhlan knew how to captivate her,
an uhlan by her soul is loved;
and lo! with him already at the altar
she modestly beneath the bridal crown
12 stands with bent head,
fire in her lowered eyes,
a light smile on her lips.

XI

My poor Lenski! Beyond the grave,
in the confines of deaf eternity,
was the dejected bard perturbed
4 by the fell news of the betrayal?
Or on the Lethe lulled to sleep,
blest with insensibility, the poet
no longer is perturbed by anything,
8 and closed and mute is earth to him? . . .
'Tis so! Indifferent oblivion
beyond the sepulcher awaits us.
The voice of foes, of friends, of loves
12 falls silent suddenly. Alone over the estate
the angry chorus of the heirs
starts an indecent squabble.

XII

And soon the ringing voice of Olya
stopped sounding in the Larin family.
A captive of his lot, the uhlan
4   had to rejoin his regiment with her.
Bitterly shedding floods of tears,
the old dame, as she took leave of her daughter,
seemed scarce alive,
8   but Tanya could not cry;
only a deadly pallor covered
her sad face.
When everybody came out on the porch,
12   and one and all, in bidding farewell, bustled
around the chariot of the newly wed,
Tatiana saw them off.

XIII

And long, as through a mist,
she gazed after them. . . .
And now Tatiana is alone, alone!
4   Alas! Companion of so many years,
her youthful doveling,
her own dear bosom friend,
has been by fate swept far away,
8   has been from her forever separated.
She, like a shade, roams aimlessly;
now into the deserted garden looks. . . .
Nowhere, in nothing, are there joys for her,
12   and she finds no relief
for suppressed tears,
and her heart breaks in twain.

XIV

And in the cruel solitude
stronger her passion burns,
and about far Onegin
4 the heart to her speaks louder.
She will not see him;
she must abhor in him
the slayer of her brother;
8 the poet perished . . . but already him
remembers none, already to another
his promised bride has given herself.
The poet's memory has swept by
12 as smoke across an azure sky;
for him two hearts, perhaps,
still grieve. . . . What is the use of grieving?

XV

'Twas evening. The sky darkened. Waters
streamed quietly. The beetle churred.
The choral throngs already were dispersing.
4 Across the river, smoking, flamed already
the fire of fishermen. In open country
by the moon's silvery light,
sunk in her dreams,
8 long did Tatiana walk alone.
On, on she went. . . . And suddenly before her
sees from a hill a manor house,
a village, a grove below hill
12 and a garden above a bright river.
She gazes, and the heart in her
faster and harder has begun to beat.

XVI

Doubts trouble her:
"Shall I go on? Shall I go back? . . .
He is not here. They do not know me. . . .
4   I'll glance at the house, at that garden."
And so downhill Tatiana walks,
scarce breathing; casts around
a gaze full of perplexity . . .
8   and enters a deserted courtyard.
Dogs toward her dash, barking.
At her cry of alarm
a household brood of serf boys
12   has noisily converged. Not without fighting
the boys dispersed the hounds,
taking the lady under their protection.

XVII

"I wonder, can one see the master house?"
asked Tanya. Speedily
the children to Anisia ran
4   to get the hallway keys from her.
Anisia came forth to her promptly,
and the door opened before them,
and Tanya stepped into the empty house,
8   where recently our hero had been living.
She looks; in a reception room forgotten,
a cue reposed upon the billiard table;
upon a rumpled sofa lay
12   a riding crop. Tanya went on.
The crone to her: "And here's the fireplace;
here master used to sit alone.

XVIII

"Here used to dine with him in winter
  the late Lenski, our neighbor.
  This way, please, follow me.
4 Here is the master's study;
  he used to sleep here, take his coffee,
  listen to the steward's reports,
  and in the morning read a book. . . .
8 And the old master lived here too;
  time was, with me on Sundays,
  here at the window, having donned his glasses,
  he'd deign to play 'tomfools.'
12 God grant salvation to his soul
  and peace to his dear bones
  in the grave, in damp mother earth!"

XIX

Tatiana with soft-melting gaze
  around her looks at all,
  and all to her seems priceless,
4 all vivifies her dolent soul
  with a half-painful joyance:
  the desk with its extinguished lamp,
  a pile of books, and at the window
8 a bed covered with a rug,
  and through the moon gloam the view from the
  and this pale half-light,   [window,
  and Lord Byron's portrait,
12 and a small column with a puppet of cast-iron,
  under a hat, with clouded brow,
  with arms crosswise compressed.

XX

Long does Tatiana in the modish cell
as one enchanted stand.
But it is late. A cold wind has arisen.
4   It's dark in the dale. The grove sleeps
above the misted river;
the moon has hid behind the hill,
and for the youthful pilgrimess
8   it is time, high time to go home;
and Tanya, her excitement having hid,
not without having sighed,
starts out on her way back;
12   but first she asks permission
to visit the deserted castle
so as to read books there alone.

XXI

With the housekeeper Tatiana parted
beyond the gateway. A day later,
early at morn this time, again she came
4   to the abandoned roof,
and in the silent study,
to all on earth oblivious for a while,
she finally remained alone,
8   and long she wept.
Then to the books she turned.
At first she was not in a mood for them,
but their choice appeared
12   to her bizarre. To reading fell
Tatiana with an avid soul;
and a different world revealed itself to her.

XXII

Although we know that Eugene
had long ceased to like reading,
however, several works
4   he had exempted from disgrace:
the singer of the Giaour and Juan,
also with him, two or three novels
in which the epoch is reflected
8   and modern man
rather correctly represented
with his immoral soul,
selfish and dry,
12   to dreaming measurelessly given,
with his embittered mind
boiling in empty action.

XXIII

Many pages preserved
the trenchant mark of fingernails;
the eyes of the attentive maiden
4   more eagerly upon them are directed.
Tatiana with a flutter sees
by what thought, observation
Onegin used to be struck,
8   what he agreed with tacitly.
In their margins she encounters
the dashes of his pencil.
Everywhere Onegin's soul
12   itself involuntarily expresses
here by a brief word, there a cross,
or interrogatory crotchet.

XXIV

And by degrees begins
my Tatiana to understand
more clearly now—thank God—
4   the one for whom to sigh
she's sentenced by imperious fate.
A sad and dangerous eccentric,
creature of hell or heaven,
8   this angel, this arrogant fiend,
who's he then? Can it be—an imitation,
an insignificant phantasm, or else
a Muscovite in Harold's mantle,
12   a glossary of other people's megrims,
a complete lexicon of words in vogue? . . .
Might he not be, in fact, a parody?

XXV

Can it be that she has resolved the riddle?
Can it be that "the word" is found?
The hours run; she has forgotten
4   that she is long due home—
where two neighbors have gathered,
and where the converse dwells on her.
"What should one do? Tatiana is no infant,"
8   quoth the old lady with a groan.
"Why, Olinka is younger. . . .
Forsooth, to get the girl established,
'tis time; but then—what *can* I do with her?
12   She turns down everybody flatly with the same
'I will not marry,' and keeps brooding,
and wanders in the woods alone."

XXVI

"Might she not be in love?" "With whom, then?
  Buyanov offered: was rejected.
  Same thing with Ivan Petushkov.
4 There guested with us a hussar, Pïhtín;
  my, how he was with Tanya taken,
  how lavishly he coaxed, the imp!
  Thought I: perchance, she will accept;
8 far from it! And again the deal was off."
  "Why, my dear lady, what's the hindrance?
  To Moscow, to the mart of brides!
  One hears, the vacant places there are many."
12 "Och, my good sir! My income's scanty."
  "Sufficient for a single winter;
  if not, just borrow—say, from me."

XXVII

The old dame was much taken with
  the sensible and sound advice;
  reckoned—and there and then resolved
4 in winter to set out for Moscow;
  and Tanya hears this news. . . .
  Unto the judgment of the exacting *monde*
  to present the clear traits
8 of provincial simplicity,
  and dated finery,
  and dated turns of speech;
  of Moscow fops and Circes
12 the mocking glances to attract . . .
  O terror! No, better and safer,
  back in the woods for her to stay.

XXVIII

With the first rays arising
she hastens now into the fields
and, with soft-melting eyes
4   surveying them, she says:
"Farewell, pacific dales,
and you, familiar hilltops,
and you, familiar woods!
8   Farewell, celestial beauty,
farewell, gay nature!
I am exchanging a dear quiet world
for the hum of resplendent vanities! . . .
12   And you, my freedom, farewell, too!
Whither, wherefore, do I bear onward?
What does my fate hold out for me?"

XXIX

Her walks last longer.
At present, here a hillock, there a brook,
cannot help stopping
4   Tatiana with their charm.
She, as with ancient friends,
with her groves, meadows,
still hastens to converse.
8   But the fast summer flies.
The golden autumn has arrived.
Nature, tremulous, pale,
is like a victim sumptuously decked. . . .
12   Now, driving clouds along, the North
has blown, has howled, and now herself
Winter the sorceress comes.

XXX

She came, scattered herself; in clusters
hung on the limbs of oaks;
in wavy rugs lay down
4   amid the fields, about the hills;
the banks with the immobile river
made level with a puffy pall.
Frost gleamed. And we are gladdened
8   by Mother Winter's pranks.
By them not gladdened is but Tanya's heart:
she does not go to meet the winter,
get a breath of frostdust,
12 and with the first snow from the bathhouse roof
wash face, shoulders, and breast.
Tatiana dreads the winter way.

XXXI

The day of leaving is long overdue;
the last term now goes by.
Inspected, lined anew, made solid,
4   is the—cast to oblivion—sledded coach.
The usual train of three kibitkas
carries the household chattels:
pans, chairs, trunks,
8   jams in jars, mattresses,
feather beds, cages with cocks,
pots, basins, et cetera—
well, plenty of all kinds of goods.
12 And now, among the servants in the outhouse,
there rises noise, the farewell weep:
into the courtyard eighteen nags are led.

XXXII

These to the master coach are harnessed;
the men cooks prepare lunch;
on the kibitkas loads are piled up high;
4   serf women, coachmen brawl.
Upon a lean and shaggy jade
sits a bearded postilion.
Running, retainers at the gate have gathered
8   to bid their mistresses farewell. And now
they've settled, and the venerable sleigh-coach,
sliding, creeps beyond the gate.
"Farewell, pacific sites!
12   Farewell, secluded refuge!
Shall I see you?" And a stream of tears
flows from Tanya's eyes.

XXXIII

When we to good enlightenment
more limits move aside,
in due time (by the computation
4   of philosophic tabulae,
in some five hundred years) roads, surely,
at home will change immeasurably.
By chaussées Russia here and there
8   will be united and traversed;
cast-iron bridges o'er the waters
in ample arcs will stride;
we shall part mountains; under water
12   dig daring tunnels;
and Christendom will institute
at every stage a tavern.

XXXIV

At present roads at home are bad;[42]
forgotten bridges rot;
in the stagehouses the bedbugs and fleas
4   do not give one a minute's sleep.
No taverns. In a cold log hut,
high-flown but hungry,
a bill of fare hangs for display
8   and teases one's vain appetite,
while the rural Cyclopes
in front of a slow fire
treat with a Russian hammer
12   Europe's light article,
blessing the ruts
and ditches of the fatherland.

XXXV

Per contra, in winter's cold season
driving is agreeable and easy.
As in a modish song a verse devoid of thought,
4   smooth is the winter track.
Alert are our Automedons,
our troïkas never tire,
and mileposts, humoring the idle gaze,
8   before one's eyes flick like a fence.[43]
Unluckily, Dame Larin dragged along,
fearing expensive stages,
with her own horses, not with posters,
12   and our maid tasted
viatic tedium in full:
they traveled seven days and nights.

XXXVI

But now 'tis near. Before them
already white-stoned Moscow's
gold crosses, ember-bright,
4   burn on her ancient tops.
Ah, chums, how pleased I was
when of the churches and the belfries,
of gardens, of palazzos the half-circle
8   before me opened all at once!
How often in sorrowful separation,
in my wandering fate,
Moscow, I thought of you!
12   Moscow! . . . How much within that sound
is blended for a Russian heart!
How much is echoed there!

XXXVII

Here is, surrounded by its park,
Petrovskiy Castle. Gloomily
it prides itself on recent glory.
4   In vain Napoleon waited,
intoxicated with his last success,
for kneeling Moscow
with the old Kremlin's keys:
8   no, did not go my Moscow
to him with penitential head;
not revelry, not a welcoming gift—
a conflagration she prepared
12   for the impatient hero.
From here, in meditation sunk,
he watched the formidable flame.

XXXVIII

Good-by, witness of fallen glory,
Petrovskiy Castle. Hup! Don't stop,
get on! The turnpike posts already
4   show white. Already on Tverskaya Street
the sleigh-coach sweeps over the dips.
There flicker by: watch boxes, peasant women,
urchins, shops, street lamps,
8   palaces, gardens, monasteries,
Bokharans, sledges, kitchen gardens,
merchants, small shacks, muzhiks,
boulevards, towers, Cossacks,
12   pharmacies, fashion shops,
balconies, lions on the gates,
and flocks of jackdaws on the crosses.

XXXIX

.   .   .   .

XL

In this exhausting promenade
passes an hour, another, and now
in a lane by St. Chariton's
4   the sleigh-coach at a gate before a house
has stopped. To an old aunt,
for the fourth year ill with consumption,
at present they have come.
8   The door is opened wide for them
by a bespectacled, in torn caftan,
gray Kalmuk, with a stocking in his hand.
There meets them in the drawing room the cry
12   of the princess prostrated on a divan.
The old ladies, weeping, embraced,
and exclamations poured:

XLI

"Princess, *món ange!*" "Pachette!" "Aline!"
"Who would have thought?" "How long it's
"For how much time?" "Dear! Cousin!" [been!"
4 "Sit down—how queer it is!
I'd swear the scene is from a novel!"
"And this is my daughter Tatiana."
"Ah, Tanya! Come up here to me—
8 I seem to be delirious in my sleep.
Coz, you remember Grandison?"
"What? Grandison? Oh, Grandison!
Why, yes, I do, I do. Well, where is he?"
12 "In Moscow—lives by St. Simeon's;
on Christmas Eve he called on me:
got a son married recently.

XLII

"As to the other . . . But we'll tell it all
later, won't we? To all her kin
straightway tomorrow we'll show Tanya.
4 Pity that paying visits is too much for me—
can hardly drag my feet.
But you are worn out from the journey;
let's go and have a rest together. . . .
8 Och, I've no strength . . . my chest is tired . . .
Heavy to me is even gladness,
not only melancholy. My dear soul,
I'm no good any more in any way . . .
12 In old age life is such a horrid thing."
And here, exhausted utterly,
in tears, she broke into a coughing fit.

XLIII

The invalid's caresses and rejoicing
move Tatiana; but in her
new domicile she's ill at ease,
4   used as she is to her own chamber.
Beneath a silken curtain,
in a new bed, she cannot sleep,
and the early peal of church bells,
8   forerunner of the morning tasks,
arouses her from bed.
Tanya sits down beside the window.
The darkness thins; but she
12   does not discern her fields:
there is before her a strange yard,
a stable, kitchen house, and fence.

XLIV

And now, on rounds of family dinners
Tanya they trundle daily
to grandsires and to grandams to present
4   her abstract indolence.
For kin come from afar
there's an affectionate reception everywhere,
and exclamations, and good cheer.
8 "How Tanya's grown! Such a short while
it seems since I godmothered you!"
"And since I bore you in my arms!"
"And since I pulled you by the ears!"
12 "And since I fed you gingerbread!"
And the grandams in chorus keep repeating:
"How our years do fly!"

XLV

But one can see no change in *them*;
in them all follows the old pattern:
the spinster princess, Aunt Eléna,
4   has got the very same tulle mob;
still cerused is Lukéria Lvóvna;
the same lies tells Lyubóv Petróvna;
Ivan Petróvich is as stupid;
8   Semyón Petróvich as tightfisted;
and Palagéya Nikolávna
has the same friend, Monsieur Finemouche,
and the same spitz, and the same husband—
12   while *he* is still the sedulous clubman,
is just as meek, is just as deaf,
and eats and drinks the same—enough for two.

XLVI

Their daughters embrace Tanya.
Moscow's young graces
at first survey in silence
4   from head to foot Tatiana;
find her somewhat bizarre,
provincial, and affected,
and somewhat pale and thin,
8   but on the whole not bad at all;
then to nature submitting,
they make friends with her, lead her to their
kiss her, squeeze tenderly her hands,   [rooms,
12   fluff up her curls after the fashion,
and in their singsong tones impart
the secrets of the heart, secrets of maidens,

XLVII

   conquests of others and their own,
   hopes, capers, daydreams.
   The innocent talks flow,
4   embellished with slight calumny.
   Then, in requital for their patter,
   her heart's confession
   they touchingly request.
8   But Tanya in a kind of daze
   their speeches hears without response,
   understands nothing,
   and her heart's secret,
12   fond treasure of both tears and happiness,
   guards silently the whilst
   and shares with none.

XLVIII

   Tatiana wishes to make out
   the colloquies, the general conversation;
   but there engages everybody in the drawing room
4   such incoherent, banal rot;
   all about them is so pale, neutral;
   they even slander dully.
   In this sterile aridity of speeches,
8   interrogations, talebearing, and news,
   not once does thought flash forth in a whole day
   even by chance, even at random;   [and night,
   the languid mind won't smile,
12   the heart won't start even in jest,
   and even some droll foolishness
   in you one will not meet with, hollow *monde*!

XLIX

The "archival youths" in a crowd
look priggishly at Tanya
and about her among themselves
4   unfavorably speak.
One, some sort of sad coxcomb,
finds her "ideal"
and, having leant against a doorpost,
8   prepares an elegy for her.
At a dull aunt's having met Tanya,
once V[yazemski] sat down beside her
and managed to engage her soul;
12   and, near him having noticed her,
about her, straightening his wig,
seeks information an old man.

L

But there where turbulent Melpomene's
protracted wail resounds,
where flourishes a tinsel mantle
4   she in front of the frigid crowd;
where dozes quietly Thalia
and hearkens not to friendly plaudits;
where at Terpsichore alone
8   the young spectator marvels
(as it was, too, in former years,
in your time and in mine),
toward her did not turn
12   either jealous lorgnettes of ladies
or spyglasses of modish connoisseurs
from boxes and the rows of stalls.

274

LI

To the Sobránie, too, they bring her:
the crush there, the excitement, heat,
the music's crash, the tapers' blaze,
4 the flicker, whirl of rapid pairs,
the light attires of belles,
the galleries motleyed with people,
of marriageable girls the ample hemicycle,
8 at once strike all the senses.
Here finished fops display
their impudence, their waistcoats,
and negligent lorgnettes.
12 Hither hussars on leave
haste to appear, to thunder by,
flash, captivate, and wing away.

LII

The night has many charming stars,
in Moscow there are many belles;
but brighter than all her celestial sisters
4 is the moon in the airy blue;
but she, whom I dare not
importune with my lyre,
like the majestic moon,
8 'mid dames and maids glitters alone.
With what celestial pride
the earth she touches!
How full of sensuousness her breast!
12 How languorous her wonderful gaze! . . .
But 'tis enough, enough; do cease:
to folly you have paid your due.

275

LIII

Noise, laughter, scampering, bows,
galope, mazurka, waltz . . . Meantime,
between two aunts, beside a column,
4   noted by none,
Tatiana looks and does not see,
detests the agitation of the *monde*;
she stifles here . . . she in a daydream
8   strains toward the campestral life,
the country, the poor villagers,
to that secluded nook
where a bright brooklet flows,
12   toward her flowers, toward her novels,
and to the gloam of linden avenues,
thither where *he* used to appear to her.

LIV

Thus does her thought roam far away:
high life and noisy ball are both forgotten,
but meantime does not take his eyes off her
4   a certain imposing general.
The aunts exchanged a wink
and both as one nudged Tanya with their elbows,
and each whispered to her:
8   "Look quickly to your left."
"My left? Where? What is there?"
"Well, whatsoever there be, look. . . .
In that group, see? In front. . . .
12   There where you see those two in uniform. . . .
Now he has moved off . . . now he stands in
"Who? That fat general?"   [profile."

LV

But on a conquest here we shall congratulate
my dear Tatiana
and turn our course aside,

4   lest I forget of whom I sing. . . .
And by the way, here are two words about it:
"I sing a youthful pal
and many eccentricities of his.

8   Bless my long labor,
O you, Muse of the Epic!
And having handed me a trusty staff,
let me not wander aslant and askew."

12   Enough! The load is off my shoulders!
To classicism I have paid my respects:
though late, but there's an introduction.

CHAPTER EIGHT

Fare thee well, and if for ever,
Still for ever, fare thee well.

Byron

Chapter Eight

I

In those days when in the Lyceum's gardens
I bloomed serenely,
would eagerly read Apuleius,
4   while Cicero I did not read;
in those days, in mysterious valleys,
in springtime, to the calls of swans,
near waters radiant in the stillness,
8   to me the Muse began appearing.
My student cell
was suddenly alight: in it the Muse
opened a feast of young devices,
12   sang childish gaieties,
and glory of our ancientry,
and the heart's tremulous dreams.

II

And with a smile the world received her;
initial success gave us wings;
the aged Derzhávin noticed us—
4   and blessed us while descending to the grave.

. . . .
. . . .
. . . .
. . . .
. . . .
. . . .
. . . .
. . . .
. . . .
. . . .

III

And I, setting myself for law
only the arbitrary will of passions,
sharing emotions with the crowd,
4   I led my frisky Muse
into the noise of feasts and riotous discussions—
the terror of midnight patrols;
and to them, in mad feasts,
8   she brought her gifts,
and like a little bacchante frisked,
over the bowl sang for the guests;
and the young people of past days
12   would riotously dangle after her;
and I was proud 'mong friends
of my volatile mistress.

IV

But I dropped out of their alliance—
and fled afar . . . she followed me.
How often the caressive Muse
4   for me would sweeten the mute way
with the bewitchment of a secret tale!
How often on Caucasia's crags,
Lenorelike, by the moon,
8   with me she'd gallop on a steed!
How often on the shores of Tauris
she in the murk of night
led me to listen the sound of the sea,
12   Nereid's unceasing murmur,
the deep eternal chorus of the billows,
the praiseful hymn to the sire of the worlds.

V

And having forgotten the far capital's
glitter and noisy feasts
in the wild depth of sad Moldavia,
4   the humble tents
of wandering tribes she visited,
and among them grew savage,
and forgot the speech of the gods
8   for scant, strange tongues,
for songs of the steppe dear to her.
Suddenly everything around changed,
and lo! in my garden she
12   appeared as a provincial miss,
with woeful meditation in her eyes,
with a French book in her hands.

VI

And now my Muse for the first time
I'm taking to a high-life rout;[44]
at her steppe charms
4   with jealous apprehensiveness I look.
Through a dense series of aristocrats,
of military fops, of diplomats
and proud ladies she glides;
8   now quietly she has sat down and looks,
admiring the clamorous crush,
the flickering of dress and speech,
the coming of slow guests
12   in front of the young hostess,
and the dark frame of men
around ladies, as about pictures.

VII

She likes the stately order
of oligarchic colloquies,
and the chill of calm pride,
4   and this mixture of ranks and years.
But who's that in the chosen throng,
standing silent and nebulous?
To everyone he seems a stranger.
8   Before him faces come and go
like a series of tiresome specters.
What is it—spleen or smarting morgue
upon his face? Why is he here?
12   Who is he? Is it really—Eugene?
He, really? So, 'tis he, indeed.
—Since when has he been brought our way?

VIII

Is he the same, or grown more peaceful?
Or does he still play the eccentric?
Say, in what guise has he returned?
4   What will he stage for us meanwhile?
As what will he appear now? As a Melmoth?
a cosmopolitan? a patriot?
a Harold? a Quaker? a bigot?
8   Or will he sport some other mask?
Or else be simply a good fellow
like you and me, like the whole world?
At least here's my advice:
12   to drop an antiquated fashion.
Sufficiently he's gulled the world . . .
—He's known to you?—Both yes and no.

IX

—Why so unfavorably then
do you refer to him?
Because we indefatigably
4   bestir ourselves, judge everything?
Because of fiery souls the rashness
to smug nonentity
is either insulting or absurd?
8   Because, by liking room, wit cramps?
Because too often conversations
we're glad to take for deeds,
because stupidity is volatile and wicked?
12   Because to grave men grave are trifles,
and mediocrity alone
is to our measure and not odd?

X

Blest who was youthful in his youth;
blest who matured at the right time;
who gradually the chill of life
4   with years was able to withstand;
who never was addicted to strange dreams;
who did not shun the fashionable rabble;
who was at twenty fop or blade,
8   and then at thirty, profitably married;
who rid himself at fifty
of private and of other debts;
who fame, money, and rank
12   in due course calmly gained;
about whom lifelong one kept saying:
N. N. is an excellent man.

XI

But it is sad to think that to no purpose
youth was given us,
that we betrayed it every hour,
4   that it duped us;
that our best wishes,
that our fresh dreamings,
in quick succession have decayed
8   like leaves in putrid autumn.
It is unbearable to see before one
only of dinners a long series,
to look on life as on a rite,
12   and in the wake of the decorous crowd
to go, not sharing with it
either general views, or passions.

XII

When one becomes the subject of noisy com-
it is unbearable (you will agree with that) [ments,
among sensible people
4   to pass for a sham eccentric
or a sad crackbrain,
or a satanic monster,
or even for my Demon.
8   Onegin (let me take him up again),
having in single combat killed his friend,
having lived without a goal, without exertions,
to the age of twenty-six,
12   oppressed by the inertia of leisure,
without employment, wife, or business,
could think of nothing to take up.

XIII

A restlessness took hold of him,
the urge toward a change of places
(a property most painful,
4   a cross that few deliberately bear).
He left his countryseat,
the solitude of woods and meads,
where an ensanguined shade
8   daily appeared to him,
and started upon travels without aim,
accessible to one sensation;
and journeys to him
12   tedious became as everything on earth.
He returned and found himself,
like Chatski, come from boat to ball.

XIV

But lo! the throng has undulated,
a whisper through the hall has run. . . .
Toward the hostess there advanced a lady,
4   followed by an imposing general.
She was unhurried,
not cold, not talkative,
without a flouting gaze for everyone,
8   without pretensions to success,
without those little mannerisms,
without imitational devices. . . .
All about her was quiet, simple.
1 2   She seemed a faithful reproduction
du comme il faut . . . ([Shishkóv,] forgive me:
I do not know how to translate it.)

XV

Closer to her the ladies moved;
old women smiled to her;
the men bowed lower,
4   sought to catch the gaze of her eyes;
the maidens passed more quietly
before her through the room; and higher than
lifted both nose and shoulders   [anyone
8   the general who had come in with her.
None could a beauty
have called her; but from head to foot
none could have found in her
1 2   what by the autocratic fashion
in the high London circle
is called "vulgar" (I can't—

XVI

—much do I like that word,
but can't translate it;
with us, for the time being, it is new
4   and hardly bound to be in favor;
it might do nicely in an epigram. . . .
But to our lady let me turn.)
Winsome with carefree charm,
8   she at a table sat
with glittering Nina Voronskóy,
that Cleopatra of the Neva;
and, surely, you would have agreed
12   that Nina with her marble beauty
could not eclipse her neighbor,
though she was dazzling.

XVII

"Can it be possible?" thinks Eugene.
"Can it be she? . . . But really . . . No . . .
What! From the wild depth of steppe
4   and a tenacious quizzing glass   [villages . . ."
he keeps directing every minute
at her whose aspect vaguely has recalled
to him forgotten features.
8   "Tell me, Prince, you don't know
who is it there in the *framboise* beret
talking with the Spanish ambassador?"
The prince looks at Onegin:
12   "Aha! Indeed, long have you not been in the
Wait, I'll present you."   [*monde.*
"But *who* is she?" "My wife."

XVIII

"So you are married! Didn't know before.
    How long?" "About two years."
"To whom?" "The Larin girl." "Tatiana!"
4 "She knows you?" "I'm their neighbor."
    "Oh, then, come on." The prince goes up
    to his wife and leads up to her
    his kin and friend.
8 The princess looks at him . . .
    and whatever troubled her soul,
    however greatly she might have been
    surprised, astounded,
12 nevertheless nothing betrayed her,
    in her the same *ton* was retained,
    her bow was just as quiet.

XIX

Forsooth! It was not merely that she didn't start,
    or suddenly grow pale, or red—
    even one eyebrow never stirred,
4 she didn't so much as compress her lips.
    Though he most diligently looked,
    even traces of the former Tatiana
    Onegin could not find.
8 With her he wished to start a conversation—
    and . . . and could not. She asked:
    Had he been long around? Whence came he—
    and, peradventure, not from their own parts?
12 Then on her spouse she turned
    a look of lassitude; glided away. . . .
    And moveless he remained.

XX

Can it be that the same Tatiana
to whom, alone with her,
at the beginning of our novel
4 in a stagnant, far region,
in righteous fervor of moralization
he had preached precepts once;
the same from whom he keeps
8 a letter where the heart speaks,
where all is out, all unrestrained;
that little girl—or is he dreaming?—
that little girl whom he
12 had in her humble lot disdained—
can she have been with him just now
so bland, so bold?

XXI

He leaves the close-packed rout,
he drives home, pensive;
by a dream now melancholy, now charming,
4 his first sleep is disturbed.
He has awoken; he is brought
a letter: Prince N. begs the honor of his presence
at a soirée. Good God—to her?
8 I will, I will! And rapidly
he scrawls a courteous answer.
What ails him? What a strange daze he is in!
What has stirred at the bottom
12 of a soul cold and sluggish?
Vexation? Vanity? Or once again
youth's worry—love?

XXII

Once more Onegin counts the hours,
once more he can't wait for the day to end.
But ten strikes: he drives off,
4   he has flown forth, he's at the porch;
with tremor he goes in to the princess:
he finds Tatiana alone,
and for some minutes together
8   they sit. The words come not
from Onegin's lips. Ill-humored,
awkward, he barely, barely
replies to her. His head
12 is full of a persistent thought.
Persistently he gazes: she
sits easy and free.

XXIII

The husband comes. He interrupts
that painful tête-à-tête;
he with Onegin recollects
4   the pranks, the jests of former years.
They laugh. Guests enter.
Now with the large-grained salt of high-life
the conversation starts to be enlivened.   [malice
8   Before the lady of the house, light tosh
sparkled without a stupid simper,
and meantime interrupted it
sensible talk, without trite topics,
12 without eternal truths, without pedanticism,
and did not shock anyone's ears
with its free liveliness.

XXIV

Yet here was the flower of the capital,
both high nobility and paragons of fashion;
the faces one meets everywhere,

4   the fools one cannot go without;
here were elderly ladies,
in mobcaps and in roses, wicked-looking;
here were several maidens—

8   unsmiling faces;
here was an envoy, speaking
of state affairs;
here was, with fragrant hoary hair,

12   an old man in the old way joking—
with eminent subtility and wit,
which is somewhat absurd today!

XXV

Here was, to epigrams addicted
a gentleman cross with everything:
with the too-sweet tea of the hostess,

4   the ladies' platitudes, the *ton* of men,
the comments on a foggy novel,
the badge two sisters had been granted,
the falsehoods in reviews, the war,

8   the snow, and his own wife.

. . . .
. . . .
. . . .
. . . .
. . . .
. . . .

XXVI

Here was [. . .], who had gained
distinction by the baseness of his soul,
who had blunted in all albums,
4   Saint-P[riest], your pencils;
in the doorway another ball dictator
stood like a fashion plate,
as rosy as a Palm Week cherub,
8   tight-coated, mute and motionless;
and a far-flung traveler,
an overstarched jackanapes,
provoked a smile among the guests
12   by his studied deportment,
and a gaze silently exchanged
gave him the general verdict.

XXVII

But my Onegin the whole evening
is only with Tatiana occupied:
not with the shrinking little maiden,
4   enamored, poor and simple—
but the indifferent princess,
the inaccessible goddess
of the luxurious, queenly Neva.
8   O humans! All of you resemble
ancestress Eve:
what's given to you does not lure,
incessantly the serpent calls you
12   to him, to the mysterious tree:
you *must* be offered the forbidden fruit,
for Eden otherwise is not Eden to you.

XXVIII

How changed Tatiana is!
Into her role how firmly she has entered!
Of a constricting rank
4 the ways how fast she has adopted!
Who'd dare to seek the tender little lass
in this stately, this nonchalant
legislatrix of salons?
8 And he her heart had agitated!
About him in the gloom of night,
as long as Morpheus had not flown down,
time was, she virginally brooded,
12 raised to the moon languorous eyes,
dreaming someday with him
to make life's humble journey!

XXIX

All ages are to love submissive;
but to young virgin hearts
its impulses are beneficial
4 as are spring storms to fields.
They freshen in the rain of passions,
and renovate themselves, and ripen,
and vigorous life gives
8 both lush bloom and sweet fruit.
But at a late and barren age,
at the turn of our years,
sad is the trace of a dead passion. . . .
12 Thus storms of the cold autumn
into a marsh transform the meadow
and strip the woods around.

XXX

There is no doubt: alas! Eugene
in love is with Tatiana like a child.
In throes of amorous designs
4   he spends both day and night.
Not harking to the stern reprovals of the mind,
up to her porch, glassed entrance hall,
he drives up every day.
8   He chases like a shadow after her;
he's happy if he casts
the fluffy boa on her shoulder,
or touches torridly
12   her hand, or separates
in front of her the motley host of liveries,
or else picks up her handkerchief.

XXXI

She does not notice him,
no matter how he strives—even to death;
receives him freely at her house;
4   elsewhere two or three words with him ex-
sometimes welcomes with a mere bow, [changes;
sometimes does not take any notice:
there's not a drop of coquetry in her,
8   the high world does not tolerate it.
Onegin is beginning to grow pale;
she does not see or does not care;
Onegin droops—and almost,
12   in fact, is phthisical.
All send Onegin to physicians;
in chorus these send him to spas.

XXXII

Yet he's not going. He beforehand
is ready to his forefathers to write
of an impending meeting; yet Tatiana
4 cares not one bit (such is their sex).
But he is stubborn, won't desist,
still hopes, bestirs himself;
a sick man bolder than one hale,
8 with a weak hand to the princess
he writes a passionate missive.
Though generally little sense
he saw, not without reason, in letters,
12 but evidently the heart's suffering
had now passed his endurance.
Here you have his letter word for word.

ONEGIN'S LETTER TO TATIANA
I foresee everything: you'll be offended
by a sad secret's explanation.
What bitter scorn
4 *your proud glance will express!*
What do I want? What is my object
in opening my soul to you?
What malevolent merriment
8 *perhaps I give occasion to!*

By chance once having met you,
a spark of tenderness having remarked in you,
I did not venture to believe in it:
12 *did not let a sweet habit have its way;*
my loathsome freedom
I did not wish to lose.

297

Another thing yet parted us:
16   *a hapless victim Lenski fell. . . .*
From all that to the heart is dear
then did I tear my heart away;
to everyone a stanger, tied by nothing,
20   *I thought: liberty and peace*
are a substitute for happiness. Good God!
What a mistake I made, how I am punished!

No—every minute to see you;
24   *follow you everywhere;*
the smile of your lips, movement of your eyes,
to try to capture with enamored eyes;
to hearken long to you, to comprehend
28   *all your perfection with one's soul;*
to melt in agonies before you,
grow pale and waste away . . . that's bliss!

And I'm deprived of that; for you
32   *I drag myself at random everywhere;*
to me each day is dear, each hour is dear,
while I in futile dullness squander
the days told off by fate—
36   *they are, in fact, quite heavy anyway.*
I know: my span is well-nigh measured;
but that my life may be prolonged
I must be certain in the morning
40   *of seeing you during the day.*
I fear in my humble appeal
your austere gaze will see
designs of despicable cunning—
44   *and I can hear your wrathful censure.*

If you but knew how terrible it is
to languish with the thirst of love,
to be aflame—and hourly with one's reason
48 *subdue the agitation in one's blood!*
wish to embrace your knees
and, in a burst of sobbing, at your feet
pour out appeals, avowals, plaints,
52 *all, all I could express,*
and in the meantime with feigned coldness
arm both one's speech and gaze,
maintain a placid conversation,
56 *glance at you with a cheerful glance! . . .*

But let it be: against myself
I've not the force to struggle any more;
all is decided: I am in your power,
60 *and I surrender to my fate.*

XXXIII

There's no reply. He sends again a missive.
To the second, third letter—
there's no reply. To some reception
4   he drives. Scarce has he entered, toward him
she's heading. How austere!
He is not seen, to him no word is said.
Ugh! How surrounded now
8   she is with Twelfthtide cold!
How much to hold back indignation
the obstinate lips want!
Onegin peers with a keen eye:
1 2   where, where are discomposure, sympathy,
where the tearstains? None, none!
There's on that face but the imprint of wrath . . .

XXXIV

plus, possibly, a secret fear
lest husband or *monde* guess
the escapade, the casual foible,
4   all my Onegin knows. . . .
There is no hope! He drives away,
curses his folly—
and, deeply plunged in it,
8   the *monde* he once again renounced
and in his silent study
he was reminded of the time
when cruel chondria
1 2   pursued him in the noisy *monde*,
captured him, took him by the collar,
and locked him up in a dark hole.

XXXV

He once again started to read without discern-
He read Gibbon, Rousseau,   [ment.
Manzoni, Herder, Chamfort,
4   Mme de Staël, Bichat, Tissot.
He read the skeptic Bayle,
he read the works of Fontenelle,
he read some of our native authors,
8   without rejecting anything—
both "almanacs" and magazines
where sermons into us are drummed,
where I'm today abused so much
12   but where *such* madrigals
to me addressed I met with now and then:
e sempre bene, gentlemen.

XXXVI

And lo—his eyes were reading,
but his thoughts were far away;
dreams, desires, woes
4   kept crowding deep into his soul.
He between the printed lines
read with spiritual eyes
other lines. It was in *them* that he
8   was utterly immersed.
These were the secret legends
of the heart's dark ancientry;
dreams unconnected with anything:
12   threats, rumors, presages;
or the live tosh of a long tale,
or a young maiden's letters.

XXXVII

And by degrees into a lethargy
of both feelings and thoughts he falls,
while before him Imagination
4   deals out her motley faro hand.
Either he sees: on melted snow,
as at a night's encampment sleeping,
stirless, a youth is lying,
8   and hears a voice: "Well, what—he's dead!"
Or he sees foes forgotten,
slanderers and wicked cowards,
and a swarm of young traitresses,
12   and a circle of despicable comrades;
or else a country house, and by the window
sits *she* . . . and ever she!

XXXVIII

He grew so used to lose himself in this
that he almost went off his head
or else became a poet.
4   (Frankly, that would have been a boon!)
And true: by dint of magnetism,
the mechanism of Russian verses
at that time all but grasped
8   my addleheaded pupil.
How much a poet he resembled
when in a corner he would sit alone,
and the hearth flamed in front of him,
12   and he hummed "Benedetta"
or "Idol mio," and would drop
into the fire his slipper or review.

XXXIX

Days rushed. In warmth-pervaded air
winter already was resolving;
and he did not become a poet,
4   did not die, did not lose his mind.
Spring quickens him: for the first time
his close-shut chambers,
where he had hibernated like a marmot,
8   his double windows, inglenook—
he leaves on a clear morning,
fleets in a sleigh along the Neva.
Upon blue blocks of hewn-out ice
12 the sun plays. Muddily thaws
in the streets the furrowed snow:
whither, upon it, his fast course

XL

directs Onegin? You beforehand
have guessed already. Yes, exactly:
arrives apace to her, to his Tatiana,
4   my unreformed odd chap.
He walks in, looking like a corpse.
There's not a soul in the front hall.
He enters a reception room. On! No one.
8   A door he opens. . . . What is it
that strikes him with such force?
The princess before him, alone,
sits, unadorned, pale,
12 reading some letter or another,
and softly sheds a flood of tears,
her cheek propped on her hand.

XLI

Ah! Her mute sufferings—who
would not have read in this swift instant!
The former Tanya, the poor Tanya—who
4   would not have recognized now in the princess?
In the heartache of mad regrets,
Eugene has fallen at her feet;
she started—and is silent,
8   and at Onegin looks
without surprise, without wrath. . . .
His sick, extinguished gaze,
imploring aspect, mute reproof,
1 2   she takes in everything. The simple maid,
with dreams, with heart of former days
again in her has resurrected now.

XLII

She does not bid him rise
and, not taking her eyes off him,
does not withdraw from his avid lips
4   her insensible hand. . . .
What is her dreaming now about?
A lengthy silence passes,
and finally she, softly:
8   "Enough; get up. I must
frankly explain myself to you.
Onegin, do you recollect that hour
when in the garden, in the alley, we
1 2   were brought by fate together and so humbly
your lesson I heard out?
Today it is my turn.

XLIII

"Onegin, I was younger then,
I was, I daresay, better-looking,
and I loved you; and what then?
4   What did I find in your heart?
What answer? Mere austerity.
There wasn't—was there?—novelty for you
in the love of a humble little girl?
8   Even today—good God!—blood freezes
as soon as I remember your cold glance
and that sermon. . . . But you
I don't accuse; at that terrible hour
12   you acted nobly,
you in regard to me were right,
to you with all my soul I'm grateful. . . .

XLIV

"*Then*—is it not so?—in the wilderness,
far from futile Hearsay,
I was not to your liking. . . . Why, then, *now*
4   do you pursue me?
Why have you marked me out?
Might it not be because in the *grand monde*
I am obliged now to appear;
8   because I'm wealthy and of noble rank?
because my husband has been maimed in battles;
because for that the Court is kind to us?
Might it not be because my disrepute
12   would be remarked by everybody now
and in society might bring
you scandalous prestige?

XLV

"I'm crying. . . . If your Tanya
you've not forgotten yet,
then know: the sharpness of your scolding,
4   cold, stern discourse,
if it were only in my power
I'd have preferred to an offensive passion,
and to these letters and tears.
8   For my infantine dreams
you had at least some pity then,
at least consideration for my age.
But *now*! . . . What to my feet
12   has brought you? What a little thing!
How, with your heart and mind,
be the slave of a trivial feeling?

XLVI

"But as to me, Onegin, this pomp,
the tinsel of a loathsome life,
my triumphs in the vortex of the World,
4   my fashionable house and evenings,
what do I care for them? . . . At once I would give
all this frippery of a masquerade,   [gladly
all this glitter, and noise, and fumes,
8   for a shelfful of books, for a wild garden,
for our poor dwelling,
for those haunts where for the first time,
Onegin, I saw you,
12   and for the humble churchyard, too,
where there's a cross now and the shade of
over my poor nurse.   [branches

XLVII

"Yet happiness had been so possible,
so near! . . . But my fate
already is decided. Rashly
4   perhaps, I acted.
With tears of conjuration, with me
my mother pleaded. For poor Tanya
all lots were equal.
8   I married. You must,
I pray you, leave me;
I know: in your heart are
both pride and genuine honor.
12   I love you (why dissimulate?);
but to another I've been given away:
to him I shall be faithful all my life."

XLVIII

She has gone. Eugene stands
as if by thunder struck.
In what a tempest of sensations
4   his heart is now immersed!
But a sudden clink of spurs has sounded,
and Tatiana's husband has appeared,
and here my hero,
8   at an unkind minute for him,
reader, we now shall leave
for long . . . forever. . . . After him
sufficiently we on one path
12   roamed o'er the world. Let us congratulate
each other on attaining land. Hurrah!
It long (is it not true?) was time.

XLIX

Whoever you be, O my reader—
friend, foe—I wish with you
to part at present as a pal.
4   Farewell. Whatever you in my wake
sought in these careless strophes—
tumultuous recollections,
relief from labors,
8   live pictures or bons mots,
or faults of grammar—
God grant that you, in this book,
for recreation, for the daydream,
12   for the heart, for jousts in journals,
may find at least a crumb.
Upon which, let us part, farewell!

L

You, too, farewell, my strange traveling com-
and you, my true ideal,   [panion,
and you, my live and constant,
4   though small, work. I have known with you
all that a poet covets:
obliviousness of life in the world's tempests,
the sweet converse of friends.
8   Many, many days have rushed by
since young Tatiana,
and with her Onegin, in a blurry dream
appeared to me for the first time—
12   and the far stretch of a free novel
I through a magic crystal
still did not make out clearly.

LI

But those to whom at friendly meetings
the first strophes I read—
"Some are no more, others are distant,"
4   as erstwhiles Sadi said.
Finished without them is Onegin's portrait.
And she from whom is fashioned
the dear ideal of "Tatiana" . . .
8   Ah, fate has much, much snatched away!
Blest who life's banquet early
left, having not drained to the bottom
the goblet full of wine;
12   who did not read life's novel to the end
and all at once could part with it
as I with my Onegin.

THE END

PUSHKIN'S NOTES TO
EUGENE ONEGIN

Notes to Eugene Onegin

[*These are Pushkin's notes, pp. 281–93 of the 1837 edition. My own notes to them will be found in the Commentary, to which refer the bracketed citations.*]

1. Written in Bessarabia. [One : II : 14.]

2. Dandy [Eng.], a fop. [One : IV : 7.]

3. Hat à la Bolivar. [One : XV : 10.]

4. Well-known restaurateur. [One : XVI : 5.]

5. A trait of chilled sentiment worthy of Childe Harold. The ballets of Mr. Didelot are full of liveliness of fancy and extraordinary charm. One of our romantic writers found in them much more poetry than in the whole of French literature. [One : XXI : 14.]

6. "Tout le monde sut qu'il mettoit du blanc, et moi qui n'en croyois rien je commençai de la croire, non seulement par l'embellissement de son teint, et pour avoir trouvé des tasses de blanc sur sa toilette, mais sur ce qu'entrant un matin dans sa chambre, je le trouvai brossant ses ongles avec une petite vergette faite exprès, ouvrage qu'il continua fièrement devant moi.

Je jugeai qu'un homme qui passe deux heures tous les matins à brosser ses ongles peut bien passer quelques instants à remplir de blanc les creux. de sa peau."
(*Les Confessions de Jean-Jacques Rousseau.*)

Grimm was ahead of his age: nowadays people all over enlightened Europe clean their nails with a special brush. [One : XXIV : 12.]

7. The whole of this ironical stanza is nothing but a subtle compliment to our fair compatriots. Thus Boileau, under the guise of disapprobation, eulogizes Louis XIV. Our ladies combine enlightenment with amiability, and strict purity of morals with the Oriental charm that so captivated Mme de Staël (*Dix ans d'exil*). [One : XLII : 13.]

8. Readers remember the charming description of a Petersburg night in Gnedich's idyl:

> Here's night; but the golden stripes of the clouds
> do not darken.
> Though starless and moonless, the whole remoteness
> lights up.
> Far out in the gulf one can see the silvery sails
> Of hardly discernible ships that seem in the blue
> sky to float.
> With a gloomless radiance the night sky is radiant,
> And the crimson of sunset blends with the Orient's
> gold,
> As if Aurora led forth in the wake of evening
> Her rosy morn. This was the aureate season
> When the power of night is usurped by the summer
> days;
> When the foreigner's gaze on the Northern sky
> is captivated
> By the magical union of shade and sweet light
> Which never adorns the sky of the South:
> A limpidity similar to the charms of a Northern
> maiden
> Whose light-blue eyes and bright-red cheeks
> Are but slightly shaded by auburn curls
> undulating.

Then above the Nevá and sumptuous Petropolis
     you see
Eves without gloom and brief nights without
     shadow.
Then, as soon as Philomel ends her midnight songs
She starts the songs that welcome the rise of the
     day.
But 'tis late; a coolness has breathed on the
     Nevan tundras;
The dew has descended; . . .
Here's midnight; after sounding all evening with
     thousands of oars.
The Nevá does not stir; town guests have dispersed;
Not a voice on the shore, not a ripple astream, all
     is still.
Alone now and then o'er the water a rumble runs
     from the bridges,
Or a long-drawn cry flies forth from a distant
     suburb
Where in the night one sentinel calls to another.
All sleeps. . . .

     [One : XLVII : 3.]

9   Not in dream the ardent poet
       the benignant goddess sees
       as he spends a sleepless night
       leaning on the granite.

Muravyov, "To the Goddess of the Neva." [One :
XLVIII : 1–4.]

10. Written in Odessa. [See Translator's Introduction:
"The Genesis of *Eugene Onegin*."]

11. See the first edition of *Eugene Onegin*. [One : L :
10–11; see Appendix I.]

12. From the first part of *Dneprovskaya Rusalka*.
[Two : XII : 14.]

13. The most euphonious Greek names, such as, for
instance, Agathon, Philetus, Theodora, Thecla, and
so forth, are used with us only among the common
people. [Two : XXIV : 1–2.]

14. Grandison and Lovelace, the heroes of two famous novels. [Two : XXX : 3–4.]

15. "Si j'avais la folie de croire encore au bonheur, je le chercherais dans l'habitude." Chateaubriand. [Two : XXXI : 14.]

16. Poor Yorick!—Hamlet's exclamation over the skull of the fool (see Shakespeare and Sterne). [Two : XXXVII : 6.]

17. A misprint in the earlier edition [of the chapter] altered "fly home" to "fly in winter" (which did not make any sense whatsoever). Reviewers, not realizing this, saw an anachronism in the following stanzas. We venture to assert that, in our novel, the chronology has been worked out calendrically. [Three : IV : 2.]

18. Julie Wolmar, the new Héloïse; Malek-Adhel, hero of a mediocre romance by Mme Cottin; Gustave de Linar, hero of a charming short novel by Baroness Krüdener. [Three : IX : 7, 8.]

19. *The Vampyre,* a short novel incorrectly attributed to Lord Byron; *Melmoth,* a work of genius, by Maturin; *Jean Sbogar,* the well-known romance by Charles Nodier. [Three : XII : 8, 9, 11.]

20. *Lasciate ogni speranza, voi ch'entrate.* Our modest author has translated only the first part of the famous verse. [Three : XXII : 10.]

21. A periodical that used to be conducted by the late A. Izmaylov rather negligently. He once apologized in print to the public, saying that during the holidays he had "gone on a spree". 'Three : XXVII : 4.]

22. E. A. Baratïnski. [Three : XXX : 1.]

23. Reviewers wondered how one could call a simple peasant girl "maiden" when, a little further, genteel misses are called "young things." [Four : XLI : 12.]

24. "This signifies," remarks one of our critics, "that the urchins are skating." Right. [Four : XLII : 8.]

25.   In my rosy years
  the poetical Ay
  pleased me with its noisy foam,
  with this simile of love,
  or of frantic youth . . .

("Epistle to L. P.") [Four : XLV : 1—7.]

26. August Lafontaine, author of numerous family novels. [Four : L : 12.]

27. See "First Snow," a poem by Prince Vyazemski. [Five : III : 6.]

28. See the descriptions of the Finnish winter in Baratïnski's "Eda." [Five : III : 14.]

29.   Tomcat calls Kit
  to sleep in the stove nook.

The presage of a wedding; the first song foretells death. [Five : VIII : 14.]

30. In this manner one finds out the name of one's future fiancé. [Five : IX : 6—13.]

31. Reviewers condemned the words *hlop* [clap,] *molv'* parle, and *top* [stamp] as indifferent neologisms. These words are fundamentally Russian. "Bova stepped out of the tent for some fresh air and heard in the open country the parle of man and the stamp of steed" ("The Tale of Bova the Prince"). *Hlop* is used in plain-folk speech instead of *hlópanie* [clapping] as *ship* is instead of *shipénie* [hissing]: "he let out a hiss of the snaky sort" (*Ancient Russian Poems*). One

should not interfere with the freedom of our rich and beautiful language. [Five : XVII : 7–8.]

32. One of our critics, it would seem, finds in these lines an indecency incomprehensible to us. [Five : XX : 5–7.]

33. Divinatory books in our country come out under the imprint of Martin Zadeck—a worthy person who never wrote divinatory books, as B. M. Fyodorov observes. [Five : XXII : 12.]

34. A parody of Lomonosov's well-known lines:

> Aurora with a crimson hand
> from the calm morning waters
> leads forth with the sun after her, etc.

[Five : XXV : 1–4.]

35.   . . . . Buyanov, my neighbor,
. . . .
called yesterday on me: mustache unshaven,
tousled, fluff-covered, wearing a peaked cap.
(*The Dangerous Neighbor*)

[Five : XXVI : 9.]

36. Our critics, faithful admirers of the fair sex, strongly blamed the indecorum of this verse. [See n. 23 above.]

37. Parisian restaurateur. [Six : V : 13.]

38. Griboedov's line. [Six : XI : 12.]

39. A famous arms fabricator. [Six : XXV : 12.]

40. In the first edition Chapter Six ended in the following:

> 5 And you, young inspiration,
> excite my fancy,
> the slumber of the heart enliven,
> 8 into my nook more often fly,
> let not a poet's soul grow cold,
> callous, crust-dry,
> and finally be turned to stone

12   in the World's deadening intoxication,
    amidst the soulless proudlings,
    amidst the brilliant fools,

    XLVII
    amidst the crafty, the fainthearted,
    crazy, spoiled children,
    villains both ludicrous and dull,
4   obtuse, caviling judges;
    amidst devout coquettes;
    amidst the voluntary lackeys;
    amidst the daily modish scenes
8   of courteous, affectionate betrayals;
    amidst cold verdicts
    of cruel-hearted vanity;
    amidst the vexing emptiness
12 of schemes, of thoughts and conversations;
    in that slough where with you
    I bathe,·dear friends!

[Six : XLVI : var. 13–14.]

41. Lyovshin, author of numerous works on rural economy. [Seven : IV : 4.]

42.   Our roads are for the eyes a garden:
    trees, a turfy bank, ditches;
    much toil, much glory,
    but it's a pity, there's at times no passage.
    From trees that stand like sentries
    the travelers derive small profit;
    the road, you'll say, is fine—
    and you'll recall the verse: "for passers-by!"
    Driving in Russia is unhampered
    on two occasions only: when
    our McAdam—or McEve—,
    winter accomplishes, crackling with wrath,
    her devastating raid
    armors the roads with the cast iron of ice,
    and powder snow betimes
    with fluffy sand covers her tracks;
    or when the fields are permeated
    with such a torrid drought

> that through a puddle wade across
> a fly can with closed eyes.
>   (*The Station*, by Prince Vyazemski)

[Seven : XXXIV : 1.]

43. A simile borrowed from K., so well known for the playfulness of his fancy. K. related that, being one day sent as courier by Prince Potyomkin to the Empress, he drove so fast that his *épée*, one end of which stuck out of his small traveling carriage, rattled against the verstposts as along a palisade. [Seven : XXXV : 7–8.]

44. Rout [Eng.], an evening assembly without dances; means properly crowd [*tolpa*]. [Eight : VI : 2.]

FRAGMENTS OF
ONEGIN'S JOURNEY

Fragments of *Onegin's Journey*

[*Pushkin's Comments and Text on pp. 295–310 of the 1837 edition*]

The last [Eighth] Chapter of *Eugene Onegin* was published [1832] separately with the following foreword:

"The dropped stanzas gave rise more than once to reprehension and gibes (no doubt most just and witty). The author candidly confesses that he omitted from his novel a whole chapter in which Onegin's journey across Russia was described. It depended upon him to designate this omitted chapter by means of dots or a numeral; but to avoid equivocation he decided it would be better to mark as number eight, instead of nine, the last chapter of *Eugene Onegin*, and to sacrifice one of its closing stanzas [Eight : XLVIIIa]:

> 'Tis time: the pen for peace is asking;
> nine cantos I have written
> upon the glad shore carries out
> the ninth billow my boat
> Praise be to you, O nine Camenae, etc.

"P[avel] A[leksandrovich] Katenin (whom a fine poetic talent does not prevent from being also a subtle critic) observed to us that this exclusion, though perhaps advantageous to readers, is, however, detrimental to the plan of the entire work since, through this, the transition from Tatiana the provincial miss to Tatiana the *grande dame* becomes too unexpected and unexplained: an observation revealing the experienced artist. The author himself felt the justice of this but decided to leave out the chapter for reasons important to him but not to the public. Some fragments [XVI–XIX, 1–10] have been published [Jan. 1, 1830, *Lit. Gaz.*]; we insert them here, subjoining to them several other stanzas."

[*For the expunged stanzas and lines that fill the gaps between these fragments, see my Comm. on the fragments of Onegin's Journey, vol. 3, pp. 259–66. For the notes commenting on the following stanzas, see ibid., pp. 267–310.*—V. N.]

[I–VIII]

E. [sic] Onegin drives from Moscow to Nizhni
Novgorod:

[IX]

. . . .
. . . . before him
Makariev bustlingly bestirs itself,
4   with its abundance seethes.
Hither the Hindu has brought pearls,
the European, spurious wines;
a taboon of cast steeds
8   the breeder from the steppes has driven,
the gamester brought his decks
and fistful of complaisant dice,
the landowner, ripe daughters,
12 and daughterlings, the fashions of last year;
each bustles, lies enough for two,
and everywhere there's a mercantile spirit.

[X]

Ennui! . . .

Onegin fares to Astrahan [XI], and from there to the
[Caucasus:

[XII]

He sees: the wayward Térek
erodes its scarpéd banks;
before him soars a stately eagle,
4   a deer stands, with bent antlers;
the camel lies in the cliff's shade;
in meadows courses the Circassian's steed,
and round nomadic tents
8   the sheep of Kalmuks graze.
Afar are the Caucasian masses.
The way to them is opened. War broke through
beyond their natural divide,
12   across their perilous barriers.
The banks of the Arágva and Kurá
beheld the Russian tents.

[XIII]

By now, the waste's eternal watchman,
compressed around by hills,
Beshtu stands up, sharp-peaked,
4   and, showing green, Mashúk,
Mashuk, of healing streams dispenser;
around its magic brooks
a pallid swarm of patients presses,
8   the victims, some of martial honor,
some of the Piles, and some of Cypris.
The sufferer thinks that the thread of life
will strengthen in the wonder waves;
12   the coquette—that the wicked years' offenses
will be left at the bottom, and the oldster,
that he'll grow young—if only for a moment.

[XIV]

Nourishing bitter meditations,
amidst their woeful tribe,
with a gaze of regret Onegin
4   looks at the [smoking] streams,
and thinks, bedimmed with melancholy:
Why by a bullet in the breast am I not wounded?
Why am I not a debile oldster
8   like that poor farmer-general?
Why like a councilman from Túla
am I not lying paralyzed?
Why do I not feel in the shoulder
12   at least some rheumatism? Ah, Lord,
I'm young, life is robust in me,
what have I to expect? Ennui, ennui! . . .

Onegin then visits the Tauris:

[XV]

.   .   .   .
.   .   .   .
.   .   .   .
.   .   .   .
.   .   .   .
.   .   .   .
.   .   .   .
.   .   .   .

9   land sacred unto the imagination:
there with Orestes argued Pylades;
there Mithridates stabbed himself;
12   there sang inspired Mickiéwicz
and in the midst of coastal cliffs
recalled his Lithuania.

[XVI]

Beauteous are you, shores of the Tauris,
when one sees you from the ship
by the light of morning Cypris,
4   as for the first time I saw you.
You showed yourselves to me in nuptial lustre.
Against a blue and limpid sky
were radiant the amassments of your mountains.
8   The pattern of valleys, trees, villages
was spread before me.
And there, among the small huts of the Tatars . . .
What ardency awoke in me!
12   With what a magic yearning
my flaming bosom was compressed!
But, Muse, forget the past!

[XVII]

Whatever feelings lurked
in me then—now they are no more:
they went or changed. . . .
4   Peace unto you, turmoils of former years!
To me seemed needful at the time
wastes, pearly rims of waves,
and the sea's rote, and piles of rocks,
8   and the ideal of "proud maid,"
and nameless sufferings. . . .
Other days, other dreams;
you have become subdued, my springtime's
12   high-flown daydreamings,
and unto my poetic goblet
I have admixed a lot of water.

[XVIII]

Needful to me are other pictures:
I like a sandy hillside slope,
before a small isba two rowans,
4   a wicket gate, a broken fence,
drab-gray clouds in the sky,
before the thrash barn heaps of straw,
and a pond beneath dense willows,
8   the franchise of young ducks.
I'm fond now of the balalaika
and of the trepak's drunken stomping
before the threshold of the tavern;
12   now my ideal is a housewife,
my wishes, peace
and "pot of *shchi* but big myself."

[XIX]

The other day, during a rainy period,
as I had dropped into the cattle yard—
Fie! Prosy divagations,
4   the Flemish School's variegated dross!
Was I like that when I was blooming?
Say, Fountain of Bahchisaray!
Were such the thoughts that to my mind
8   your endless purl suggested
when silently in front of you
Zaréma I imagined? . . .
Midst the sumptuous deserted halls
12   after the lapse of three years, in my tracks
in the same region wandering,
Onegin remembered me.

[xx]

I lived then in dusty Odessa. . . .
There for a long time skies are clear.
There, hustling, an abundant trade
4   sets up its sails.
There all exhales, diffuses Europe,
all glistens with the South, and is motleyed
with live variety.
8   The tongue of golden Italy
resounds along the gay street
where walks the proud Slav,
the Frenchman, Spaniard, Armenian,
12   and Greek, and the heavy Moldavian,
and the son of Egyptian soil,
the retired Corsair, Moralí.

[xxi]

Odessa in sonorous verses
our friend Tumanski has described,
but he with partial eyes
4   gazed at it at the time.
Upon arriving, he, like a regular poet,
went off to roam with his lorgnette
alone above the sea; and then
8   with an enchanting pen
gloried the gardens of Odessa.
All right—but the fact is
that there's around it a bare steppe;
12   in a few places recent toil has forced
young branches on a scorching day
to give compulsory shade.

[XXII]

But where, pray, was my rambling tale?
"Dusty Odessa," I had said.
I might have said "muddy Odessa"
4 —and, really, neither there would I have lied.
For five-six weeks a year Odessa,
by the will of tempestuous Zeus,
is flooded, is stopped up,
8 is in thick mud immersed.
Some two feet deep all houses are embedded.
Only on stilts does a pedestrian
dare ford the street.
12 Coupés, people sink in, get stuck,
and to a droshky hitched, the ox, horns bent,
takes the place of the debile steed.

[XXIII]

But the hammer already breaks up stones,
and with a ringing pavement soon
the salvaged city will be covered
4 as with an armor of forged steel.
However, in this moist Odessa
there is another grave deficiency,
of—what would you think? Water.
8 Grievous exertions are required. . . .
So what? This is not a great grief!
Especially when wine
has been imported free of duty.
12 But then the Southern sun, but then the sea . . .
What more, friends, could you want?
Blest climes!

[XXIV]

Time was, the sunrise canon
no sooner from the ship had roared
than, down the steep shore running,
4   already to the sea I'd make my way.
Then, with intensely hot chibouk,
enlivened by the briny wave,
like in his paradise a Moslem,
8   coffee with Oriental grounds I quaff.
I go out for a stroll. Already the benignant
Casino's open: the clatter of cups
resounds there; on the balcony
12   the marker, half asleep, emerges
with a broom in his hands, and at the porch
two merchants have converged already.

[XXV]

Anon the square grows motley.
All is alive now; here and there
they run, on business or not busy;
4   however, more on businesses.
The child of Calculation and of Venture,
the merchant goes to glance at ensigns,
to find out—are the heavens sending
8   to him known sails?
What new wares
entered today in quarantine?
Have the casks of expected wines arrived?
12   And how's the plague, and where the con-
and is not there some famine, war, [flagrations,
or novelty of a like kind?

[XXVI]

But we, fellows without a woe,
among the careful merchants,
expected only oysters
4   from Tsargrad's shores.
What news of oysters? They have come. O glee!
Off flies gluttonous juventy
to swallow from their sea shells
8   the cloisterers, plump and alive,
slightly asperged with lemon.
Noise, arguments; light wine
is from the cellars brought
12   by complaisant Automne* onto the table.
The hours fly by, and the grim bill
meantime invisibly augments.

* Well-known restaurateur in Odessa [Pushkin's footnote].

[XXVII]

But darker grows already the blue evening.
Time to the opera we sped:
there 'tis the ravishing Rossini,
4   the pet of Europe, Orpheus.
Not harking to harsh criticism
he's ever selfsame, ever new;
he pours out melodies, they seethe,
8   they flow, they burn
like youthful kisses,
all sensuousness, in flames of love,
like, at the fizzing point, Ay's
12   stream and gold spurtles . . .
but, gentlemen, is it permitted
to equalize do-re-mi-sol with wine?

[XXVIII]

And does that sum up the enchantments there?
And what about the explorative lorgnette?
And the assignments in the wings?
4   The prima donna? The ballet?
And the loge where, in beauty shining,
a trader's young wife,
conceited and languorous,
8   is by a crowd of thralls surrounded?
She harks and does not hark
to both the cavatina and the pleadings
and to the banter blent halfwise with flattery,
12   while, in a corner behind her, her husband naps,
half-wakes up to cry "Fuora!",
yawns, and snores again.

[XXIX]

There thunders the finale. The house empties;
with noise the outfall hastes;
the crowd onto the square has run
4   by the gleam of the lamps and stars.
The sons of fortunate Ausonia
sing light a playful tune,
involuntarily retained—
8   while we roar the recitative.
But it is late. Sleeps quietly Odessa;
and without breath and warm
is the mute night. The moon has risen,
12   a veil, diaphanously light,
enfolds the sky. All's silent;
only the Black Sea sounds.

[XXX]

As said, I lived then in Odessa . . .

· · · · · · · · · · · · · ·